The Madness of
Eamon Moriarty

NOVELS BY THE SAME AUTHOR
(Published by Valley Press)

The Deserted Village
Amerigo Vespucci
The Intelligence Man

http://www.angelfire.com/on/valleypress/books.html

The Madness of Eamon Moriarty

Barry Swan

Valley Press

First published in 2000
by Valley Press
236 Tokyngton Avenue, Wembley,
Middlesex HA9 6HJ

Copyright Barry Swan

Typeset in Stone by LaserScript Ltd, Mitcham, Surrey
Cover design by LaserScript Ltd
Printed and bound by TJ International, Padstow, Cornwall

ISBN 0 9530768 3 0

Dedicated To
The Anti-Defamation Society

A History of the World, Discovered in the Ruins of an Ancient Shebeen

Note - It is believed that the author of this manuscript was very drunk or mad (though inspired) when he wrote it but it is mooted by experts at the University of County Cork to be the book from which the Bible, the works of Karl Marx and every single human political or social doctrine ever advanced, or even practiced, can find their meaning. These experts have worked for decades deciphering the strange, illegible hieroglyphic writing and have come up with this translation, which will enable the Censorship Board to make its decision. A word of warning is given that this book is not to be considered as Divinely inspired, as some people and 'sects' have been making out – but that is another story.

Further note - The identity of the character who goes by the name of Economy is a central puzzle as the writer gives no name to the said person in the original text, leaving a blank where the name should be. As the author obviously wishes to minimise his (or her) own role in the document's production, it was decided by a panel of independent experts to substitute the name 'Economy'. However, it is apparent from an attempt to spell his name at one place in the text that possibly his actual name is Eamon. The Galway school would agree, as they believe that they know who the author is. As regards the actual text's content, it is believed that the experience of discovering that one is 'hard up' is central to every human and indeed religious experience. The Cork School is adamant that being hard up is the explanation for the course of human events. This can take the form of being short of a few pence or – in a more fundamental way – providing a reason for whacking your neighbour over the head in pursuit of some unspoken revenge.

Note of dissent - The experts at the Galway University have insisted upon this note of dissent from the majority report being included in the official report.

We, of the Galway University, dissent from the Cork school (who for understandable reasons of local pride claim that no Cork person could have written it) and insist that 'A History of the World' is none other than the writings of one Eamon Moriarty of somewhere near Ballynamona (known as Ballyhilty in some manuscripts) in the County Cork, a failed scholar at the local school, a noted cause of troubles in the community and who was eventually incarcerated in the Mental Asylum at Cork where it is believed he still is, a very old man. How and where the young chap learned to write is a mystery that one day we hope to solve.

Note - Dr Crane of the Mental Health Board.
It is given as a warning that reading this manuscript can be a danger to the mental health of the vulnerable. It can be stated as an absolute truth by me that the writer of the words contained in the 'History' suffers from a severe mental disorder, as evidenced by the slope of his writing, and it is yet to be proved that Mental illness is not contagious.

chapter one

It was through his left eye that he could see that everything was in chaos, for he did not trust what he saw out of his right eye.

It had been raining for many months. The deluge came down in a heavy thunder so that the mice panicking in the fields were more adept at swimming than running and the water-birds, such as the plumes and the giant sea-gills, were uncontrollably a-swim, their webs and water-appendices made useless in the unending cataclysm. The distraught people stared in awe at the violence of the black clouds, entrapped helplessly below the oceanic crescendo of despair, and wondered when the rains would cease. At rare intervals the sun's orb would appear through its halo in the heavens, observing the disorder below. When blue patches of sky appeared on these occasions there was initial hope and expectation that the inclement weather would end, but to no avail did they cherish these happy moments for the rain poured down nonetheless. It was after a period of this that Halo, a madman on the capital Balhop's corner, came out with talk of a miracle.[1]

As the storm and rain continued, certain wise men began to notice changes taking place in the natural paraphernalia around them. There was the breaking down of the tall bember trees and the removal of the foliage of the elilahs and the evergreen bubs, the twisting and turning of the whole density of forests and the ruin of crops of centuries of long-standing. The diminution of all farming activity was a

2 The Madness of Eamon Moriarty

sudden fact and a wonder to them, as they in bewilderment watched diverse folk begin to partake in all sorts of queer, unprecedented commercial activities. The sky and the air had a different aura about them and the sea, which for aeons had lain like a soft blanket around the island now rose to unite with the sky in a dreadful encroach, and the practitioners of the art of wave-riding fell back in despair, no longer passing on the secrets of ocean-going to their progeny. These fat fishermen, the patriarchs of the shore regions, withdrew in abject horror at the inescapable fact of the sea's rejection of them. They turned inland to the Wither Woods where, for a time, the previously eschewed, easily gathered wild woodland plants and berries were an insurance against starvation. The Tennit folk, a hardy, masculine tribe of a different religious persuasion to the rest of the island folk who, when they had pursued their old occupations in the crafts and lower arts, were considered aloof and reclusive, (and whose status had also lately become downgraded to that of a nomadic group of apple dealers), resented this invasion of their area by the more effeminate fisherfolk, and there was a long period of bitter internal dispute amongst the Tennits over whether they should make a stand, or head off somewhere else.[2]

The odd thing was that when the fishermen and the Tennits inevitably met in the interior fastness they soon, despite initial mutual suspicion, became quite friendly due to some similarities in their new ways of life, especially both now being dependent on an unreliable source of income, (some had even taken to begging). Their present hardships and mutual physical attraction, accentuated by the contrasting colours of their skins, enabled the rise of a strong bond between them, seen in their going for long walks together, often in pairs, when they would discuss intensely the intricacies of their new situation, so much so that although a few Tennits went off to distant lands, (where they became known as Ex-Tennits and were later written out of most history books and social commentaries when they finally lost their roots), the majority stayed put with their new-found friends.[3]

The farmers, who were the most multitudinous and polyglot category of people over the entire land, lived on the fat and wealth of their stored-up crops believing, as they held themselves to be the only people who really understood nature, that the unnatural times would soon pass. The town dwellers of Balhop and Inisbay were fortified against hunger and floods by their elevation on cliff-tops and their decades' supply of preserved foods. A strong ship came every month from Assaland with cargoes of cheap ludge that were issued in return for some precious minerals and a promise to allow in a 'regular' group of missionizing Lasdiacs when the rains stopped.[4] These experts on everything that was modern and advanced in the world believed (which was anathema to the independent-minded islanders) in the uniting of all the mainland and the islands under that great, one, all-wise, technocratic chief who had brought unending prosperity to all who lived under his rule, and proved his immense wisdom by never setting foot on the island or any of the other outlying islands but living grandly and proudly, seen, heard and spoken to by no one, his supremacy unchallenged, in Assaland,

They said madness ran in his family. All the uncles and aunts were bound together in some secret, silent conspiracy. They denied knowledge of him or his parents and rejected, sometimes hysterically, the manuscript. They would not accept requests to come to the Social Services annexe and talk about some legal matters concerning his incarceration. They went mute at any mention of his name, or else simply walked rapidly away.

4 The Madness of Eamon Moriarty

There was also a problem with interpreting the case notes, due to the interference of reputed 'experts' in the text, with personal opinions and supposedly relevant footnotes added at odd points along the way, and even the very substance of what he wrote was sometimes twisted to change the meaning.

Halo too had ominous talk about these visits from the ships, and said that salvation lay only in flight from doomed, conceited Balhop. He warned that things would never be the same again if they didn't all leave the decadent city at once, flee into the hills and forested interior, camouflage themselves in cheap, second hand ragged clothes and meditate on what had gone wrong with their lives.

The soils of the mountain lands were washed down to enrich further the fertile plains which, with a sort of cosmic and quite unfair providence, were a virtual reservoir of abundance and ripe pickings for the lazy city folk. To the surprise of bewildered mountain hermits, amateur climbing enthusiasts and terrestrial scholars who now abandoned their misleadingly glamorous guide books, the mountains themselves, gigantic fortresses as far as the inhabitants of the island were concerned but only 'hills' to visitors from superior Assaland, had become worn down and wasted overnight so that they were left only a semblance of their former selves.[5] The sun, according to Mouth Merrick The Astronomer, had changed too with strange islands crossing its face and a decidedly faded aspect appearing on its cooled, yellow features. The birds appeared to give up their once-constant praising of the skies and to go into cloud-like mourning instead.[6] The rivers, which had once been gentle and often irregular in attendance to their earthly tasks in the dry, sunny days of the halcyon, mythic past became more swollen now, like huge liquid vampires sweeping across exposed and vulnerable lands, their speed being as immense as their

The Madness of Eamon Moriarty 5

breadth and depth. They were now no longer sources of liquid honey to be treasured but gaping, hungry mouths bent on destruction, putting folk and chattels to flight.

"Oh no, oh no," cried the people who lived in the valleys, "our mountains grow ever smaller, and our rivers ever larger. Our leader Top Carrot is wet, and the poor people fret."

This was their way of saying that their leader had broken an unbreakable taboo, using the euphemism, or analogy of a fool standing out in the rain, when he had said that things were not too bad.

It was Halo who noticed major changes taking place in the soil.[7] He pointed excitedly at it one day as he stood in the pouring rain and although the townspeople took no notice of him, and certainly they were not people to be interested in the soil very much, it became evident to them nevertheless that the soil was taking on a red colour. At the same time it looked sickly and was quite unlike the soil they had known as children. Halo said that the people from Assaland were letting in underground poisons to ruin the country by spoiling the land, but Professor Sammy told a quickly-assembled gathering of uninterested scholars (most schools had closed temporarily for the duration of the heavy rains but the soldier-scholars, a select caste of professional thinkers, remained on duty) that the volcano and molten ash that underlay their island was letting out some of its interior essences, most likely in response to all the other changes in the natural environment that were taking place around them.

"It means, I think, that we will have to re-educate the farmers," said a leader.

"The farmers are unchangeable," replied a disillusioned scholar.

"Be that as it may, the mountains and skies are changing, and our farmers have to change with the times," went on the leader.

6 The Madness of Eamon Moriarty

There was a moment of silence at this unfathomable, unprecedented and quite unthinkable idea.

"Change may be forced upon them," continued the leader philosophically, if also with some vindictive satisfaction.

"And upon us too," put in a sensitive, very religious soldier-scholar.[8]

In the following days a chill, or harshness, came into the air and there was a strange freshness about the morning and daytime now that made them all rub their hands and wear warmer clothing (if they could find any). Jalosp, the priest-official, commented enthusiastically on this new atmosphere, or 'sting' (his own word) more frequently than he did on any other topic; more so even than he discoursed on the major features of the turbulent events and unearthly and catastrophic restructuring of the order of nature in that place. He said that it, the chill, was good for the people and it was something that had been needed for a long time. That is, as far as he was concerned, there might be earthquakes and volcanoes and tidal waves and such things but the unchanging character of the people would never change, or be changed, and the chill would keep everybody happy and cool, sensible and levelheaded. This truth he strongly recommended that everyone deeply and steadfastly believe, as even a simple reflection on it would immune them against hardships in the future and make them feel better.

A very fat retired fisherman who had been used to spending his days and evenings walking around the sea-front smoking a great okra pipe and telling yarns to sprokrels and now could no longer do so, had taken to weaving the freshwater variety of web-fish (the sight of these excuses-for-fish made the old seamen weep) in the interior and passing these on to his many sons who were reduced to the, for them, shameful, lower grade occupation of food selling in public market places. It was he who first calculated the seasons since it had

The Madness of Eamon Moriarty

last ceased to rain for any length of time. In that time, he said in the rich hum of his experienced, aged voice, there had been more changes take place in the country than in his own and his father's lifetimes, as well as all of their previous lifetimes. None of these changes had been caused by any human agency. Everybody who heard him speak thus, or who had heard someone else who had heard him, or who had heard someone who had heard someone else who had heard someone who had heard him, did not doubt his word in any way. But there were no means or opportunity for the folk in the interior for comparing his words on these matters with those of the soldier-scholars.

And the birds in the air had an entirely different view of the situation and a different tale to tell. They were becoming angry and menacing, causing much consternation as they blamed man for their misfortune and gathered themselves in swirling flocks to persistently and flagrantly land on the famished, neglected fields and snatch the roden berries which until then had been the community's most valued commodity of exchange in the once-fully, now less-well replenished, market places. This lately ample fruit was becoming as rare as appletans and its scarcity served to worsen further the rigidity of food supplies over the land. So it was that when the alarmed sons went to the fisherman to tap his once-rich source of wisdom which had flowed like oil-gold from old river-beds, the man had replied in an offhand manner and said nothing meaningful except that the birds were simply behaving in their natural fashion much like the star-fish that used to snatch his fish-catch, when he wasn't looking.

"As sharp as sharks,
the star-fish took the lot,
if I wasn't looking;
these birds now behave in the same way."
He looked at them with dead, sad eyes.

8 The Madness of Eamon Moriarty

"Nothing is changed," he said glumly.

The sons wondered at this and shook their heads in impatience at the seeming end of the old man's wisdom.

So it was that after being taken to the Old Wise Sage, in fact just a local, money-making quack, (for the community G.P. had declared him untreatable and barred him from his surgery for fear of driving away his other patients), by liaison officers for help with his psychological problems, Eamon was assured that 'all was okay', that only nature was to blame for his seeming lack of normal development, with rogue hereditary elements the chief culprits. Nobody in the community or Social Services dared to face the unpleasant fact of a possible congenital 'weakness-in-the-head' in the 'problem child', for such an admission of ultimate powerlessness and defeat would have made their on-going theories of social progress, and thus much of their work, redundant. All were strangely relieved that Eamon had come out of the session laughing uncontrollably. In fact to their surprise the conversation seemed to have been mainly about birds and fish; woods and horse racing came into it, too, sometimes. People of that era, in the words of an eminent social critic, 'chose to ignore the realities of rational reasoning as applied to everyday life', easily mistaking it for insanity, as when faced with its unavoidable manifestation in one of their own community who, by his inability to conform to local life (or even to attend the local educational institution), showed that there seemed to be an inexplicable, irrational streak in human nature that rejected all that was set up for its own good.

The changes and revolutionary events were first noticed by Economy, a lad in the hinterland, who dwelt in an enclave on the other side of the Wither woods, a hilly district in the foothills of the Chasemeup Mountains. It was a backward place frequented at different periods by all the mendicant, irascible or migratory people and occupations to be found in

The Madness of Eamon Moriarty 9

that land. Sitting on a waving branch and holding his end up with the grip of strong, red hands, he sat quietly and contemplated eternity in the natural, unending flux of daily events as they moved like memories through some old, familiar dream, each banal or drab sight and sound like that of a dead thought returning from out of its ancient grave to a new, unexpected, but still drab life whose unending gyrations in ever-renewing circles he had once overheard a scholar say was to be the destiny of all on the island.

As he looked out through the pouring drizzle at the bleakness of everything he wondered, for he was feeling very perplexed about the nature of existence at that moment, what it was he was doing there, in that place, at that particular moment in time?[9]

Economy was a young man who had been born on the same day that the country's first illegally elected government, that had fooled the electorate by pretending that all the candidates were out for the good of the country, had publicly declared its own loss of faith in itself and called a general election, offering the country up to any and all-comers who, regardless of credentials or reputation, would take responsibility for it. That this had happened on the very day that Economy was born was taken as a sure sign of his forthcoming, calamitous destiny.[10]

Economy was born at such an ebb tide in the country's affairs that his own mother and father had disowned him immediately and left him out in the open to be devoured by the wild oins.[11] His crib, a long wooden box of tanwood, was rescued from the creatures by his aunt Na, a now-elderly lady who had lost a leg in an oin-bite sometime back in her unrecorded but clearly hapless (to have been anywhere near oins) youth. Economy was reared by this eccentric, one-legged lady in the belief that his own extra leg was abnormal;(perhaps the awkward presence of this leg was

The Madness of Eamon Moriarty

why he also came to believe that everything seen through his right eye was abnormal). He learned to adapt to life by hobbling and pretending that he had just one foot. Life was a burdensome affair for him as well as for his aunt, who spent a lot of her time sticking factory-made pins (cheap, though easily breakable) into a multitude of hereditary dolls, her most prized possessions, and sometimes, shamefully, into other more unmentionable things as well. Her relationship with her nephew was determined by his usefulness as a stick-gatherer. She was implacably talkative whenever he brought in a good bunch, but would be unremittingly hostile if he returned empty-handed. She had developed a piercing cry for the purpose of calling him home. It was said by the neighbours that her shouts of ECONOMY, unfailingly imparted throughout day and night for most of the island's recent history, could be heard many thousands of tall stories away. They became part of daily life, as regular as an early employer-rooster call in the dawn, the roll of the oppressor's thunder at mid-day, the wasteful, sickly, pleasure-fun-seeking coo's cry at dusk, one indeed with all the shimmering cries of the wild beasts and irremediable, plaintiff moaners of that land.

Nowadays Economy's backchat with his aunt was being adversely affected by the decline in the number of trees and the consequent shortage of stick-wood all over the place. The coldness of the days and nights made the absence of a good fire even more distressful, and Na came to communicate only in grunts and shouts, saying over and over again how glorious life would be if only she had not rescued him from the wild oins when he was a baby. He in turn did his best to ignore her ill humour and to throw in the door any old bit of wood he was able to find, hoping that her ladyship might find something to keep her contented, if only for a single moment in the day. This woman had once meant everything to him,

The Madness of Eamon Moriarty

whom he had always called 'mother' until one morning as he lay under a bember tree when he was approximately ten years old with a friend by the name of Ivan, who was indeed his greatest enemy whilst masquerading as his best friend, who told him that everybody around was of the firm impression that he was adopted, that *old Na was certainly not his mother.* This revelation had greatly shocked Economy, as Ivan had meant it to, and it took him a long time to get used to the idea that Na had really nothing to do with his coming in the world at all and that she was only, at most, a distant or even non-blood relative. He became very quiet with her for a while after this and did not call her 'mother' again for quite some time. He eventually came to feel some gratitude towards her when she told the story of his rescue from the oins, and after a while he got used to this idea of having been 'adopted' and became a little proud of the story of his origin and even occasionally called his aunt Na 'mother' again. He always tried to do his best by her and would have defended her in the event of, say, an oin attack being made on her person or an Ebit snatch on her meagre possessions.[12] Nevertheless, their relationship was stormy even at the best of times and Economy spent much effort in an attempt to keep the peace in the household, trying to placate her constant complaining and dodging her wilder outbursts of 'missile' throwing as much as possible.

Now there came a shout through the wood and he heard his name being called and he felt irritated, as an idea had been slowly forming in his mind concerning what he was doing up in the tree, an idea that also gave him an important insight on the country's turbulent history and its present, disastrous plight.[13] Her cries disrupted his flow of thought and brought a temporary confusion to him. He knew that unless he replied, or went home straight away, she would only continue shouting, awakening the island to his prodigal wandering and undermining that special secrecy that he liked to have.

The Madness of Eamon Moriarty

He got down from the tree and hobbled a few paces over to the side, an action he assumed would make a little bit more difficult the discovery of his exact location.

"I'm getting sticks," he shouted.

"There is an oin in the barn," she cried.

There was absolutely no hint in her voice that anything out of the ordinary was happening in the home, which was about the call-carrying distance of one minute's shout (or even a minor, scathing anecdote) through the forest. It only meant that she wanted him back, perhaps to perform some new, meaningless chore to keep him out of the trouble she was ever imagining he was getting into, like talking to strangers who would lead him away on strange, wondrous, fulfilling adventures or, worse still, being hoodwinked into doing unpaid jobs by local, unscrupulous farmers. Oins were the great scapegoats for everything in that island. Their ominous presence lurked behind every aspect of life and thought. Many times in the childhood of the population oins had been called upon as ultimate threats and sanctions against misdemeanours, and as the children of this place were exceptionally naughty so the threat of oins was frequently called upon. It was to the regret of some assiduous people that the number of these hairy, blunt-clawed and toothed, dull-eyed creatures who lived on chewing up the island debris was diminishing throughout the land, due to the removal of the excess woodland and the flooding of sanctuary places. This was indeed something that had been causing a rethink not only among the nannies of the land, and among the unspeakable Ebits who liked to take the foul-smelling furs off the bodies of dead oins, but also by concerned soldier-scholars who, in contrast to the more humble, ordinary scholars who simply liked to read and with whom they were in competition, (the latter were secretly glad for any sign of social or educational deterioration in society which could be blamed on the soldier-scholars), had held this decline of oin-wildlife storytelling to be a symptom of the inevitable decline of a civilization which, against all the odds and contrary to public opinion, they had been trying so hard to improve and bring to perfection.

"I will be back as soon as I have enough sticks," Economy shouted back and then returned, hobbling, to his tree and his meditative pose. From his vantage point he was able to see over a huge part of the surrounding area, and indeed he felt at that moment, in his solitariness, that he was the undisputed, powerful lord of the world.

Eamon had by now reached the natural age of fourteen, although his social isolation in living away from the mainstream of knowledgeable civilization, as did many in those days, meant that he was not fully aware of the latest psychological theories and physical facts on growing up, or even that comfort might be taken in the fact that these were simply mental disturbances accentuated by his body undergoing certain, unfathomable changes whereby the limbs and senses competed to take over each other's roles. It is true to say, along with the experts, that his 'hiding out' was as much an introverted act of (normal) psychological withdrawal as any overt social, economic or political statement initiated by such mechanisms as the benign and invisible 'economic hand' or any blind, irrational distrust or fear for society occasioned by the threat of some subversive, alien power. At the end of the day, as one sensible person asserted, countryside living is very much a solitary experience, and the mind is allowed to expand to its farthest dimensions in the timeless hours one spends there with silent, insidious Mother Nature.

Three Tennits wearing their felt-cap hoods were passing down the rock and boulder strewn roadway, followed at close quarters by two ex-coastal fishermen. Each one had on his shoulder a bag containing some illicitly obtained goods. The liaison between the Tennits and the fishermen had not escaped the notice of all decent folk in the region and this phenomenon was held by them all to be a mystery and a bit of a scandal.

Economy studied the five figures with curiosity. The fishermen, he noticed, being fatter were finding it difficult to keep up with the pace set by the Tennits. He knew of the dislike and suspicion with which the Tennits and fishermen were held by the farmers and everybody in the world but this only strangely increased the esteem he felt for them. He experienced an inner glow at the thought that peace and friendship could exist in society between two such disparate groups whilst all everyone else seemed to do was fight with their kith and kin. He felt he even wanted to call out a greeting to them. He was constrained from doing so by the fact that his position in the woods would then immediately become known. Wisely, and showing a political awareness beyond his years, he held his silence.

The group took a short respite from the drizzle, which was ever-increasing in intensity, under a bullwash tree at the side of the track and they stared out over the region, not speaking to one another at all. Economy thought they must be very tired after a long walk. Eventually they moved off again and went around a bend, going very quietly. There was a strange air of timelessness about their movements in that glade that made him feel that time itself, and the whole world, was coming to a full stop.

Economy was now able to go back to what he had originally been doing. He surveyed the distant bushes once more, checking the lay out of the local farmers' plots and observing where there was any sign of activity. Dark, wet smoke was rising from a number of damp fires in the distance and he could hear the chopping of firewood. He now concentrated his attention on a grassy bank, for it was here that the chickens were accustomed to wander. In particular, he devoted most attention to the area of nettles near Farmer McCrachan's property, a man noted for the plumpness of his fowl. With some excitement he heard a prideful crowing and spotted a fat bird ambling over in his direction. His excitement mounted, slowly at first and then at a rapidly increasing rate so that he was scarcely able to control himself.

He prepared his net, which was attached to a series of long strings with stones at the end, which he took out from under his scandalously unfashionable oin hair-skin jacket. He lay in wait, slithery like a tree snake, on a lower limb of the strong branch overlying the track along which the bird was approaching. Then in a flash he silently dropped the net and hauled in the bird.[14]

Eamon was filled immediately with deep shame and loathing at another impetuous act of his guilt-ridden, ignorant, damnable life. He vowed to himself that he would resist temptation the next time. It was as if nature herself was deliberately tempting him with this prize, filling him with an urge he could not control. And what would happen if his right-living, most virtuous uncle, Tom Curran, who he always imagined was watching over his life, if only at a distance, ever get to hear of his lack of self-control and his criminal deeds?

Top Carrot, the soaked, popular valley people's leader, called a meeting that evening in his run-down barn that was the driest place in the whole region.[15] He called all his own people, a clan of insecure small farmers who had become increasingly bellicose and impatient due to the economic decline, as well as all the surrounding hillside peasants who were considered by the lower valley people to be a class of poorer relations. It was a general characteristic of the island people, as beheld by

The Madness of Eamon Moriarty

Assaland observers, that they were a people addicted to leaders. There were great leaders and sub-leaders with many other kinds of leaders in between, all attempting to have the first say or the last word on everything. Frequent, undeclared elections, 'coups' and counter-coups, carried out by the 'have you heard the latest' gossips in society were a great tradition and no other nation on the planet could boast of such a preponderance and proliferation of leaders of different kinds. It was a way of life that nobody had ever explained properly or discovered the origins of; they had a word for it, 'democracy', which when said out loud had a way of shutting people up if they were making nuisances of themselves. It was totally different to the Dictatorial system in Assaland, where ordinary people were not allowed any say and leadership of any kind was forbidden. The highest development of this tradition was reached in Economy's own hinterland, where in one small hamlet all of the inhabitants had been appointed, by themselves, as leaders with only one exception, a poor river labourer who was the solitary, resigned subject in that mini-kingdom. But even this village owed some begrudging allegiance to Top Carrot, whose name had become widely known by continual repetition, and was often mentioned in places outside that immediate district. Indeed talk of his great reputation had extended to the capital, Balhop, and accounts of his supposed achievements and follies were repeated there; (there had been a snowballing process, petty boasts growing into legendary achievements, and acts of minor charity becoming myths of miraculous generosity). On one occasion he had even been visited by important people from the capital and his opinion sought on a matter of rural etiquette, necessitated by a visit from a wealthy, gift-bearing Ex-Tennit they were all anxious to impress, who had come back looking for his lost roots. Top had shown him around all the hovels in the district.

The Madness of Eamon Moriarty 17

Top Carrot, (*Uncle Top, as he was known to the hero-worshipping Economy*), spoke roundly and squarely to everybody, completely unaware of the hypnotic effect he was having on the lad hiding away in one corner of the building. He spent three-quarters of the speech greeting people and then eventually disclosed, in a sorry voice, the shocking news that the honour and rights of an honest small farmer had been abused again that day and another fine fowl had mysteriously disappeared. The rash of thieving had become a distressful problem that made Heaven itself cry out for vengeance! Despite his reluctance to think ill of others, and as a politician it was his duty to foster good community relations, it was now apparent to him that the Tennits and the fishermen had been up to no good and were making the rest of the community pay for their own economic failure, their personal impurities and anti-social deviltry. Five of these folk were seen walking through the district that day and, in the course of a canvassing campaign for the forthcoming election, a united attack under his command had been made on them. One of their number, whom they had held for the purpose of filling in a questionnaire, had been 'accidently' killed despite Top's best efforts to make sure that things did not get out of hand. The fatality had been no-one's-fault-in-particular. The killing of the slower Tennit, a weak, seedy sort of individual, might admittedly be seen as 'an act against one's fellow man' (murder of one's neighbour was still considered immoral at that time), but then again it might serve as a warning to others. In future these strangers might, hopefully, refrain from passing down their way. There was an air of hopelessness and depression in the region now, said Top Carrot, such as he himself had never felt before and petty back-biting and party jostling (even among complete strangers who were just passing each other on the trackways, upsetting people who were keeping themselves to themselves and minding their own business) were increasing all over the place.

"I will have to go to Balhop without further delay," said the leader solemnly, his head hurting with the guilt of delivering a falsehood and knowing that he was betraying all that he had ever stood for (at least in his speeches) by concealing his real motives for wanting to depart 'temporarily' for the capital; "in order to find out from our learned men and leaders what it is that's happening in this land and why it is that the peace of the old days has gone and it rains without cease and the rivers and mountains are tumbling down and the moon and the sun are hidden as are the stars and food is scarce and strange characters walk up and down our village roads."

The assembled multitude, in order to show their distress at Top's departure and also to demonstrate their sense of communal guilt at the accident to the stranger, were laughing and smiling and drinking their bubble drinks in a great commotion and sing song and, all being leaders in their own right, stood up and shouted acclaim together for Top Carrot and wished him well on his journey and told him he could stay away as long as he liked.

Eamon left the hall at the community centre where he had been hiding behind a tall trestle as the implications of his own criminal act came to him. He now realised that he had been the cause of a murder, and would now be responsible for all consequent communal troubles, including the imminent outbreak of war. The crack of doom sounded in his head and he found it difficult to see clearly even through his good eye. He could not retain his bodily balance or sense of direction with the weight of guilt and foreboding as he departed, leading others to notice his strange mannerisms and comment with whispers and sideway looks on the deteriorating condition of the lad.

Notes

1 - The early part of the book seems to revolve around the childhood experiences of the author. While the Cork professors believe that this 'deluge' refers to The Flood, Dr Crane is of the opinion that the young Eamon/Economy was depressed by the weather a lot and might have been left out in the rain as a very young child. But the Corkonians are clearly determined that their county is not slandered in any way.

Great controversy centres on the identity of Balhop. Dr Crane and Galway hold firmly that it is Cork City, whilst the eminent Corkonians state that it is none other than Ur, the first great city of the world. There are indeed similarities between the two cities. Ur was on the great river Euphrates and it too had a favourable position for commerce and political dominance. Ur was the centre for Moon worship, whilst references to the Moon in Eamon's text are certainly not innocent. Both Cork and Ur had three dynasties of rulers. Although Cork's Ziggurat has not yet been unearthed, there is clear evidence for an almighty Flood both in Ur's archaeological ruins and in the moss-festooned buildings in and around Cork.

2 - This paragraph raises a number of points. The author's design in calling his land 'the island' is a puzzle until we remember that the civilised or literate world tends to look upon any barbarous region as an 'island', and this derogatory appellation would probably have impressed itself on the writer's sub-conscious. Another anomaly is Eamon's habit of giving strange nicknames to his neighbours, and indeed this inability to use the correct name for many ordinary objects or even normal people is symptomatic of his condition. In reference to the author's aversion to the sea, Dr Crane also points to a probably apocryphal story that, on the occasion of his being taken on a day-trip to the seaside by 'social workers' for the first time, Eamon had been greatly frightened by the overwhelming sight of the ocean, to the unsuppressed amusement of all concerned.

It is possible that the 'infighting' here and between various groups mentioned elsewhere in the text are coded references to the traumatic conflicts between, and eventual defeat of, the Sumerians by the Babylonians. However it may also be pointed out that frequent infighting amongst different Gaelic football teams in the area had a dramatic effect on the impressionable Eamon (these village blood feuds went on for years, often from generation to generation), who was quite unable to distinguish between the game and the bloodshed, as was discovered later when attempts were made at the school (and later asylum) to have him 'play Gaelic'.

3 - Here, in Crane's opinion, we have not so much an intermixing and fusion of significant, disparate cultures as Eamon's first impressions of the man-woman relationship, perhaps inadvertently stumbled across in some back field or gripe under a lay-by, something basically natural to human beings but which he was never really to come to grips with in his life. The doctor's exploration of his patient's unconscious jabberings (observed whilst the chap was under the influence of a new, experimental rehabilitation programme called 'speaking in the national language', a therapy probably derived from the Viennese School) revealed many such mismatches and wrong identifications in his appreciation of the normal goings on of life, as shall be seen.

4 - The Galway professors and the doctor concur that Assaland could refer to the Dublin Pale, whilst in those days it was easier to go by sea from Dublin to Cork. The Cork people insist it refers to the perfidious 'Empire' of whatever hue, such oppressive encumbrances as have always dominated human history at every age. The mineral referred to is probably the Cork stone, useless to the Corkonians themselves.

5 - Deep psychoanalysis revealed this to be a misunderstanding of a geography lesson Eamon once attended. As we shall soon see the existence of a school nearby did far more harm than good to Eamon, even in the short period he spent therein. Needless to say the Cork university people hold that this piece refers to the gigantic geomorphologic movements over millions of years that affected not only Cork but the whole world.

6 - Disturbances amongst the bird population are a constant feature of Eamon's pre-occupations and could be a motif reflecting the dark forces and fears in his own mind. University of Cork experts have very little to say about erratic bird behaviour.

(A Junior lecturer claims that it could have something in common with The Plague Of Locusts).

7 - The matter of the changed constituents of the soil, which recurs in this book, is a reflection of a deep inner insecurity amongst a mainly rural people.

The Madness of Eamon Moriarty

However it must be said that there was a belief that when land was appropriated by the invader it somehow changed its very nature, reflected in the superstition about the requirement to 'dig with the other foot'. But it is also an illustration of the dangers of a little (in this case geological) education, furthering the case for the banning of all science and technical education in the schools in the region, as put forward later by the Lasdiacs.

8 - Farmers have been seen as heralds of civilization throughout history. But, to the likes of Eamon a landless, roving stick collector (or 'hedge-shatterer', in the parlance of the farmers), their narrow-mindedness and anti-social intolerance as experienced during many run-ins and vindictive pursuits made it hard to see any virtue in their much spoken of, traditional-farmer's-robust-resistance-to-change or any disruption in society. Anti-farmer gloating was not beyond the ken of even this wayward lad, a certain satisfaction seemingly being taken in seeing the onset of that which hits the farmer hardest – bad weather.

9 - This coming to critical consciousness, reputedly (according to the Cork School) similar to that experienced by the first human being, Adam, as he sat up and looked around for the first time; could also be seen as the start of Eamon's adolescent problems as he began 'to think for himself' in what was clearly the beginning of what was going to be an unusually difficult transition from childhood to adulthood.

10 - As Franz Fanon has illustrated in his linking of all psychiatric problems to the phenomenon of colonialism, (he would have a deep insight into madness for by constantly trying, and failing, to cure it in subject people he would have finally exposed his own judgement to those deep, questioning doubts about reality that threatens one's own sanity; that is, if he wanted to retain even a semblance of self-respect as a practising professional), there is a profound relationship between the guilt and self-blame of the lower classes, and the shame of the conquered.

11 - In relating this tale of his origins to her 'adopted' child it is not to be assumed that Na necessarily understood all the biological facts of life either. Meanwhile, Cork members of the committee have not failed to point out the similarities with the story of the infancy of Moses.

12 - Ebits were an outcast sect classified as sub-human so that nobody in the island would ever have to admit to being related to them. They were avoided

at all times by the people – that is if they valued their sense of self-worth or even their powers of rational discrimination.

13 - It is here that we begin to see Eamon confusing his own psychological state, his numerous and increasingly difficult personal problems in an intimate, intricate way with the political and socio-economic history of his country. Later on it would become difficult for him to distinguish between the two.

14 - Some of Academia, motivated by Religious Orthodoxy, say that the 'capturing of the rooster' was Eamon's Original Sin, equivalent to the eating of the forbidden fruit in the Garden of Eden. Needless to say the age-old conflict in the Near East between the settled agricultural communities (Cain) and the nomadic pastoral tribes and their camp following brigands (Abel), could also be related to this. However, most medical experts conclude that a sexual sin is involved and critical analysis has shown that 'Rooster Stealing' was probably a euphemism for some other more serious, taboo-ridden crime of the time.

15 - Top Carrot (or Tom Curran), a protector-uncle figure in Eamon's life, though his real kinship to the lad is obscured in the mist of mystery.

chapter two

*E*conomy rested in the interior of his bed and felt relaxed after the attainment of bodily satisfaction. To soothe the increasingly intense phantom pain of his second leg he had imagined that he was walking like any other normal person through the woodlands and glades, and at a moment that was unpredictable and instantaneous, he was totally relieved of the pain. Peace fell in a silent, gentle stillness around him, in the manner in which blessed relief comes after the release of much tension. He relaxed his muscles and breathed contentedly and was unperturbed in the quiet surroundings of the old house that was the abode of Economy and Na. As he lay there he wriggled his toes in his fur socks and hummed to himself (Aunt Na had been out when he came back, so all the shouts had been a diversion by her.) He welcomed the quiet of the house at moments like these. How much he preferred solitude to the irksome company of people and the hustle and bustle of the world.

He rested and through his mind there went images of the things that gave him happiness (lately they were becoming more scarce): the noise of whistling trees and falling sticks; the sweet smell of the sun rising in the morning and the glow and crackle of its evening setting; the pale rise of his old friend moon over the magical ear-chorus of the fields and the heavenly message-sounds of the bird-carried, visiting wind: these were a greater happiness to his senses than either the vain-glorious sound of men's chatter or the sight of their handiwork. It was the woody lane or the quiet byway that was

Economy's walking ground rather than the busy highways and tracks that men frequented. The ditch or solitude of a peaceful field was of more interest to him than the noisy and public village street or busy, people-crowded crossroads. It was a sleep under a wild bember tree that was a refreshment to him rather than a night's joviality over bubble drink in a barn.[1]

Occasionally Economy felt the need of some other company. A strange pang of sadness and loneliness would seize him and he would approach a person on a lane or thoroughfare or even go into a barn where people were in revelry inside; but he was always ejected on such occasions and a cruel, debased pleasure taken in giving him 'a right trashing' (the favourite expression of island disciplinarians), on such occasions. He assumed that his troubles were due to their disquiet at the sight of his cumbersome, awkward, useless extra leg, as well as perhaps his lack of social 'finesse' caused by, amongst other things, the absence of a proper schooling.[2] Everybody else in the world had attended the schools. How he wished that he had been accepted there, and had not been thrown out after an unsuccessful, single day of supposed 'learning' in the much-vaunted institution.

He sighed, thinking of a great, lost opportunity. In the lauded and respected learning places, where every young islander was expected to attend in his or her youth, they picked up the rudiments of island carving and mud bashing and they also learned the National Song of the country. Economy had not stayed there long enough for any of this and he had been out stick collecting from an early age. So he did not even know the National Song. For much of his life (until recently when his more evident unsightliness and strange walk made others a little more circumspect about openly mocking him), the youths and lassies had laughed whenever they saw him. Such he had believed to be the case, as they were always standing around in talkative, chortling groups whenever he passed by. It was only later that he realised that that they did not even see him at all, for whenever he tried to catch their attention by a wave or a 'hello' they never gave any response. Aunt Na explained it was because he was 'not all there', that he did not have the 'brains' to learn anything and that he was only good for stick collecting and breaking firewood.[3] He was puzzled by what she meant. What did it mean to be 'not all there'? What were 'brains'? Was their absence a curse like his bad leg, something that had been an oversight in the making of him? Perhaps he had misplaced his brains somewhere and they were just lying around waiting to be picked up again? But he did not ask Aunt Na about these or other things for too often her answers simply raised more questions. Instead he dwelt on the problems in his own head and tried to examine them from every angle, turning the questions each way, inside, outside, up and down in search of enlightenment. As the last tiny bit of peace he had been enjoying left him now sadness overcame him and he wondered if indeed it really would have been any use to have gone regularly to a school. Would it have meant that his 'bad' leg might be giving him less trouble now, that he would have obtained those 'brains' which would have made up for what else there was missing in him? He felt the strain of a strange force battering behind his eyes and as the sadness dulled his face and a shadow seemed to dissolve his whole appearance he was once more trapped in that dejection which was as familiar to him as the onset of the day and seemed to forever hold him in its twilight world.

Eamon, as so often when he returned from his rustic forays, had lain on his bed and as the dark clouds of despondency came over once again and he felt a great pain and disquiet in his body he found himself ruminating over another disconcerting puzzle – how it had been that he had seen Na with water coming out of her eyes one day as she had sat in the corner, emitting a strange wailing sound. He had observed this disturbing event again since, especially after she had spent some time staring at him in a curious way. What was this inexplicable behaviour? And why could he not shed those same 'globules of water'? Then the worry left him as he fell into a dream in which he was walking through the darkness of a womb-like wood and then suddenly exiting, with a feeling of peace and relief, into the sunlit happiness of a bright glade.

In place of its usually placid, sleepy countenance his face now had an open, wide-eyed look. He shivered as he felt a chill. Three or four sticks were lying on the floor, in the spot where in that once-tropical land (they always talked about the days when their ancestors had basked under an unblemished tropical sun. The country's unfortunate displacement from its previously happy location to its now desultory position in the cosmos had been explained to him by the teacher in that geography lesson on the single day he had spent in school, in terms of a story of eviction of some people called Adam and Eve from a place named the Garden of Eden. He said that this was why the island had all that rain now), fires were traditionally lit for cooking; though now it was more often the case that such a fire was for the heating of cold flesh rather than the preparation of nourishing food. He was feeling too lethargic and disinterested to move; he just lay there and indulged in one of the tricks of the imagination and saw the incipient sparks of a newly-lit fire begin in his inner eye and already he felt the glow of its magical flames and felt the warmth of its invisible heat. These were better than ordinary fires for they were less effort to start and were warmer. His sticks would burn for a long time as some quality in them provided great longevity in burning; (in fact they seemed to burn without end, a phenomenon cynical scholars would say was caused simply by the amount of dampness in the wood rather than any magical quality) though now it seemed that the constitutional dampness was affecting even these metaphysical fires, making them dimmer and more smoke-infested lately, just like ordinary fires in fact, despite the best efforts of the imagination. Yet the fires that Economy initiated from his resting place sometimes had a spiritual quality, softly glowing in their heat, rising like prayer as a comfort, a relief from the coldness of the world.

In this warmth he luxuriated and he listened with his best ear to the falling rain and a sort of temporary contentment entered into him again. After a short period, measured by the brief spate of a chorus of insect-wing beatings to the number of three complete beats, the thud of an equal quantity of branch-drops outside, and the intake of three complete sighs he heard the clatter of Aunt Na's foot approaching the door. Normally he would have felt the warmth that simply comes from familiar habit, which consisted of listening with a deep resignation to the erratic approach of her bag-carrying, swearing, inevitably disruptive company but he felt, strangely, greatly indifferent to her now. This, in its way, was uncharacteristic, his new independence of outlook, although the immediate cause had been her annoying diversionary tactic earlier in the day. He was disdainful as she hobbled in on one leg through the leafy doorway, dripping wet in her oin coat-skin and with a discarded Tennit's sack over her head and her briny face hidden in a net made of wood-spiders' web in order to protect it from the biting insects and the evil spells of the Astronomical monks whom she had a particular fear of. She did not seem to be all that pleased to be home from another day's shopping expedition and it was with irritation that she dumped her heavy bag on the floor with a clatter.

She spoke in a shrill voice, saying that in the bag were three roden berries that she had found lying on the side of the road on the way to Dumnill. Somebody must have dropped them there and it was her good fortune to have found them. She lifted the sack with her root-like hands and out of it tumbled all manner of things: old nut-seeds, frazzles, bean sprouts, a good-sized chip off an old block and one curious item, a fisherman's boot. Economy for his part pointed to a corner of the room where lay a pile of his own day's takings. In addition to the sticks there was one roden berry and a few bones that, he said, he had found outside a barn. Na's face crinkled up with satisfaction at the sight of the sticks. She sat down without a word on her one good hunker and rested her limbs. She was silent with pleasure at the prospect of hopefully soon seeing the lad light up a nice warm fire. She spoke at the end of this moment of happy anticipation:

"I saw some good trees standing down on the Dumnill road today. I believe you could do worse than to go down there tomorrow and chop some branches off them. We will build up a huge pile of wood if you concentrate on the trees instead of picking up measly stick specimens from the ground, and forget your foolish fear of being caught by the farmers. The way things are going to be we will be the richest people in the whole district one day and they will all be coming to beg little bits of twigs off us and we will not let them have any."

Economy put away his anger and impatience with Na for a while and grinned at her, saying that it was a stroke of luck finding the three berries and now they had four and they could make roden soup. He just might take a look at the trees down that way tomorrow. He didn't think that he had been over in the Dumnill direction in a long time. On the last occasion, before the big rains, when he had been down that way he had come across an old witch who lived in a house with a black cat. This cat, he said in voice now suddenly trembling, appeared to have strange powers that its mistress put to no-good use. It had sat in the middle of the road and

The Madness of Eamon Moriarty

spat at him, refusing to let him pass. He had turned and ran away in the opposite direction. He would certainly give the house a miss if he happened to pass that particular way again. He would have to find a roundabout route and hope he wouldn't be seen by her cat. He would report the witch and her cat to Top Carrot the next time he saw him.

"That was no witch, you fool," shouted Na, "but it was your old sweet Aunt Rosie who was most overjoyed at your coming. She sent out a great welcome to you and you hurled insults at her in return, you dunderhead. To this day she has not got over it; she says you turned into the devil himself. I was up there again today trying to make my peace with her and to get her to welcome us once more into her home. There will be nobody left to speak to us soon. Oh, the day I took you in was the blackest day of my life!"

Economy shook his head.

"Aunt Na. There is nobody in the Dumnill direction who we are related to. We do not have one friend up that way and there is no such person as Aunt Rosie. It was a dangerous witch with a black cat."

"The amount of trouble you have brought me is sufficient for many lifetimes. Only that fraudster Top Carrot ever comes here and all he is after is a good bunch of sticks. I hope that you are not thinking of emulating *him* in life?"

Eamon, after an anxious and difficult day, asked his mother whether she had heard the recent news about Uncle Tom, that he was leaving the district and going to the city for an indefinite period. Who was going to come to their aid now? It was Uncle Tom who had always given them advice, especially when Economy was in serious trouble, such as the time he was accused of chasing young girls. Tom Curran had been able to explain everything to the satisfaction of all. Eamon was worried at the thought of Top going away. It was true that T.C. never actually said that he was his uncle, or even that he was related at all to either of them, but there is no doubt that he was an altruistic benefactor, a sole friend in a friendless world, a giant among the giants of philanthropy, a credit to his own mother and father and not least, to the Creator Himself.

Economy sighed and listened to Na's criticisms and thought that nothing he ever did would be correct in her sight. Lately he had become more aware of her scorn for him, making him the scapegoat for everything. He spoke now with the strength of a new inflection in his voice:

"I bring you sticks every day, I protect you from the oins and the unruly neighbours when they come by. I find wild berries and leftover bones for you and many is the bonus I bring for your diet. Drink I have on many occasions taken for you from unwatched barns, yet you say I am not your son."

"Is it any wonder? You were born that day when the government was disastrously elected, and your birth was a disaster for the general social and economic welfare of the country."[4]

She gave a bitter cackle, as of one who has somehow been put upon in life.

"Your parents' departure was unlamented, and they were never seen again by anybody. Their instruction was that you should never receive any schooling, that you be hidden out of sight and that you see and hear as little of the outside world as possible. Only as much as is required for stick gathering was to be your sum. I have done my best to carry out their wishes, (even if I failed that day you sneaked off to the school). It has done you well to be living such a safe life here in the woods with your old Aunt Na looking after you, collecting sticks every day and not bothering about other things. But now you are beginning to annoy me by asking questions that are not like the questions you asked in the past. Today your questions make sense, and that is worse."

Her words were spoken in a high-pitched tone that was both angry and fearful.

"Tell me again how it was that you found me and took me in with the gold that is in your heart," he said softly, trying to placate her; "do you still regret it even when I tell you of the mighty dreams that I have?"

Na hobbled towards him and for a moment he thought that she was actually going to touch him. He felt that if she did he would die from gratitude and joy. For, as far as he could remember, she had never once had physical contact with him in his life. But nothing happened as she simply walked past him and sat in the corner.

She put down the stick she had been inspecting on the catmat at her foot and tapped the ground with her toes in impatience both at the raindrops that still were attached to them and at Economy's childish and despicable request. From his earliest days he had asked strange questions, seemingly possessing great ideas of himself and of his 'destiny' in the world. He was always wondering about where he came from and where he would 'end up'. She remembered his childhood days when he would chase the elusive beagle-moths in the sky, or try vainly to catch the wild rat cats in the topmost branches of the bullwash trees, and looking extremely foolish on such fruitless quests; or else, as was another habit, staring at the ground for hours seeing nothing in particular there; and she had laughed at his childishness and silliness and shaken her head, wondering what went on in his head.

She now, surprisingly, told him more about the parents about whom she had said she knew nothing.

"Your dad left you with not a tear in his eye, and went back to Balhop because he could not prevent your birth. Your ma was a hopeless lady; she wished to go with your dad but couldn't because all the stars in the sky were fixed firmly against her. She tried to move the stars and make them go to a different place in the heavens but they would not go. For many long, hopeless days and nights I watched her desperate efforts. Your dad was a man of rich blood, but your ma's blood was poor ditchwater. At the time everybody blamed on your birth not only the mishap of the new government, but the excess rains of that year (as well as the last great drought the year before) on the absence of any hair on your head; the demise of the tireless patriarch fisherman king who had brought great fish wealth to the shores on the weakness of your eyes; and the nuisance of the government's new economic and social policy on your large ears and ungainly feet. That is the reason I took you in, for after hearing the judgement of the whole country your ma tried to have you taken away by the Ebits, and when they refused to have you, eaten by the wild oins. But I took you in for your usefulness in stick gathering. That is your story."

Economy was mystified by the whole story. He thought now of a recent comment of Ivan's, made as they accidentally met for a moment on the local trackway, to the effect that 'to consider your birth as that of a normal human being is generally considered sacrilegious around these parts'. This remark was delivered in the superiority and confidence imparted by all the new knowledge and erudite pronunciation Ivan had gained from his time in the school.

"Is it true that my mother is far away and forbidden from ever returning to this region?"

"It is true that she has gone and has vanished. She has changed her garments and appears now as a butterfly does after it has left the state of being a caterpillar. She has become an entirely different person in the turn of the years and the glooms. You would not know her now if you saw her, and she would not know you at all. And your father may be anywhere."

These words about his other mother hurt Economy so that his neck became riveted with the strain of keeping his head from separating from the rest of his body and it was with some effort that he maintained all his body in a normal position.

"One day I will go to Balhop and maybe I will run into my father in that place. Is Balhop like any place that I know of?[5]

Economy wondered to himself what it was that Uncle Top and all the others saw in that city, the Big Smoke as it was sometimes called by those who had come back boasting of having visited it. Why was it that so many people left their homes and kinfolk and headed for that destination? Was it just the glum hills and the sinister woods they were fleeing from, or was there something cursed and malign about living in the countryside that made everybody there obstreperous and vindictive? He thought again of all the evil signs that, he had been told, had accompanied his birth and life up to now.

"Balhop", said Na, opening her mouth wide in an annoyed intake of noisy breath and twisting her nostrils at the strong odours and wisps of the (still imaginary) smoke that were in the room, "is a dark place in a spot that was first chosen by the younger, ne'er-do-well gods for the locating of water troughs for their unicorn chariots (and the goat carts of their hangers-on) and hence it will always be a shifty and treacherous locality that is meant to be visited by country folk only on urgent, impending matters and otherwise better left to the tramps and upper class of wayfarers. But because the weather there is exceptionally rich with winds and choice mushrooms grow well in the ground travellers are loath to leave it and it has become a place of some prosperity with a strange fame throughout the land. However the wisest country folk usually are very unwilling to go into Balhop as, for one thing, it is most likely that they will get lost in the huge cavities that exist there and never return to their beloved homes. It is a fearsome place for many of our neighbours and relatives have been known to vanish behind its high boundary walls, and when a few have occasionally returned to the world outside they are individuals unknown to their mothers and carry strange smells and hawk obnoxious goods with a strange banter of unknown words. It is very hard to understand all about Balhop and it would be better that the mention of the town does not come to your lips. It is said that there are many entryways into Balhop but there is only one way out again. Few are those who can find this way out and those who do escape are marked in the struggle by a great twitching in the fingers that are made useless thereafter for countryside tasks. There also comes on them an unquenchable wish to return to the terrible place, a wish that gives them no peace and never leaves them thereafter. One man told me of the buildings in Balhop. He said, and his voice sounded terrible as he said it, that there was nothing more frightening than those buildings anywhere else, for they were more like great, underground caverns than buildings and he was always afraid to enter them. There was a spot of trouble on the main highway in Balhop once and he found himself pushed into one of these buildings against his will and this experience had affected him badly for weeks, for he had not been able to find his way out for a long time. He had found himself inside a cage, like what they keep wild animals locked in, and there was a man with a key who would not let him out. Also, he said, the people there are very noisy and they are not able to get on with one another for they all have different opinions on every topic under the sun. They even go into special buildings where they place money on the truth or falsehood of these opinions. They have an exceptional hostility for people like yourself – they do not like to see your type wandering in the streets. Now, will you go to the pit and get me a drop of something to drink and you can have a taste yourself, just a sip mind you, for bringing in the sticks and don't be troubling me with questions. I have enough worries as it is."

Notes

1 - It has not escaped the notice of critics that here we have the author writing in that peculiar style that is to be found in ancient Gaelic scripts. The two schools of thought diverge here. The Cork people hold that his mode of expression represents the subconsciously entrapped language of a rural and ancient people, in this instance the Celts, here emerging in a statement of primitive, basic needs and fetishes reduced to an even cruder form by centuries of poor education; the Galway school say that there is no such thing as a quantifiable 'race consciousness', that Eamon had copied all this from an old book he found somewhere. Some clues as to the identity of this old book are to be found in the text, they say.

2 - Eamon's peculiar physical appearance and mental anguish was one of the factors that cast for him a role not unlike that of an afflicted Biblical prophet in that community. This, at any rate, was the theory of the religious branch of the Cork school that was anxious to push the idea that Eamon was some sort of 'holy idiot'. Galway insists that Eamon was already simply and plainly mad or at the very least, an unreconstructed 'anti-social' as evidenced by his stubborn belief that the beatings and ostracising were sure signs that the local community was rejecting him.

3 - Wild berry and stick collecting represent man's earliest, indeed primeval, form of economic behaviour. The idea that such a livelihood remained extant in the county of Cork in the twentieth century has been a source of much emotional denial; hence the Cork thesis that this manuscript's origin could only have a date in primeval times (before the age of printing – editor). Independent experts have definitively proven that the paper it was written could only have existed from the beginning of the twentieth century onwards. Galway gives a date of 1946.

4 - These misconceptions are probably a result of the faulty information dissemination system that prevailed in the country at the time, with simple people being harangued by the many leaders on the dire state of the country, and the blame being placed on obscure and innocent scapegoats.

5 - The migration to Balhop, which is a key event in this narrative, reflects in many ways the many, great world wide treks that have so dominated history, leading to the downfall of great civilizations and empires and the rise of new ones. A dominant theme is the purging of that civilization which has become soft and ineffective in its townie, lazy, often coastal (allowing access to easy pickings) way-of-life to be replaced by that of a more uncouth, mountain or country people who, initially and awkwardly, such as by means of the example of raucous behaviour in public and private places, but later more subtly by marrying the man-hungry ladies of the effeminate society, impose their own unrefined ways on the population.

chapter THREE

Na went to a corner of the room and disappeared behind a high canvas curtain. A little later Economy dragged himself across the floor like an old sack of potatoes, as he had not the energy to walk on his good leg. He went outside and after some time came back with two bottles of coaloil; not the common bubble drink but a most inaccessibly sourced liquor; it was a natural drink that fermented deep within the volcanic bowels of that country. It was held by the wise to be a good cure for thinking, feeling or worrying about life, family, job or one's eternal fate. Although its effects were such as to make some wary of it, (these people never did well in life; it was also significant that the Assalanders themselves never touched it), for it was said to cause madness, death, violent crime, physical abuse of one's nearest and dearest and neglect of duties, this was not seen as an impediment for the advantages of passing long periods of time out of this world in a stupor far outweighed the disadvantages. Economy and Na consumed large amounts and there were no side effects of any kind resulting from their indulgence of it. As the oin-wax candle was lit to show in its smudge light the shadows of the old house and the new night's creamy darkness was creeping in through every nook and cranny and the sounds of buckets' wings beating and the hand-claps of oily-owls chattering increased in crescendo to fill the night and the soft thud of the rain continued in its tap dance they drank their fill from the bottles, feeling its warmth so that they did not need the imaginary fire anymore.

After a while Na became more amenable. She asked Economy if he had lately dreamed one of his big dreams. He had a way of revealing curious knowledge through these night-time reveries. Indeed it was this shutting down of his normal faculties in sleep that Na thought probably explained this acquiring of an unconscious wisdom.

Economy said that he did have a big dream a few nights before.

"I do not know what it means, yet," he said in a sullen voice, for he never liked to reveal the details of his dreams. When he did recount one it was always with a strict censoring of the more outlandish details. "I was on a high mountain, but I felt myself to be even bigger, and the mountain became smaller and smaller so that I looked down the mountain and saw all the island below me like a little dot in a large expanse of water. It was surrounded by the whole world. The longer I stared the smaller did the dot become so that it was on the point of disappearing altogether and I had a great feeling of power. It lifted me up much higher so that I felt I could easily go to wherever I wanted. I thought to myself, I do not have to live in this tiny spot forever! I took off, flying right across the world and over a huge expanse of water. I went through the night and was not afraid of dropping into the ocean's great depths. My hands and foot kept me up and this seemed perfectly natural to me. I saw another high mountain in the night in a southern land where I landed. A man with one red eye, who spoke a language I did not understand, chased me until I flew away and found myself in an even stranger distant place that was covered with many buildings. These were very tall and made of red bricks. He was still behind me and shouted for money. I had to leave the ground again in order to escape. I did not know for what purpose I was in those places, although it may have been that I had arrived there by accident. Then I came down to see you, Na, who are still my mother, and I held you tightly in the joy at having escaped that red-eyed man, and I rose up again before you could set an eye on me. By that time light had come back into the world and I had a clear view of the island again. It was blue in the sunlight and all the rain had stopped and it was clear again and very dry."

Na had a startled look and her voice was very high:

"What?" she cried, "there were red marks on my throat this morning and I dreamt I was being suffocated by a great, big ugly ogre and I nearly expired for lack of breath."

She went silent for a moment with the shock. Then, with wonder, she cried:

"But you say you saw the island dry again? That is most important, celebratory news."

"Yes, it was just like it used to be, dry and bright and the sun was a sight for sore eyes."

Na spoke in a mood of excitement, her distress at having being nearly suffocated to death by Economy the night before temporarily forgotten:

"Should the rains stop soon, it will be of immense benefit to us both. We will have food again in abundance and there will be dry sticks aplenty. People will not blame us for the destruction anymore, and we will not be chased out of so many districts! I will now be able to go and tell everyone that the rains are soon to end. I will get gifts, and much respect and friendship for that good news and we will not remember these days again. You must not say anything about this dream to anybody. I will be the harbinger of the Good News!"

"Aunt Na, it was only a dream. What if the rains do not stop? Then you will be stoned."

"Your big dreams always come true, son. You dreamed of the great rain's arrival, of the collapse of the big, proud mountain at Outer-Resh, the vomiting of the rivers and the flight of the seamen from the raging ocean; of my discovery of a great eagle-spider in my bed as of my attaining of wisdom from that swamp viper's bite; also my luck in finding a huge ogre-stone down the well. All of these you dreamed of, as also of the appearance last year of those strange visitors in white who you say, when they return, will cause the weather to change once again and the winds to take an entirely new course and the Civil Service to introduce many new checks on all. What will happen when the rains stop? What will the island be like then?"

Economy's reply was obscure.

"When the island-weather fortune turns,
the farmers will happily go to fish
and the fishermen contentedly to farm,
and Economy will sit on his own bench
in the schools . . . ."[1]

"That is a riddle that makes no sense to me," said Na, annoyed, "and it is far too late for you to go to the schools now. It is time that you learnt your place in the world and was glad for what you are. At least your life is better than that of the Ebits'!"

He thought on the tedious existence of the Ebits and the many beliefs about them. They were not human beings, and to speak or associate with them would rot your tongue and damn your soul. Even normally placid dogs chased them down the roads and by-ways if they came seeking rats' tails which is what they were said to like in their favourite soup. They were believed to be the very first exiles put out into the world, cursed for having laughed at their original great ancestor when he was in a drunk and disorderly state. This is why they were said to be descended from the Hams or Canaanites. They had landed on the island, wearing a disguise that had never yet been seen through, in the days of the Ancestors. They had travelled around ever since in other people's clothes. Their skin had turned to an unhealthy yellow from drinking rainwater and their open air way-of-life and overall elusiveness was a deliberate ploy to demoralize farmers, all respectable members of society and in particular those sedentary, serious, introspective followers of the official Astronomical religion, by the example of their sheer cussedness and lack of responsibility.

"It is true that the Ebits do not have the freedom that we have but, as we are told by the monks, are possessed by the spirits of wild animals and are content in their misery. All the same, I would not like, either, to have to go through the rituals that the educated men suffer, or to have to sit down in their bare dens," said Economy quietly.

He thought of the infamous life of a scholar or soldier; the grim taxes that they had to pay of enforced and regular speeches to ensure that their privileged positions continued, as well as the compulsory, tiresome, head-nodding courtesies that they had to give to all those around them in order to retain the friendship of their equals and the respect of their inferiors.

"It is also true that I live an existence free from the dangers of the outside world here in the woods, though the hardships and troubles have increased of late. I do not wish to live as the farmers or the soldier-scholars or as the Great Men live. But sometimes I wish I knew what the world is really like, like when I see a faraway view from a tree top, or when I spy a scholar reflecting his face in a book on a leisurely stroll. Then I know that there are things that are barred to my knowledge and the secret thoughts inside my head fill me with wonder at what things there must be, what they are, and where they are."

His voice had dropped to a wondering whisper.

He pondered why it was that some were born to be rich and powerful, like farmers and the silver businessmen, others to be poor and unsuccessful, yet others to be afflicted like the Ebits, while some were destined to be mere animals or even

The Madness of Eamon Moriarty

inanimate things, objects like trees or pieces of dead wood or bits of decaying matter that float around in the rivers and swamps going nowhere in particular. He wondered about these things. The thoughts went round in his head and he looked like a philosopher sitting there on his legless stool. But all his aunt could see were the dreaminess and idleness of a lazy fellow as he squatted on one leg in his peculiar manner.

Eamon was not to be left for long even in that measure of privacy that was his, for due to reports of his accosting and intimidating an old woman in a country lane, as well as persistent absconding from school, Big Brother, in the form of the caring agencies of the State, was to intrude into his domestic situation. Civilization had advanced so far that even those who were not registered in the Volume of Good Citizens were, these days, not beyond the reach of at least some government department. Thus was occasioned the visit of a group of social workers who had somehow been alerted to the circumstances of Eamon's life, either by his non-attendance at school from which in fact he had been indefinitely suspended for poor behaviour, having being accused (it was not he) of throwing at the teacher's head a piece of slate which was what they wrote and drew pictures on in those days, for no apparent reason. (If there had been a reason the incident would have been understandable and quickly forgiven, as slate throwing was a feature common to school life there). It had also come to their attention that certain unpleasant incidents in relation to young girls had been occurring thereabouts, which had all happened around the same time, and in the same general locality, where Eamon had been reportedly seen wandering somewhat aimlessly about.

There was a knocking on the door which at first they did not notice, or at least paid no attention to as they contented themselves in the darkness of their drink-instilled thoughts. Economy was amusing himself by staring at the twigs on the

The Madness of Eamon Moriarty

floor, examining them intently until their shapes changed and they became aggressive snakes and darting insects making all manner of fantastic movements. It was to Eamon's and Na's astonishment that they eventually heard the hammering and shouting outside, and then they saw the door burst open and a crowd of people rush in.

First there was a gross farmer, followed closely by two indigent shopkeepers and a water-clerk. A collection of wives with red scarves over their heads and a relapsed monk also appeared, as well as a tree-feller and a man wearing a goose hat. Two navvies followed along with one small, plump musician who was followed by a thin doggerel. At the back of the group was a relative of the well-known farmer who had both lost, yet not lost (as the public sympathy and government compensation far outweighed the loss) a prime bird recently and which relative's name was McNabb. At the tail-end (officially overseeing procedures but probably for safety in case of fighting) was a man whom Economy and Na recognised as the current deputy leader of the district, Top Carrot in his 'alter persona', the gruff and rascally Old Gobhook.[2] This assorted group stood around talking their heads off and shouting at one another. Economy and Na could not understand a word that they were saying. Then Old Gobhook waved his arms and put on a mad face, encouraging all the visitors to encircle the pair and place their hands on them. They then pulled the two astonished individuals up from the floor and proceeded to drag them across the room.

"Let me go, you officious fools," screamed Na as she waved an arm to stop the intruders manhandling her, "I'll put you in the pot that has roasted many a scamp before you."

A few of the people laughed and said, 'Aha, see, we told you so' and they increased rather than diminished their exertions by jerking their victims. Economy thought it best to say nothing, just to let them do what they wanted. The captives were pulled outside into the darkness (the 'cooling down' stage in the professional parlance) where the dreary rain only made the two more distressed, (a deliberate ploy). Their persecutors were of course well clad against the elements and they took added pleasure in seeing the abject misery of their victims, for which they felt the two had only themselves to blame. The visitors maintained throughout a light heartedness that could only have been the product of having had to deal with such difficult and painful situations many times before.

Old Gobhook spoke again, like one who knew well beforehand what he was going to say, in the attitude and manner of a leader.

"I told ye what we would find! For far too long we have put up with these unruly people. Did ye not see all the evidence on the floor, the bones, the sticks and the bit and pieces? There is evidence of contact with Tennits, and I know that the boy has been seen in close proximity to the interlopers. Their defiance of local custom, wandering around interfering with fences, protected natural areas and private property must be stopped. It has only been the soft-heartedness, the do-good ineptitude of Top Carrot that has saved them from their punishment. Top Carrot has protected his favourites (what is *he* getting out of it?) for too long, thinking he was doing good in society by maintaining the Pax Carrota and covering up many dark things. Well, have you ever known him to make a sensible decision?"

Eamon never understood why Tom Curran had come with these local government officials, but he guessed it was to do with his new political ambitions. He was so different from his usual self. His face was red and all squeezed up in a kind of anger and he thought they were seeing the other side of him, the bad T.C., without a doubt. He remembered his mum warning him once, that Tom Curran was 'not all there' either, that he had a queer side to him (though you wouldn't think it). It was all very upsetting for Eamon, who had been accustomed to his 'uncle's' good side. He was confused by the intimate questions the Social Workers were asking and their poking into every corner of their personal lives and belongings, (they were going through the room in a very thorough search). Eamon suddenly fell on the floor in a fit, his limbs kicking violently and a lather coming out of his mouth.

"Hold him down, don't let go of him," shouted Old Gobhook; "while I tell you a few more things about Top Carrot."

Gobhook was one of those who saw the solution to every problem of life and public policy in an interminable discussion of the character defects of his antagonists. Such defects were, in his opinion, the great hindrance to everything that had to be achieved in the world, the bane of human progress as well as his own great plans.

"He agrees with everything you say, but he never puts his money where his mouth is. He does his deeds behind the people's backs. But I think that he will not dare to return now, for he is a coward also. The Tennit folk hold him responsible for the killing of their relative. No, he will not wish to involve himself in the wars that will soon commence. If he does ever return, it will be to face the consequences of his dishonest actions. For the first time in his life he will have to face up to the truth about himself! All right, hang them."

"Hooray, hooray," shouted the others and pulled the two under the arms of a big tree. Economy had to be supported by three of the strongest men, whilst Na just stared at the ground.

"I think I know now how it is done. Haul them over that branch," said Gobhook, pointing at the lower arm of the tree.

"It's the best way," said the gross farmer.

"It's how it's done in Assaland," said the first shopkeeper, "a pity the method took so long to come over here. We are always miles behind them."

"There always has to be a first time," said the water-clerk.

"Why don't they plead for mercy?" one of the wives asked.

"They just don't know what is good for them," answered Gobhook.

"We shouldn't hang them for too long," said the relapsed monk solemnly; "we should get it over with as soon as possible and not prolong the spectacle. It is not morally right to enjoy a hanging."

"We haven't got all day to stand here, moralizing and discussing what is best for society. We should be getting on with the job," said Gobhook.

Whilst they all nodded in agreement there were a few there who did not go along with everything Old Gobhook said or did, and who thought he was a bit of a fool. They felt that they themselves would make a better hand of things. One day, a more sophisticated way would be found for choosing leaders. Thus thoughts of rebellion are to be found in the most acquiescent of folk, even as they diligently go about their mundane daily duties.

They tied the rope around Na's neck and pulled her over the branch. She kicked her legs and a grimace came on her face. They asked her some questions, which apparently she did not understand, and her reply was very strange.

"Economy's dream tells all –
the rain no more will fall."

"A witch!" they all said aloud.

This last prophecy of a stick-gatherer in the last days of an archaic, landed plantocracy was enough to make them all feel justified in the tough approach they were taking for only monks, astronomers and to a certain limited extent soldier-scholars were supposed to make prognostications. It was clear to them that Economy and Na were somehow involved in malpractices that touched upon the realm of the supernatural, for how else could they have this preternatural knowledge of future weather patterns?

(Definition of the supernatural – called the affairs of the place where the island loses its solid consistency and human decisions their relevance and have no significance or reality whatsoever and there are no such things as questions or answers, knowledge or learning. A privileged place where no Assalander ever sets foot, where each man sits on a bonny box and the women finally undo all the tedious, delicate needlework at last, free of a task that had always been unfit for them, whilst placing their feet in comfort up in the air whistling catchy tunes which make their relieved-to-be-single-again husbands forget all the bad old times, though also perhaps with a kind of nostalgia for them, and where nobody is encumbered by life or death or any sort of hauntings of a religious or even earth-bound nature and the old fisherman has no pipe to smoke nor bothers people with tedious reminiscences; with baskets upon baskets of pepper drinks-which they drink without cease not by taking it down into delicate stomachs but just never-endingly pouring it into their open mouths while they at the same time speak wordless words in the emptiest of peaceful, non-contentious silences, their faces strangely resplendent with the ease of not having to tell any more old stories; where the well-known monk leader number one reckons all his ancestors originate from and where all leaders are destined to become great men. Ebits (some say also Soldier scholars) will never go there and will never know what it is to see heavenly visions or to dream pleasant dreams or to eat fresh bread. Where tempests of previously unknown pleasure and yet-to-be-discovered true island wit run rampage, creating storms of golden nuggets of imminent laughter, effortless, suppressed mirth, irony and satire along the gullies and eddies of the omniscient elbows of lucid, over-benevolent, if unpredictable giants as well as occasional, simple, ordinary jokes and laughter falling from above on to the sporting little people who can but marvel at the incandescent splashes of higher wit lighting up the heavens high above their heads. It is there too that proud or cruel men become much reduced in size, and in their miniature form are chased in great fun by brightly-coloured butterflies, evil, ugly spiders and darting, poisonous insects on the God-given task of giving them a very bad bite as a punishment for all their previous disdain of inferior creatures. A land where the early morning hours' wakening of doubting, disillusioned islanders are spent trembling as their sins rain down on them or as they despair over their inadequate personal virtues which are now become unfortunately almost completely redundant in the supernatural world; and all the while the amused, omnipotent, invisible, highest deities overlook it all, dishing out slapstick dashes of great, running streams of rich legendary stories and delicious food for the imagination that, unlike earthly stories, are not boring or tedious in any way, distributing them with generous handshakes and with much carefree advice; where the grey dim edge of the boring old island gives way with a shiver of anticipation, or even a proud shrug, to places of unimaginable complexity of understanding, a secret, private fantasy world which it is blasphemous to be heard discussing and shameful to be found even imagining its suspect pleasures).

The words of Na, resonant with a politically and even religiously charged content, viz. forecasting the future state of the weather, only added fuel to their zeal.

"Up with her, up she goes!" cried Old Gobhook triumphantly and Na kicked her one leg and with a painful look on her face closed her eyes in what was a deep struggle to find a single word or expression with which to make a reply that would end the torment.

Economy was still shaking uncontrollably as he looked at Na hanging lifeless from what appeared to be a political hanging tree. As he watched with wide-open eyes he felt the noose being tightened around his own neck with many strange questions and incomprehensible words being put to him. He listened with distress to the queer talk.

"He is just an eejit," said the man with the goose-hat, who was a disgraced barber, making sure that everyone knew to whom he was referring by pointing to Economy, thereby removing the possibility that he might have been referring to Old Gobhook. Despite his past disgrace he had managed to ingratiate himself again with his customers by shaving off his beard and his hair and going away to Water Bird Island for a certain period to live among the geese. He came back repentant and reformed, wearing a wide smile that asserted that all shame and guilt were gone, as well as an impressively foolish goose hat;

"I'd just say that he can't help not being able to answer our questions. He has probably no idea how to, or is even aware that he has gone astray. As I discovered myself when I fell out with the customers, when you go astray it is no easy matter to see at first your terrible mistake. Or be humble enough to come back and admit it."

Gobhook spoke haughtily:

"That may be, and there may be a place in society for the reformation of character, not to mention also for true repentance and forgiveness, as our penal institutions are always trying to impress on those who pass through their austere and hallowed walls. Rehabilitation schemes, such as those on Water Bird Island, prepare people to re-enter the world with a new wisdom, i.e. that it is not worth going to prison and that it is not worth coming back into the world either. But at the same time if someone like the young man here should no awareness of his own wrongdoing, then we have to take a stricter line."

"What is his crime again? I've forgotten," asked one of the wives.

This was followed by a medium length silence in which nobody thought, or bothered, to give a reply.

"There is nothing for it then but the long arm of the law above," said the gross farmer eventually, with McNabb applauding his words.

They saw Economy's face change from red to blue and the sight made them all stand back with awe. The next thing that happened surprised everybody. His neck broke through its bonds and he fell to the ground with a loud shout. Some inner strength or power had caused the rope to come apart and he fell from the tree. Before anyone could do anything he was 'up and away swearing like a trooper', as was afterwards reported to the Report Keeper. They watched helplessly as he disappeared into the bush, the words 'Ye'll never catch me' dying away in the distance.[3]

They all stood there looking at Gobhook who was rather shamefaced, and there was a small hint of gratification in their eyes, which emotion was on the point of accusation and even mockery.

"Do you think," asked the water-clerk in a mercenary vein, "that they might have some drinks in the house. It's a cold night and we have come a long way."

The relapsed monk now spoke for the second time.

"Dare I say, it is typical that a hames has been made of the job, and now you must go and immediately have a drink to recover. Your questions have as good as killed them both. Sure you scared the life out of them with your daft questions. You are all as foolish and incapable as scholars recklessly drunk in a barn! If Top Carrot had been here things would have been different, you know. We will be a laughing stock for years to come."

This open criticism of accepted, standard policy brought the usual establishment backlash.

"Oh do you hear the rascal?" shouted Gobhook – "you just love it when things go wrong! It makes you feel that it's not

The Madness of Eamon Moriarty

only you who has made a mess of things. Yes, we have all heard of how you ran away from your wife and children. Of how you let everybody down by absconding from your post on the top of Holy Mountain the day the big ship came. How you illicitly washed yourself by accidentally falling into the Ebit's ritual washing river near Inisbay. And all the other things they say about you. You are a disgrace to every monk on this island, past, present and future!"

"Just you wait till Top Carrot gets back," muttered the relapsed monk.

"It is true," said Gobhook, "that Top Carrot has gone soft in his ripened years. He may still be known as a master curer of apple curds and blue bees, a renowned taster of cawls and sips and a cultivated judge of tans and establishment flowers such as Crowstoes, Thespian and Howmuchchangehaveyougots as well as a master of bonus friendships. But today he seems to be more interested in going off to visit old senators and soldiers and gossiping on the lawn of Island House amongst the mottled tea parties and stroppleblossoms than doing what needs to be done around here. I must say that, even though he is of my own flesh and blood, I now abhor him. He lets rascals like these strip trees, often down to the bark, something not even Ebits normally do, and cast spells of destitution over the whole countryside. And who has not heard the rumours of other things that have been occurring under Top Carrot's reign? Tennits' secret leagues with fishermen, conspiracies against farmers, the breakdown of law and order, visitors from Assaland who propose a total destruction of our culture and way of life with their education schemes? It's no wonder that many people are scandalized and no longer want to go to work, or send their children to school."

"You two-faced old git," muttered the tree feller quietly.

By this time the water-clerk had gone inside and given the place a thorough examination, making notes as he went around.

The Madness of Eamon Moriarty

"Would you look at what I've found here," he cried out.

"It's a piece of parchment with things scribbled on it, lines and scrawls such as the monks and scholars make." As these intruders ransacked the house, Economy ran through the woods until he came to a cave. He rested there. He was not the same Economy of a few hours before. He was a much more angry person. He wept tears over the old woman, and this time he thought he knew what tears were, and why he was weeping.

Notes

1 - The riddle of these lines has been pondered upon in great depth. The learned academics of Iar and the other part of Connacht say that they detect here an ancient practice by worldly-wise countryside people of keeping a number of different occupations going in order to benefit from different sources of funding. Cork rejects this, needless to say, and shows us in the report that here we have an idealized society imagined by a visionary brain where **one step beyond Communism** is to be attained by all its members.

2 - It had long been suspected by Na and Eamon that there were two sides to the same Tom Curran, his good side and his bad side. Eamon was aware of this conflict and tension between the two personalities inside the man, even though Uncle Tom usually managed to keep the best side out whilst in important company or when visiting supporters. Only on the one occasion, when he helped himself to a share of the coleoil in their hut did the balance shift and T.C. treated the woodland couple to an abusive tirade in which even his physical appearance had utterly changed. It was not known if T.C. himself was aware of this inner conflict going on inside him; that an ugly, destructive character was threatening to take over (had in fact now completely taken over) from the calm, politic person.

3 - Quoting from the official Social Services report would be useful here – "... **the subjects in order to calm down the situation. A minimum of physical force was used to restrain the old woman who, at the end of the day, was the prime suspect in a serious case of child abuse and a potential candidate for the juridical process. It has been claimed in mischief-**

making quarters that it was as a direct result of our severe questioning subsequent events took a turn for the worst. Nothing could be further from the truth. The unfortunate accident to the foster mother was caused by her own sheer cussedness (if plain language must be used, let it be so). It was, indeed, only through our handling of the case that a veritable can of worms was opened and a serious deterioration in community relations pre-empted ... ."

chapter FOUR

Meanwhile Halo had observed the entry of Top Carrot into Balhop and had covered his eyes at the sight. It was just one more distressing sign of the impending doom which he had been telling everyone about, and it caused him great consternation to see Top Carrot on his regal carriage, the back of a boisterous, stubborn king-donkey. The rustic donkey became unhappy in the crowded, busy thoroughfare of Balhop as it was jostled by the people and the native, urban proletarian donkeys. The journey through town, after much trouble which was watched in all its vicissitudes by Halo who followed behind, was concluded with Top Carrot being deposited by the irate donkey in an untidy heap on the street to the casual if prolonged amusement of passers-by. Halo did not share in the amusement. He tried not to look at Top Carrot, and in fact did his very best to persuade himself that the rural demi-potentate was not there at all.[1]

He then thought that the best thing to do would be to confront Top Carrot directly and exorcise him from the capital with as much hue and cry and ballyhoo as possible. But instead, to his own great surprise and bewilderment, he found himself running off in the opposite direction shouting at the top of his voice and looking for one of the reclusive Astronomical monks to tell his troubles to.

Professor Sammy ran a long-term electioneering experiment in the confines of his school's science laboratory and came out with a look of puzzlement on his spotty, bearded face, as well as displaying the dark grains of dirt resulting from weeks of un-washing and various chemical reactions.

"I am already at a conclusion," he said to himself as there was no one else there, "and we are going to have to find a way of choosing a leader for our country, or face the alternative of us all having to leave this island for ever. The volcanic ash that is spoiling our roads and land, as well as the bad weather that some say is caused by the activities of this particular, as yet undiscovered and unnamed volcano, as well as by the wayward planets and even by the morose temperament of the people, are beyond our control and I think there is panic in the air. Crowds of penniless people are flocking to the capital in search of financial aid and advice. Many of these are from faraway country districts and they are a great burden on our corporate system. And worse more is taking place and our chief monks and main leaders are not doing the least thing about it, saying that all is for the best because it could be much worse, whilst pretending that their own speeches have brought about such great, ubiquitous modern progress that it is impossible to actually see it because we have become so accustomed to it. They even boast about what they are going to do about the weather, how they will reduce the amount of rainfall with some marvellous plan that they have up their sleeves, and they make brave, mocking speeches on the topic of Assalanders and their Single Leader. They dish out awards to any occasional fisherman who has somehow managed once again to make a voyage in a boat, or to proud businessmen who have enslaved some Ebits, or otherwise to boring scholars who have succeeded in educating themselves in a remote branch of astronomy. I once, by accident, found myself at a garden party at Island House and there I saw displayed the result of centuries of our futile free speech tradition, the massed representatives of every level of society in this island, gorging themselves on stroppleblossoms and acid gossip drinks, sporting themselves in their best clothes and not one of them with the sense to realise it was raining. So taken up were they with their silly chatter that they were getting soaked and making muddy holes on the best-kept island lawns, ruining their rented, expensive day-suits and none with the sense to get under cover. Contempt must have shown on my face for they all refused to talk to me. They saw me laughing out loud, and probably realised how idiotic they must have all looked.

My secret laboratory experiments have proved many things to me. If only I could get one single person to take me seriously, I could bring about much badly needed reform. I have this great vision of our own single ruler for the whole island, just like they have in Assaland! A complete change is necessary in the way we do things in this island. We need to learn how to obey and respect authority, or there will be no hope for us and we might as well all go and live in Assaland. If I could just for once get the Chief monk to take my advice and give my works the Astronomical Blessing there would be hope. Long ago, when I taught at a school in a remote country district, I met a knowledgeable man who was a minor leader in his own right. His district was a haven for all the rural vices and virtues and he had that great gift so rare in most elected representatives, a humble disposition and a complete lack of faith in his own words or opinions, with a mind open to everything an educated scholar like myself suggested to it. If someone like that was put to rule over this island (with myself as the chief government scientific expert) what a prospect! But he was only a remote country yokel unfortunately, stuck in his ways, who went by the name of something silly like 'Cabbage', I think .... "

At this point he realised that there was nobody else there and that he was in fact talking to himself.

"Oh well," he said with a shrug, and he continued to walk up the garden path, muttering to himself.

The Madness of Eamon Moriarty

It was at this moment that he saw Halo running across in front of him and the professor called out officiously:

"Hello, what are you doing in here?" for it was obvious from the garment of the intruder that he did not belong in that place. Halo imagined he heard his name being called and pulled himself up at once.

"Ah, I hear my name being called before I even reach to where I am going! My mission is known already," he said joyfully.

"Don't I recognise you as the wild man who hangs about the corners of Balhop?" asked Sammy with a mixture of unease and interest.

"You are an asker of questions, I see. If you saw me and you heard me then only you could know if that is so," said Halo enthusiastically, waving his arms.

"It is a sad case you are, for the days of listening to your kind are gone," said the professor shaking his head, with a feeling of sympathy, for he knew what it was like not to be listened to, and he thought that even mad people might have something to contribute to life or to say about the world around them. He wondered how he might get Halo out of the campus without further ado and certainly without having to compromise his own respectability.

" Mad, sad and bad that is me,
wringing my wrists, flailing my fists.
Halo, I do a little dance
to scare you out of your pants!
Dee de dee dee de dee,
lee de lee lee,"

sang Halo happily, or at least jollily, and doing a little two-step.

"That is very fine indeed," said Professor Sammy, and he stood there without a further word, not knowing what to do about Halo.

"I see that you are a wise man, a worthy man, and a man who knows how to tie up his shoelaces," said Halo with approval.

"You do?" said the professor with surprise and thinking now to himself that perhaps the man's eccentricity was a cloak for a type of genius, or perhaps for some secret knowledge of the world, said:

"Now it is very interesting that you should say that, for they are few indeed who have ever seen that possibility, or have ever even listened to my words."

"Ah, it is a blind world," agreed Halo in a strangely deep, sympathetic voice.

"You cannot be such a mad fellow after all if you are able to have such astute insight into things. We scholars may not have that monopoly of learning that we think is ours. But whatever you do, don't say I said that," was the professor's reply.

"I don't hear what I hear,
nor feel what I feel,
I don't see what I see,
nor say what I say,
dee de dee dee dee,"
said Halo loudly, reverting to his previous obscurity.

"Very fine," said the professor, and then he asked another question of Halo.

"What do you think of the present state of affairs on this island?"

"Is that a question I am supposed to answer?" asked Halo cagily.

"Don't you think matters have reached a terrible stage? Have you ever known things to be as bad as they are?"

Halo thought on this and then he answered:

"There has been a great change take place in the heavens. This has been caused by a single person, and that person is myself. I am responsible for the havoc in the sky. I have decided that I must destroy this island and everything that is in it before *they* come here. The Assalanders as you know are wicked people and they are trying to conquer those who are not like themselves. They have even poisoned the soil. They have many other plots and schemes afoot and a scholar has written a whole book about their designs that nobody has ever read, because it is hidden away. So I have devised a plan of my own that will catch them out! I am afraid that I am about to ruin their game. Hence you see this storm and the dying off of our natural plants and the consternation and bad temper of the people that have all been caused by me, and is my own way of making this place inhospitable and unattractive to these interlopers. And I caused this miracle to happen by just staring very hard at the sky one day, and then all of this took place."

"There is only one answer to the problems of this island, and that is for there to be a great leader," said Professor Sammy emphatically, even if it was without much hope of being comprehended by the unfortunate Halo.

Halo spoke now with a surprising clarity:

"A leader came into this town today. I am on my way to tell a holy man about it."

"Why would you be concerning yourself over such a matter?" asked the professor curiously.

"He is Top Ferret from behind the woods, and he threw me out of that region in my youth. He sometimes comes to town to show off and to get bandages and man-about-town things."

"Top Ferret? Would his name be something like Cabbage rather than Ferret, or something else?"

"Sometimes he is called Top Carrot."

"Top Carrot! That is his name. He is an interesting man and his name is known in official circles. I would dearly like to meet him again. Thank you for telling me that he is in town. I will go and see him. Why do you wish to tell a monk about him, and why did he throw you out of his district, if you don't mind me asking?"

"That Great Carrot is a secret agent of the Assalanders. And I could tell by the look on his face that he is up to something now, coming like that into town today. People must be warned. My magic is not very strong against him."

"Why is that indeed, and how do you know these things?"

"He is my brother."

Professor Sammy's ears pricked up at this information, but before he could enquire further Halo realised perhaps that he had already said too much and skedaddled off, humming an obscure tune that was popularised long ago by a great island classical composer in the days when nightingales sang.

That evening as Economy lay in his cave and the night time seemed to fall late and hesitantly, due to an unusual interlude of a few hours of blessed dryness, there were shenanigans all over the island owing to the temporary lull in the rainfall (though the sky remained pasty, what that once sky-admiring, idealistic community of artists in upper Balhop had come to refer to now in a derogatory way as 'the soup dish'), and airy parties in castles, with a right royal inundation of astonished revellers who flocked under umbrellas to watch the deluge of the gigantic waterfall just outside Balhop (it was hard for them to get the sound of crashing water out of their ears and this was their idea of having a good time) helped to bring a temporary jollity into the evening; while of course the more serious, business-like elements of society simply walked about on the fringes and irritably talked over all the year's dispiriting financial events. The noise of the cheerful parties was an annoyance to them, a painful contrast to the mournful mutterings of these metal business partners, rock-star quarriers and fine silvermen as they twiddled their drinks at their semi-official conference-tree tables discussing how badly business was going, concealing their deeply personal profits from even their best wives, but overall there was a mood of determined happy forgetfulness and non-regret. The activities taking place in and around Balhop were an amalgam of all the national festivals, including Big Island Day, which were once separate holidays spread throughout the seasons but now were crammed together into the first single dry day that came in the year. It was more lively this year due to a remarkable upsurge in a strange giddiness among the people, with folk alternatively aggressively argumentative and over-friendly with each other and quite unable to talk seriously or walk straight.

Outside the capital elsewhere in the island on that dry evening celebrations were more muted, and Economy in his silent cave was not aware of any special or joyous occasion. He sat in a melancholy daze. Eventually he opened his eyes again to a dream world (for that is what the world looked like to him now, as though he was waking up from reality) and the various metaphysical ingredients of the immateriality of his own existence came to him freshly mixed with a strange, new immense quiescence, a calm that was more than calmness, a silence that was timelessness itself and a deadness that was like the end of the world. This time he did not 'fly upwards or move through the air at a great speed' as was his wont, but instead the cave and the whole world and all its substance appeared to close in on him more tightly, with a sort of overbearing, oppressive power. It caused him to feel dizzy and he had a sensation similar to falling from a great height with an unusual lightness. He became short of breath, though at the same time this deprivation of air seemed not a problem but a way to a new and higher level of meaning. It was even to an extent an invigorating feeling. A thought, or an unusual emotion inside him seemed to come alive now, at first gently pulling at him and then seeming as though it would actually fly out of him and depart, taking away with it a piece of his soul. This appeared both as a frightening and a pleasurable thing. He realised that he was going to have to make a decision. It was either to call in that thought, or to let it go. He did not at that moment know which he should do.

He opened his mouth in a shortness of breath. Although he could at least hear himself breathing (he had thought for a moment that he was dead) he felt that he was partaking in the experience of another world. He felt, despite the clamour of emotions, nausea and claustrophobia, a continuing great calm as the realisation came to him that he was himself, really a separate entity, just like all those other things around him, rocks, trees, the birds, a substantial existence which could itself be called something. He could have feelings about things, emotions, and yet again different feelings about other, completely different things. Thoughts about himself, separate from each other, came to him; already he could think of a possible use for his previously unwanted leg. A revelation came to him that he did not need to return to his own district but that it would be quite a good idea for him to leave the area and go travelling. He would be able to see that world he had always wondered about. He might even succeed in meeting his parents one glorious day. In the past his pleasure, and pain, had been in imagining faraway, unreachable places. But he had been a dreamer rather than an explorer; that is, until now. With these notions emerging in his head he felt he might even follow Top Carrot and go to the most important place of all, Balhop. There was nothing to make him want to return home where his enemies would probably be waiting for him with more questions.

Eamon had run away from home and was now an official juvenile-at-risk. The police were informed but they were quick to point out that if they spent all their time chasing up cases of runaways there would be no opportunity to solve serious crimes. The young man was to roam the countryside and villages for a period of time. Every unusual incident and occasion of disruption or damage to property was blamed on this wanderer. As he was 'not wanted by the police' nobody in authority was willing to take responsibility for him, or deal with his supposed crimes. As usual it was the ordinary population that had to put up with his wanderings, an entirely innocent population which had to pay the price of his excesses.

Economy began to think of all the things he would leave behind him should he go away for good. When he thought about it there wasn't in fact all that much to regret! The hard floor, his irascible relatives, stick collecting in the rain, not to mention very poor food – he would not regret the absence of these things. There was one thing, however, that he had always liked to do in the past. He was a poor man, but he did have a gift that was all the more rare and precious for being raw and simple. He was able to communicate invisible (or at least artistic), obscure and impractical things by means of mural forming. He had carried on this secret hobby of mural forming (a form of representation of reality by means of marks engraved on plain surfaces) to counteract the hunger, poverty and boredom of the long, dark evenings. But it was an illegal, shameful activity, although he had not yet realised this. Mural forming was supposed to be the preserve of soldier-scholars alone.

The memory came to him of the day he had begun this unusual activity. He could not go to the school that was in the lane next to Abbercroppy barn, the place of most renowned learning in the district as it had a resident scholar. This was a man who, although he had never been a soldier, was still the recipient of respect because he came from a region not known to the local inhabitants and because he wore a huge sheet of transparent material, said to be glass, in front of his face through which he was able to see all ultimate wisdom. He was often prepared to share small pieces of this wisdom with ordinary people, a generosity appreciated by everyone and not commonly found in most scholars. Economy had approached this teacher of wisdom (Plain Mr Samuel as he was known to most people then) one sunlit day in his early boyhood which happened to be a public holiday (The Day of The Deliverance of The Island and Its People From The Horrible Hornets, a rare species of bee that had been stinging everybody and giving them cramps in the remote past), and had asked him to teach him something. The kind teacher had shown Economy how to put coloured dye on the bark of an Ash tree and to make rough inscriptions, first of all as a kind of decoration, and then to put the inscriptions in intelligible, colourful patterns. Economy in fact had been able to learn to make a version of the Old Island Alphabet, a code of seven secret characters that mimicked the Standard Alphabet but which had its own arcane meaning which Economy was later to make all his own. These characters, in the form of smiling and scowling faces and other human facial expressions, emotions and various bodily actions, would obsess Economy for hours on end as he tried to put them into patterns that made sense in his own head. When Economy went further and tried to tell a story he had made up using these letters the scholar, for some unknown reason, had turned hostile and had stopped his lessons and indeed the same scholar, Mr Samuel, went away from the district soon afterwards and was replaced by another, severe and much more unapproachable individual. This new man was loath to share out even the smallest bit of his knowledge; (he went on to become a Chief Soldier Scholar later).

(It was this secret learning of Economy's, which not even Na knew he possessed, that explained why it was that the hanging party found an incredible written text, and not just simple primitive letter drawings, in the house of Economy and Na).

Economy now became a little happier in his cave recollections and the anger and sadness, although still there, were joined by another emotion, something that felt like what a normal person feels on waking up in the morning – a sense of purpose. A new self-knowledge seemed to be a product of this turmoil of emotions. He felt capable of a 'spiritual flight', as though he was able to move about in his own dreams. He sat up straight, constrained by the walls of the cave, and discovered that he was still weak. He leaned against the rock wall for support. He found that his neck still hurt him, although the swelling was going down and the pain that was in his head had lessened, had become more of a regular, gentle throb. Gradually the disturbance to his thoughts and emotions ceased and a peace filled him. Then sleep descended.

His sleep was disturbed a little later by a strange noise that came to trouble him. From beyond the zone of sky and air, somewhere out over the distant edge of the world, there came a very deep sound, a hollow yet full-sounding noise that emanated from a distant source and seemed to be coming closer.[2] Economy had heard something like it on a previous occasion, when he had been in a tree on a hilltop and then he had said to Na that he had felt the approach of a great, inexplicable *thing*. Na said that she herself could hear nothing and that he should not be making up stories, or listening out for things, anyway. The sound, almost impossible to describe or properly comprehend, awoke Economy again in his dark cave and he listened to its deep, intermittent murmur, something like a growl. It seemed even louder than before and it came like a forewarning with a new, increased strength. He wondered if he was the only person in the island, or in the whole world, who heard it. In the past the sound had been soft and vague, almost uncanny, as to make him wonder if he was really hearing it. Now it was a much clearer sound, producing in Economy a feeling of ghostly wonder, like that of a surprising intuition.

Eamon at that moment felt his anxiety coming back. He had almost forgotten about the fear, for there were periods of time lately that had been without that mind-numbing sense of foreboding. For a short while out here in the wilderness in fact it was as if dread had never been part of him, so free did he feel. Now, as he sat in his hiding place the hairs at the back of his head rose again. Yet he thought that this time he detected something recognisable, something ordinary and yet impossible to understand in his mind, behind his great unease.

Notes

1 - It would seem that the arrival of the ambitious 'country bumpkin' in the chief town is not only a universally significant event but involves also an archetypal 'experience'. Just as Alexander's arrival on his mighty charger at the edge of the world was accompanied by some feeling of disappointment and anti-climax, and Dick Whittington's coming to London with his cat was also a bit of a let-down at first, so many other famous arrivals at the big smoke often took place in humiliating or odd circumstances. These, however, only portended impending, prodigious events. Galway, though, sees the main significance in that his uncle's going to 'see the lights' of the capital left the lad with a similar ambition to get to the place – the age old rural-urban migration by stages proposition.

2 - Cork and Galway had locked horns over the matter of this 'sound'. It seemed that more than academic reputations were at stake, as indirect allusions were being made to the many superstitious beliefs of a naive people, said to have been peculiar to Cork and region over the generations, and which often manifested themselves as a tendency to conduct strict moral questioning in the face of any kind of modern progress. It bespoke the

sensitivity of the thing that both groups of experts were unwilling to give ground here. They saw each and any explanation as a matter of crux and the other's interpretation as something sinister. The very vagueness of the whole matter added fuel to fire, oxygen to flame. With Galway repeating ad nauseam (after the initial Cork suggestion that it was the rolling thunder of Hephaistos, god of metalworking), that it was probably something no more controversial than Eamon's recognition of the (late) arrival of electricity in his district, this innovation being at odds with his own backwoods frame-of-mind, bringing to mind that memorable statement in The Cork Examiner that as humanity had done without electricity since time immemorial why should it be accepted now? This Galway idea was that what appeared at the time as a new, surreal power triggered a 'commotion' or 'noise' in Eamon's brain. Cork took to arms and demanded a weekend seminar on the issue at a neutral point – the Down Arms hotel in the county Limerick – at the taxpayers' expense. Here every possible interpretation was discussed, beginning with Dr Crane's explanation (delivered out of the side of his mouth as he drank a pint, in the casual style of a professional expert dispensing privileged revelations to the uninformed), of how the side-effects of tinnitus in the ear can change a person's personality and, if tinnitus be discounted, then hallucinatory events of an auditory nature as found in Schizophrenia were surely at the bottom of it all. Cork came in with a Big Bang theory, (almost literally, for they had been imbibing heavily of alcohol and smashed down the door as they came through into the conference room – the lounge bar), 'exploding' their new theory with great joy: it was that what Economy was picking up was the static associated with the phenomenon produced at the onset of Creation. Any idiot who had ever heard a wireless set crackling could have sussed this out long before its 'official' discovery in the 1960's anyway! With the Cork experts elaborating the Grand Unified Theory Explanation for everything that happened to Economy there was an inevitable reaction in the Galwegians who insisted on plumping for the simple or even banal theory. (Surely no Corkman could have discovered all by himself a valid 20th century astronomical/Physics theory – was their rub).

If, on the other hand, the Dublin Synthesists had been invited, suggested one cynic at the seminar, there is no doubt that they would have found a simple connection between everything and explained the sound in terms of The Anxiety Creation Caused Due To Electrical Impulses Leading Thereby To Both Tinnitus And Mental Illness in Susceptible Parties. There was no laughter at the critic's remarks; it seemed that nobody saw the joke.

chapter FIVE

The fisherfolk, the Follys, Crollys, Jollys and Lumps and all their kinfolk were also having a party that evening. As they stood around, some sucking appletans in their hostles, others standing on crabfish as a symbol of their old traditions and yet others sitting labelling bottles of old Smeer drink with festive slogans before drinking them back with all-sauce, it was as though everything in the island and home was normal and as happy as it had been in the shore days. Dar Folly looked around at the dancing and chatting relatives and friends and he had a pleased smile on his face. There were two reasons for his rejoicing that night; one was the prospective engagement announcement of his elder son, Val; and the other was the declaration of his own Last Will And Testament in the light of a funeral that was shortly to take place – that of himself.

A wispy, nervy, ageing Val proudly announced his engagement to Sul Jolly, who was of course related to all the Crollys, Lumps, Follys as well as the other Jollys. They had waited a long time that evening for Val to pick up the courage to make the announcement, for not until one complete bottle of smeer and two full cups of bubble drink had been drunk had he dared first approach Sul and say to her that he was ready to come into her house now and help look after their children if she would let him, as he no longer wished to live the wild hooley life with the men but would be very glad to put his feet up and acknowledge his responsibilities at last and help to provide for the family and generally see to it that everything was properly done for his own comfort. Jal, another elderly fisherman, smiled and thought back to the days of their life on the coast and of how an engagement ceremony like this would never have been called for, as only the head fisherman ever usually got married, and then it was on his deathbed that he officially took his wife to himself and acknowledged her as his own. Still, these were harder times and it made sense for the men to be looked after by the womenfolk who knew how to cook, sew, knit thriftily with dog-hair thread, make sweet-smelling slumber beds, tan the children, boil the sugar-drinks and cure all manner of ailments and loud complaints with kisses and salt herbs which they rubbed in sore spots under the nails. The most important development in recent times, which had made it even more incumbent for the men to be dependent on the womenfolk, was the latter's' ability to cure appletans and to present them in edible form at the food troughs. This had replaced the previously prosperous food trade in wild pigs, roden berries and the craft of selling weaved web-fish to outsiders, all of which had come to extremely hard times of late, and was now almost their sole source of nourishment. Appletans, although harder to obtain, were now made to last much longer, one apple going as far as three would have done previously, thanks to the marvellous cooking methods of the fishermen's women.[1]

Oh, how times had changed! So many new things they'd had to learn since they caught their last fish! Strange new friends they had had to make! No longer were their neighbours the respectable if greedy, lowland coastal farmers. Instead it was the dark Tennit who shared the district with them, and while this latter folk had shown themselves to be magnanimous in the manner they had accepted their new neighbours, there were still problems of misunderstanding and incomprehension between them. Many fishermen found

The Madness of Eamon Moriarty

it difficult even yet to be comfortable in the company of the ill clad, reserved and usually dirty (for they were always working at taking their bits and pieces of equipment apart or putting them together again) Tennits. But they grew to like the forest dwellers and to appreciate their helpful and homely company.[2] So established had the relationship become that there was present that evening with them in fact a Tennit, Firk Woodlander, who was enjoying himself quite well it seemed. Although he found the swing dancing of the fishermen to be quite alien compared to the hop-step-and-jump of the Tennit dance, he was feeling quite comfortable in the fishermen's household. He would tell his fellow Tennits later that the fishermen in their private revelries were not such a bad lot, that they were gay, chortled with a sound like thunder and were conviviality itself in the wax light, with their fair skin glistening and their blue eyes shining.

The Tennit, however, had been invited there for another reason. The fishermen were feeling a little guilty over the recent incident when they had encouraged an innocent Tennit to join one of their smuggling enterprises. This had led to the incident involving a vengeful mob of farmers. (Subsequent generations of fisherfolk had to learn to live with the guilty secret that the Tennit had in fact been taken along as a patsy in the event of any confrontation with the fanatical farmers, and they had abandoned him to his fate in the ensuing contretemps. This was the origin of the Fisherman's Day of Atonement, the one day in their year when they could talk to farmers). Outrage was still being felt in the Tennit camp and the fishermen were anxious not to lose their friendship and cooperation. Firk was being given the honour, as a representative of all the Tennits, of witnessing to the Last Will and Testament of Dar Folly. This deviation from the established custom of never allowing outsiders to be involved in the processing of family matters de jure was a startling development in legal and social affairs. It was symptomatic of the revolutionary changes, upturning the most cherished and sacred conventions, which were taking place.

There was to be another development in this strange change in customary mores. Dar called everyone in from the party room to his corner net to make the public announcement in what was a rare use of his own true voice about which there could be no dispute later on. He said that he was now ready to re-distribute his entire property which he had brought with him from the shore region; twenty five 'precious' mineral stones, the unit of currency (in fact this was valueless to the bartering inland people, but they liked to have 'money' for the prestige it bestowed) in which he had been paid for the house he sold on the coast to a lowland farmer who was desirous to use it for keeping his lowest-grade beasts in, a boat wheel, a kettledrum, an old scissors and the last of his rusting fishing gear. He made it known, to gasps of surprise, that he saw no point in continuing with the tradition of leaving everything to his youngest daughter, which was the time-honoured code of their society, in contrast to that of the farmers, who left everything to the fattest child in the family (male or female), while the Tennits were, as semi-nomads now, accustomed to having everything in common and left nothing to anyone in the end. It was next thought that he would leave it to his sons who like all fishermen's sons were shifty, carefree fellows, in the hope that this might make them settle down and perhaps take life, marriage and death a little bit more seriously. The girls themselves would in fact be happy to accept such a change in their official status, especially in view of the present harsh economic conditions and if only because it would leave them with more time to cure appletans and be about their other womanly interests in their unprecedented man-free, liberated way of life here in the interior. It was accepted that some of the ancient priorities would have to change, and that from now on each man, woman and child would have to put up with changes here and there, and make do with a little less of everything, although there were also compensations to be had. For instance, they could all safely now eat the occasional small piece of meat that came their way (at least the elders' eyes would be closed to this), when only fish had been allowed to them in the past; and they did not lose so many of their best men out on the high waves anymore. For it had been a feature of their old fishing life that the men had an obscure and mysterious attraction to going out on to the jocular waves with their heads inflamed with wild humour and be merrily outrageous and get up to all sorts of high jinks, regardless of the impending dangers. A death at sea in such a state was not even feared by them, and old, sickly men often asked to be taken out on a particularly stormy night in the hope of such a glorious end. Needless to say, however, not many fish would be caught in such a system of work and most of their food in fact had come from the inland rivers where the womenfolk were wont to go to get the evening meal which the men, as they exuberantly related their ocean exploits, did not usually realise was fish not of their own, but of their wives' catching. But those days were gone anyway, and so what if a few more cherished customs also had to go by the board?

It was to their astonishment that they heard Dar say that he was leaving all his wealth to Firk Woodlander the Tennit, and not any bit of it to his kin or friends. For a moment they could not get over the shock and they breathed their smoke inwards with the trauma and let out waves of horror through their nostrils and ears. Their eyes expanded and came out of their faces in amazement. The women reacted differently, though with a similar, disbelieving confusion. They became very sad, and bubbles of tears came out of their eyes and they felt that indeed the old and intimate bond between father and daughter had now come to an end. Dar's daughter indeed was heard to utter a sharp moan right then and she withdrew into herself in a desolate mood and collapse of spirit.

(This was how the new Fisher/Tennit religious heresy began, which held that all folk were brethren, that there should be no division between men, and that peace was better than war).

Jal was the first to speak, proving his solid leadership qualities by being the first to recover from the shock since he had never gone into shock at all, for he had understood nothing. It was almost as if he had known beforehand what would happen. He was also respected as a solid leader because he had a speech impediment which made him at least sound very silly, and everyone could respect him by being able to look down on him, and at the same time look up at him in wonderment at his strange ability to get people's attention with the same impediment. In a solemn voice he spoke:

"Whats it is,
is a token of esteem
of the fishermen for the Tennits,
and I herebys announces the engagement
of Dar's daughter to Firk,
to makes this a famous occasion
that wills makes brothers of us all."

Dar's daughter was aghast at this pronouncement of Jal's, if only because it was unheard of for a man to make a speech (and bring to reality what should otherwise have been, wisely, left hidden in the unconscious) instead of a woman on family matters or indeed on any topic of great import. The speechless girl heard loud applause greet the announcement of her engagement. Even the other women joined in the congratulations and her dad clapped too. Dar's daughter went very red in the face. The already mystified, dark face of Firk seemed perplexed by events as well. He could not tell whether it was all good or bad, but he behaved now like one who knew that there was little he might do about the complex, unprecedented situation he found himself in. If he should refuse to accept the lady's hand now offered to him in marriage, he would be breaking his own intimate Tennit social code, committing a crime of the utmost disgrace, viz. refusing the offer of a free gift, and he would no longer be able to hold his head up high as a man of honour again. It had certainly never happened before for a Tennit and one of the fisherfolk to marry, but the risks involved in that were nothing compared to the dangers a refusal would also bring from an enraged Fisherfolk society, who would be led to believe that not even all their wealth could persuade a Tennit to marry one of their daughters. It was as if he had stumbled into a 'set up' situation, from which there was no way of escape.

"You will come and live with us," said Dar's daughter in an emphatic tone (these words that would reverberate down through history as the 'blessing' that started off the mighty new heresy), and she stared at the man who now owned everything that rightly should have been her's and who did not return either her gaze or have a reply for her words, but instead he grasped the hand of his benefactor, saying that he was deeply honoured and believed that what he had made was a sound, moral, and wise decision.

"Sings, claps, dances or be's happy," shouted Jal to a hesitating, still-troubled crowd, and they restarted the celebrations with an emotionally recharged, if wondering spirit.

As the evening came to a close they all went outside for a breath of fresh air. Some of them said they were able to hear a strange sound in the air where before there had been nothing, or maybe just a confused mingling of noises like the hiss that you normally hear in your waxears and pay no attention to as it would probably be caused by your evil spirits expressing their frustration and displeasure over your stubborn lack of evil intent. Initially the sound was simply internal to each one's ear, but it became louder and more externalised like, as some said, a howl from a haunted castle or horn of a ghost-ship so that they all stopped what they were doing to listen and to bend their heads together towards the seashore which was where the noise was coming from and that itself was a relay of a good half-hour's listening, five hundred dog barks or fifty one oin roars away; and listened to the *woa woa, woa woa* of some scary, ghouly thing, and with no idea of the vast fleet of ships setting out at that moment from technologically superior Assaland. "What is it?" asked Jal junior, son of Jal, scared out of himself and his pants for he was still just a child at heart even though he was at least fifty; "it is so terrible and strange."

It was plain to see that everyone was made hugely uneasy by the noise. Jal's ensuing words did not entirely relieve their anxiety, for all the confidence of their delivery:

"I, Jal, your leader, hears this sound too, and I thinks that it belongs to a large Cockadoodledooo bird that flies with the eagles in the rainy season from Assaland to the Antibedes and it has losts its way and is flowns itself into our region. It wills soon goes away again, for there is nothing for it here."

His words were a comfort to a few, and most of them were absorbed in listening to the increasingly loud, rumble-sound. Even the marriage engagement was forgotten in the eerie, heavily laden night. Heads and hands became motionless and mouths were wide open as they watched and listened in anxious silence, slowly moving closer together.

Halo did get his message through to a strolling, idle monk in the sandlands of the lower Castle grounds, who liked to listen to mad ones and who thought Halo's an interesting enough disclosure in the light of the island-wide restlessness. But this man had a strict rule never to divulge a mad one's confidence so he kept the information as his own secret. Sammy meanwhile also reported T.C.'s arrival to monk leader number three who was his personal friend, and who was researching at that moment the chances of a previously unknown moon appearing in the sky over the island. It would, some members of the Astronomical Order held, appear below cloud level, on the horizon and be visible from the top of the castle balcony. This explained the presence of an Astronomical monk in the household castle of Jalosp himself, and that was how the Chief Monk, subordinate only to Jalosp in the hierarchy, came to hear of Top Carrot's arrival in Balhop. Since Jalosp was otherwise intellectually preoccupied, the Chief Monk took it upon himself to declare (deciding that all things, even the smallest happening, could be taken as important portents in these times) that Top Carrot's arrival in the great city, as reported by the distracted, outraged madman, might be of some significance. Such is how small events inadvertently change history. He said that both the impending discovery of this new moon and Top Carrot's coming, as well as Brother Hasit's breaking his foot against a big stone that had become dislodged from the cliffside, were all events linked. As Jalosp was too busy right at that moment to be bothered about current affairs in the island, he would himself call a conference, and he asked monk leader number three to invite Top Carrot to the castle – and every other important person in Balhop should be present too. After a word with Professor Sammy, the Chief Monk had an invitation sent all the way to Mouth Merrick the Astronomer himself, on his mountaintop in the country.

Top Carrot in the meanwhile spent the morning looking for his brother and his wife in the residential quarter of Balhop.

78 The Madness of Eamon Moriarty

They had moved from their old house and had left no forwarding address. It was ages since Top had heard from them. He asked around and was soon being directed to a street that was right on the outskirts of the town. It led up a slope that ended at the very edge of a cliff. He paused to look down on the heart of the capital. Once he had dreamed of being a leader there, living in urban splendour and hobnobbing with all the other leaders. Now, instead, he had returned to town almost as a desperate man. If the villagers ever knew of his real feelings and his real thoughts about their small-minded village, of his fascination for Balhop and of the real reason for his coming there, surprise and shock might be their chief reaction. He had come in fact without any intention of ever returning home. Quite simply, he had got fed up with life in the country, with the rainy, joyless days, the shortages, the moans and rivalries of greedy peasants, the devil-may-care outlook allied to the no-hope of the lot of them; and to top all this there was the likely break-out at any moment of a not inconsiderable barney over the walking rights of Tennits, a considerable increase in praedial larceny and other disturbances of a petty and obsessive nature that were preoccupying the community back there.

When they came to realise that he would not be coming back, Gobhook would have to take all the stick for what was happening and that served him right! What a snivelling wretch was his alter ego! Considering that Gobhook had sat back all these years and let old Top Carrot carry the can for everything, it was the least of his desserts! It was about time that the blame when things went wrong was put where it rightfully belonged. Hopefully Gobhook would stay in the country and not follow him to town in order to continue hassling him. In the past everywhere he went Gobhook went too! There was no getting rid of him. He was like a shadow, one move to the left and he'd follow, a move back again to the right and Gobhook would be there before him! He had been growing increasingly tired of the fellow and had warned him on a number of occasions to watch his step. One morning he woke up to find that Gobhook had been sleeping in his bed and then even partaking with him in joint morning toiletries in the washroom! There was no beating the fellow. The next thing was he was sitting in Top's breakfast place all dolled up and ready for the grub! That morning will be well remembered by Top's wife for the prolonged and vicious tableside argument and mental battle between himself, herself and Gobhook. There was for instance the matter of Gobhook taking out and lighting up a cigaroon which Top kept trying to grab from his mouth and put out, all to the annoyance of Mrs Top Carrot who hated smoking inside the house (there will be no more about her in this book). There you had the cigaroon moving from one side of the mouth to the other to escape Top Carrot's hand, Gobhook insisting he wasn't inhaling and Mrs Carrot generally doing her nut.

Top even tried to trick Gobhook that morning into revealing his true colours by saying that he was leaving the house for good and immediately setting off for the city, going through the pretence of this before even finishing breakfast and walking out the door, hoping that Gobhook would fall for it and leave forthwith. But when Top slipped back inside to his breakfast seat the old fellow was there right beside him again.

Another thing that had fixed his mind on leaving was the impending investigation by a government department into the case of Economy and Na. For the first time in the history of the island the ignorant, poverty stricken individuals who made up the mass of the population (the electorate) were to be asked questions and a scrutiny made of their personal situation. As it was also an investigation of fence-breaking, thieving, gossiping, the frightening of children, eating up all the roden berries, conspiring in whispers with person or persons unknown, drinking, smoking, throwing stones, causing birds to gather in flocks, mitching from school, cogging written assignments from other people's copy books and the practice of witchcraft, this could produce embarrassing disclosures, with tongues beginning to wag in his rural constituency. He decided now that he should never have involved himself with the couple in the first place, that beneficence was a mistake, to be regretted now in later life. By visiting them in their one-room shack and trying to help them out with a few friendly suggestions when they were in trouble in the days when he had been a very idealistic young leader, he had inadvertently found himself associated with their present disapprobation in the mind of the community. It might have been better for his political career to have done some more bad things, to have acted the big goat instead of trying to be the good shepherd.

La, his brother, was a disappointingly changed person when he met him. Instead of greeting Top with his customary cheery wave and bravado spirit he was indifferent to him and his arrival at the cabin. His wife stayed out of the way and he himself seemed very distant. He only talked about a new philosophy, saying that he was not at liberty to say what it was or when, where or how he had come into possession of it. It was his whole existence now. Top had never seen him look so serious in all his life, and his eyes had such a faraway expression that Top had the feeling that La was not even fully cognizant with his presence.

"I can only give you one clue to the name of this great teaching, but it is not really a clue," said La after a while in response to Top's questions.

"What is it you believe, La?" asked Top, who was by now losing all interest in La and his philosophy.

"The clue is that it has no name. There is no clue to my philosophy, which is not my philosophy. In fact it is not a philosophy at all," La said vacantly, looking at his fingertips.[3]

The Madness of Eamon Moriarty 81

Top tried asking him about the likelihood of his getting a job in Balhop, but gave up the attempt when La started rambling on about the ecological beauties of the island of which he had recently suddenly become very aware, but which he was becoming entirely indifferent to now. Top went out of the house and as he walked down towards the town centre he heard the sound of a ship's horn out on the harbour and thought about what it would be like to emigrate to Assaland.

Notes

1 - Suggestions that Cork married life did not always measure up to the standards of a decent, politic society have been faced down by the academics of the southern university. They have, they claim, proven beyond any shadow of doubt that what Eamon/Economy is referring to here is a very ancient system of family affairs as symptomatic of an archetypal, archaic society of the pre-historic world. The idea of very ancient men, i.e. old men, getting married is **not** an imputation of any Cork social trait but is in fact a reference to the biblical lifespan achieved by those patriarchs, they claim. Western academe insists that all this, especially the cavalier attitude to the opposite sex, is very much a part of everyday life in areas of what is known eponymously as Munster.

2 - Dirty Tennits, failed fishermen, lazy farmers are the neighbours of us all, says one expert. We live next door to one or other of them. We know them from their peculiar or foreign ways sometimes, from the way they speak back to us, or their personal mannerisms at other times. We can tell them from the way they decorate their houses, till their gardens, treat their children, or even the way they drink their pint in the pub.

3 - The description of La's philosophy was the cause of a particularly unpleasant dispute between the two university panels, an account of which appears in the Report. The University of Galway took the view that La represented a true breed of Corkman who is 'all philosophy and no action'; whereas the typical Galwegian is a wise sort who eschews 'philosophy' to concentrate on concrete action and good deeds. Needless to say this lifted the

roof off and there followed an unseemly slanging match unrepresentative of normal academic behaviour and more in tone with those peasant 'fights' reported by Eamon in his travels around the region. Dr Crane made matters worse by suggesting that we are looking at two different kinds of human beings in a psychological rather than a cultural sense and that 'they who indulge in imaginary abstracts of the mind' were more likely to suffer from delusions and acts of inexplicable behaviour, resulting from mental derangement, while those whose 'feet were based firmly on the ground' usually succeeded in life. Go into the two cities of Cork and Galway, he said, and you will see in the buildings and monuments, such as cathedrals for instance, examples and representations of the two kinds of mind; one extremely and unhealthily subjective, and the other broad, friendly and expansive.

'This is going too far and we are getting carried away on side issues here,' said one of the Galway scientists (true to his supposed 'character'?), 'and such groundless speculation is not called for in our brief.'

chapter six

On a ship out from Assaland was the first official missionising group of Lasdiacs for the little island. Shells, snails and flails were their lock, stock and barrel in accordance with their motto, (come unarmed, possessing nothing but your hopes and beliefs), and they went about the ship with great gusto and alertness. The captain, a veteran of many trading trips to the island, took the missionaries with him as part of an elaborate trading arrangement involving powerful merchant-men, business-partners, the sole government of Assaland and the indispensable collaboration of at least one islander. A very weak-in-the-head rural despot had once suggested in a moment of inexplicable madness to a holidaying, out-of-uniform Lasdiac that he thought it might be a good idea for Assalanders to come and 'teach these people some new ideas'. He had added that everybody in the island was tired of 'the same old faces' about the place.

The captain felt that these enthusiastic missionaries were a nuisance on his old worn out ship as they kept congregating on one side and nearly overbalancing the vessel. The overpowering gales and destructive storms, which the Lasdiacs were informed were currently lashing the island, as well as the chaos that was reported from the towns and countryside, were a providential incentive to their going and there was unabashed optimism on all their faces as to the ultimate success of their mission in that stricken land. It was the Lasdiacs' policy to find just one susceptible, influential-in-a-sort-of-way individual in a new region and concentrate on winning him over to their ways.[1] Once the fresh recruit to their cause had been obtained, they dressed him up in new clothes and used him to draw others over to their side. This raw recruit (glad for free clothes in excellent condition) would never be a monk or scholar, astronomer or clerk. Normally he would be an ordinary individual who might also be a sort of minor leader. It did not matter if he, or she, was a lower-down leader. On the island of Upper Handia, a small island next to Lower Handia, they had first converted the overall leader and this had brought them apparent success, but later their success had turned against them when the leader developed an extremely swelled head and had started singing Lasdiac hymns as he paraded around in the streets, making an embarrassing scene and creating a terrible nuisance for the old, established street singers. The result of that was a collapse of their plans as the leader became a figure of fun in musically-aware Upper Handia and he in fact never regained his proper senses after this. From that time on they had never approached a Chief Leader in the first instance, and this preference for the minor leaders became a part of their policy. The chief policymaker on the present mission was Usdiark II, a Lasdiac from the Lasdiac Centre who had been promoted over the heads of better and longer-established rivals and seniors, and given his very own mission to lead to the small, off-shore island. Usdiark II was a figure of fear to the younger Lasdiacs, whilst being an almighty pain-in-the-backside to the seniors and everybody else on the ship, and especially to the captain. For instance, he kept insisting to Captain Art that his ship really did not need its sail and steering rudder, but that it would be better and more virtuous to let the vessel find its own course, which would be a more impressive sight to the islanders, if they saw the ship coming into harbour of its own accord with the Lasdiacs up front controlling operations by their own impressive 'spirit'. When he found that he could not have his way with the captain, he turned his attention to perfecting the characters of his own men, and after a few incidents their patience too with Usdiark II began to wane a little. This discord was not visible to anybody else however, remaining covert, for one Lasdiac would never openly speak ill of another.

It would be too tedious to detail the daily schedule of the missionisers on that voyage. A brief outline of their rituals is as follows: rise at the first chink of light of day and turn their faces in the direction of the breeze or wind, thereby refreshing their spirits; a dusting of their white gowns and robes and a running of their hands over their bald heads; then after a breakfast of banana bread and feet pie, deep meditation on business and administration management at their sundry sitting-boxes, with the rest of the morning devoted to various activities, of which some of the most important were lively conversations about impending personal or career successes, always, for 'reasons of humility', conducted in pairs. The activities of the rest of the day were shrouded in secrecy, being carried on in ritualistic or ceremonial forms appertaining to hidden spiritual values (such as sales pitch, attitudes to customers, cost cutting). Even when these were observed by onlookers they remained nevertheless obscure activities, not being meant to be understood by the uninitiated. The increasing amount of rain that fell as they approached the latitude of the island dampened their spirits somewhat, and the excitement of the adventure began to diminish a little in their hearts as they contemplated the more mundane tasks of the mission that lay ahead of them. The older ones knew the tedious explanations they would be required to give to their uncomprehending hearers, and they felt a natural rebellion against having to give long, drawn-out definitions of Assaland philosophical ideas such as that of 'Hop', which in its simplest and most platitudinous version means a kind of walk, or a way to walk, and 'Pinch', which refers to a way of lifting things or of holding things in your hands, such as eating and drinking utensils. There was one young Lasdiac who was still having difficulty mastering some of these concepts, and Usdiark II discovered this fact by means of one of his routine, invigilatory questions.

"Tell me again what you said Hop was," asked Usdiark in a pretend-disinterested sort of voice.

"I didn't say anything," replied the unfortunate Lasdiac whose name was Charles.

"Oh yes you did; I heard you," said Usdiark with a sudden burst of anger.

When Usdiark got angry he usually did a little dance on his toes, which he commenced to do now with some difficulty due to the movement of the ship.

"Oh, I said that Hop was a bit of a silly thing, that was all, and I only meant by that that it would be very hard indeed for the natives to understand it," said Charles meekly.

"Who was your teacher, lad?"

"You were, sir."

Usdiark struck Charles and left a red mark on his face. Charles was mortified with embarrassment and looked around to see who was watching. To his immense shame and despair, he saw that nearly all the Lasdiacs as well as the whole ship's company had witnessed the slap, and he felt regret that he had ever come on the voyage. He decided that he would not end his days in that company, and the last person in the world he ever wanted to see him again was Usdiark II. It was a humiliation beyond bearing, for it had all happened in full view of not only the other Lasdiacs but of non-Lasdiacs. This was gross professional misconduct on the part of Usdiark! Unfortunately, it was written into their rules that a lower Lasdiac must never make a complaint against a higher one. Charles had never felt so helpless, and at the same time so angry in his life.

"What is Hop?" Usdiark repeated, while all the other Lasdiacs either looked the other way or moved further off to escape the spectacle of Usdiark's wrath.

Charles was just about in the mood to spit in Usdiark's eye, but he knew that the consequences of this would be dire for him (it would go in a report), and it would also please Usdiark by justifying him in his unprofessional slighting of a fellow-Lasdiac. Even as the spit was ripe on his tongue he held himself, and felt the anger go down his stomach and run on into his boots. He must have looked pale and strained standing there, and he thought he saw a flicker of cruel pleasure on Usdiark's face.

"Hop is what we all know it is," was his reply.

"What sort of an answer is that?" said Usdiark loudly, and Charles knew he was shouting only in order that everyone else would hear.

"Hop is ..." mumbled Charles.

"You don't know what it is, do you? I will give you one more try at an answer, and that will be it," said the master.

"I can't say what Hop is .... It is a kind of ... something. I would say it represents a mysterious quality in our way of looking at things ... ; a definite ... oh, I can't think of the word."

"Do you know what it is?" asked Usdiark.

"No. Or, what I think about it is so difficult it cannot be put into words."

"Well then."

"Can you explain to me again what it is, sir?" asked Charles, and it was hard to know whether he was being sincere or simply sarcastic in his request.

"I have heard enough. I will put this in your report," said Usdiark between gritted teeth.

For the rest of the morning the other Lasdiacs spent their time working out, reasoning and repeating to themselves what 'Hop' was, and wondering if Usdiark would be coming to question them about it too. Captain Art, in the meanwhile, was pondering why it was the heaving ship seemed to be finding it so hard to make its way through the waters which were becoming increasingly murky, and why progress through the sea seemed to be so slow. As he looked ahead through the treading waves and the driving rain, he felt that this was one of the most unpleasant, uncomfortable voyages he had ever had to make in his life. He had always found that the Lasdiacs were a nuisance when they came as individuals or small groups aboard his ship on their various 'educational trips'; they were an even bigger misery now. He looked down his beard at his protruding stomach and thought that maybe he would hang up his sails soon and retire to that small, secret island on the other side of Andovia that nobody knew about and where he had stored the gains of decades of profitable trade in ludge and astronomical theories. Perhaps, he thought, he could settle the hash of these arrogant Lasdiacs too, before he had to make his withdrawal from the scene.[2]

Economy, by this time, had thought of something else he hadn't considered before. Why not, he reasoned, walk on two legs instead of just hopping about on one? The idea was like a new light to him, like a star that appears in the sky where there had been nothing but darkness before. There was no reason why he shouldn't try to use both feet! What if people laughed? That wouldn't bother him at all. He had a glorious feeling of complete indifference to folk now. He was free! It was a grand feeling when he thought about this new ability of his to think, to make decisions of a practical, and indeed philosophical nature.

He crawled to the opening of the cave and peered outside. He saw that it was early light, about the time of first morning smoke in the island. But there was not a sound of civilization in the area. He was in the wilderness in the back of the Chasemeup Mountains and only the twitters and chirps of the fantasy birds could be heard. He breathed in the dripping mist and twitched his hairs as they irritated his skin in the clinging moistness. He thought for a moment that he detected a greater chill than was usual in the world around him.

He was ready to try out his bold experiment. He stood up cautiously and promptly hit his head against the roof of the cave. His cry rent the air and startled the birds and confirmed them in their suspicion that there was some intruder in the vicinity. Ever watchful of their roden berry preserves, they instantaneously flew together in a tightly knit group to a great height.

Economy staggered out into the open. Would he accept a new challenge? With feelings of doubt and trepidation he slowly lowered his useless leg down on to the ground. He closed his eyes with the effort and waited for the moment of contact. It seemed to take ages. He could not believe it when he actually touched the ground, for he felt no new sensation at all. It was as if he still only stood on one foot. He did not feel any better, or any worse for it. If anything he was feeling a little awkward and thought that perhaps he had been more comfortable when he had used only one foot. He felt that he might even have some greater difficulty in walking now, as doubts came to him.

But his new spirit filled him with recklessness and he strode forward. He immediately felt like one of those gigantic centipede island-spiders stepping out on a sheet of slippery, clinging water and then realising too late its presumptuous mistake. He felt that his limbs were spreading out in all directions, leaving intact nothing within himself as he wobbled this way and that way. He used his hands to keep his balance, pushing upwards at the air and he walked along feeling like he did in his flying dreams, as if he was once again taking off into the unknown. He walked at he-didn't-know-what-speed feeling a funny exhilaration, as he was not in control of the speed at which he was going. This light-headed feeling lasted precisely as long as it takes to make five steps and then suddenly, where the scrub ceased to dominate the vegetation and strips of fresh grass appeared, it was as if nothing unusual was happening and he stood erect and took another step forward on to the lushness of the meadow as though he had always walked in that manner. It was all so easy! However, the habit of using one foot had left its mark, and now there was a definite, strange distinctiveness about the way Economy walked. The stiffness in his second leg gradually eased, and as he went along he happily commenced to have a good-natured game of hop-and-jump with the playful lasso dwarf snakes that lived in the clumps of grass in that lush meadow.

At last Economy came out of the overgrown bush and on to one of those wild-man-of-the-hills tracks that led down from the highest summit, across the plateau level on which he now stood, to the plains below. And Economy did not know whether to go up or down! The indecision caused a panic in him. His legs (for there were now two of them) seemed to stop right there on the spot of their own accord. It was a case of having two ways to go. After a time, he picked up a stone and threw it down the hillside. It went a long way, and out of view further down. He then picked up another stone and flung it above his head towards the hilltop. After what he thought he heard to be a cry it came back and hit him on the head. When he had recovered his senses he thought that the stones' fate had at least given him an idea of which way to go. It would appear that the first stone went on the right track. He realised now how unpredictable life was out here in the open.

And as he sat there a realisation seemed to crystallise out of nowhere. Somewhere down on the plains below were his real father and mother. He would go and look for them. They would be surprised to see him after all these years. They would be glad to see how he had grown, how knowledgeable he was in countryside ways. He even had strange powers he could show them! He might find out why it was that they had not bothered to visit him. He could not help it as his face contorted itself into a fantastic grimace (such 'screw-up' faces of Economy were to become famous in island art motifs in later generations, their ominous details being remembered from his murals by assiduous, and somewhat morbidly inclined scribes), as he contemplated the past. He would discover the truth as to why they had left him in the first place, in the care of that old woman. He was already going down the hillside as he was perusing these questions. It was another grey kind of day and the wetness in the air and vegetation reflected a stable condition of nature. As Economy approached the plains below, with the air and clouds all around him lifting their veil away, their cultivation and civilization became clearer and more impressive. It was like one of his dreams, but now it was the case that the indefinite pinpoint of the island grew suddenly, and portentously, larger. He had a strange feeling, as if he was re-experiencing a dream in reverse, although now fully awake.

It was in fact déjà vu, a phenomenon experienced by souls of great sensitivity and long respected by the scholars and monks of the island, who were long drawn to esoteric philosophy as a reaction against cold, run-of-the-mill, everyday science. It was interpreted as some kind of camouflaged, secret wisdom. In fact déjà vu and its complex, prolonged analysis formed the whole content of the one and only philosophical school to be found in the country. Its investigation, description, break-down into constituent, innate elements, re-arrangement of segmented parts, its meaning, religious significance and astronomical value took up the whole intellectual life of a great many of the very best philosophers there. They believed, against the opinion of visiting scholars from Assaland (who held that all knowledge could, indeed should be pursued as a logical, rational process), that this reliance on dreams and intuition (of history going around in a circle) was the key to understanding existence. There was no need for schools of logic, of ethics, of abstract argument, human and physical sciences or any of the other factual fields of study that so inflate the workload, not to mention the living expenses, of school campuses in other lands. There were two streams of philosophical thought in the island regarding déjà vu, or as they preferred to term it, 'exigent-island-existence-experience'; the Extraneous or Pertinent lobby and the Subjective, Impertinent or Internal Metaphysical lobby. The former group believed in a Higher Being, whilst the latter crowd believed that 'it' was all in everyone's head. Those who were of the Extraneous Lobby were distinguished by a number of characteristics. They were very nice, eschewed loud arguments, believed that Ebits were human beings, sang in choir, tried to be helpful and generally were quite pertinent and practical. The opposing team were cocky, cynical, argumentative, believed in looking after 'number one', held that Ebits were an ethnic sub-group, never did any really hard work and refused to sing in choir. At certain times of the year the two schools of thought would play against each other in ball games or some other team sport, such as chess, during which, as at other significant times, they would not ever speak to each other and made it a rule never to look the opposition in the eye.

Because of this feeling of déjà vu that Economy himself, without all the paraphernalia of academic terminology, analysed simply as one of his dreams coming true, he now felt an increase in self-confidence. He sensed that his way was being guided by some unknown power and that he was going

The Madness of Eamon Moriarty

into territory that was somehow already familiar to him. As he observed the fields and plantations below him he imagined that it really all belonged to him, that the landscape was his own, private world. It was a grand feeling. Yet a sense of unease came back to him as he went down the slope, for he knew that all reality around him was only a facade and a disingenuous illusion. For he and Na had discussed the false appearance of reality on many occasions. They had called everyday life the 'Other Side of Real-Supernatural Reality'. Real reality, part of that unknown essence of things, which they experienced in their 'real minds' in their everyday life, which the two of them would attempt to discuss through their nets into the early hours, was in fact unknown, or hidden, whilst all that they experienced through their senses was false, or at best misleading. This was a fact of life. It was only a case of working out whether this fact of life was reality also, or whether the truest, most accepted facts of life were a camouflage for some other unreality.

(In fact, what he didn't realise as he fondly remembered now their discussions, was that all of this mad midnight talk was also totally meaningless to Na. The incessant chatter of her nephew that she had to bear with she put down to something that had happened to his thinking during his short stay at the Abercroppy school).

But now reality was to turn into unreality, or unreality into reality, as he clambered down the rough track, grabbing here and there the odd limb of a bush or angular rock to steady him on his course, or even at times to save him from a nasty, dangerous fall. At a turn on the mountainside, marked by a huge boulder which looked as if it had been put in position there by one of the legendary giant-ancestors, he came to a wild man's roden berry patch. It appeared as if the mountain hermit, perhaps a handicapped monk or some other unfortunate person condemned to be an outcast earth-tiller, was having notable success where others had none, for the berries grew profusely despite a plenitude of the monstrous grabworths. Economy rubbed his hands with anticipation as he prepared for a feast. Hiding in the shade of the grabworths, he used their large leaves to make up a bag so as to carry away the berries. When he was sure that the wild man, or hermit, was not in the immediate vicinity he crept out and started to eat and bag the tasty, mincy berries. After approximately one minute of happy plundering he was suddenly and rudely disturbed by the raucous sound of bird screeches. Before he knew what was happening he was being attacked on all sides by, it seemed, every bird in that island. In different colours, shapes and sizes they came from the left and right, above and below, flapping at him, pecking at his face so that he had to cover his eyes, landing all over him, biting and clawing whilst making the most horrendous din. He could not drive them away and as one bird pecked him grossly in the left eye he waved his arms wildly and shouted. His eye was now paining him terribly and he could see blood running between his fingers. There was no sign of any birds; it seemed as if they had gone as suddenly as they had come. He ran across the plot in the direction of the trackway, and it was while he was hastily crossing the overgrowth that he came upon the body of a man.

A large wound was wide open in the corpse's head and the body and face had been grievously disfigured by the ravages of beast or beasts. Economy could not see clearly as he was covering his injured eye with his hand, and he had long been accustomed to ignoring what he saw through the other eye. To add to his miseries it was now raining very heavily. He lay down on the wet grass and suddenly found that he was weeping again. He still could not understand what this weeping was. As well as the water coming from his eyes there was also so much mucous and unsightly expectoration coming out of his nostrils that he felt he was suffocating. All his powers seemed to have left him.

A number of individuals were found dead or injured with grievous head and other wounds throughout the region at the time of Eamon's wanderings. It was considered unlucky to ascribe these deaths to the lunatic, Eamon Moriarty, for it was a tradition, or a superstition, that one never spoke derogatorily of the mad. In any case there were other more suitable candidates for blame than the poor forest wretch. The Tennits for example, or the fisherfolk. Eamon himself, meanwhile, was disconsolate in his isolation, beginning to cry frequently and make cuts in his flesh, his right arm, face and neck, with a sharp stone that he reserved for this purpose alone. He washed himself in his own blood, and liked to run his tongue over his wounded skin to gain from it nourishment and strength. He saw too that the occasional persons he passed on the way were behaving in a manner that was increasingly unfriendly towards him, withdrawing to the side of the track and putting their heads down and ignoring him, but he paid little attention either and he certainly wished them no harm.

It was a healing, though tired Economy who arrived at the tiny hillside village a number of days later. Despite the dangers inherent in meeting people, he felt that he must inform folk of the murderous bird attacks. They would be surprised and indeed terrified to learn that a man had been killed by these once timid, chirpy, harmless songsters that had now become the deadly enemies of mankind. He did not really care if he received a hostile welcome at the hands of the villagers. Such isolated hamlets were not accustomed to visitors and sometimes they welcomed travellers and sometimes they didn't. However he felt he had to unburden himself of the terrible sights he had seen. He might even find the people grateful for being warned of a great danger.

The Madness of Eamon Moriarty

Notes

1 - Great emotion and much 'digging in of heels' over the issue of Top Carrot's reputed dalliance with Assalanders, and specifically a pre-visiting, unofficial Lasdiac delegation, have been engendered over this matter. Cork's learned stratum has denied the claim by Galway scholars that a Dermot McMorrough type figure is to be found in Cork's history.

For the benefit of ignorami, Dermot McMorrow (Diarmuid MacMurrough) was a king of Leinster whose name has been blackened for all time for his inadvertent role in the English conquest of Ireland. Brother of Enna, King of Leinster, Dermot claimed that the throne was his after Enna's death but he was foiled by another king who kept putting his own relatives in. Fracas and infighting broke out for the next thirty years (The Thirty Years War), reaching a climax when Dermot abducted another king's wife, a Mrs O'Rourke. This made him a big enemy in Mr O'Rourke who pursued him in the quest for revenge and the recovery, if not of his wife, at least of his honour. His back up against the wall what with ambitious upstarts in revolt all around him, and with Mr O'Rourke in no mood for forgiveness, Dermot left Carlow and sailed for Pembrokeshire. Here it was that he made a grave breach in Irish 'Rights and Customs', particularly in the inheritance laws, when he promised Strongbow, the Norman, that he could marry his daughter and be his heir. Dermot spent a while swanning around Bristol and then made the fatal mistake of going to see King Henry 11 in person. Arrangements were made for help to come to Leinster and eventually Strongbow arrived with his gang. After minor victories Strongbow married the daughter of Dermot, who himself had been waltzing around the country with the Norman knights, archers and troops. Hoping to make himself High King Dermot went to Dublin and forced the Dubliners out. He died soon afterwards however and Strongbow, illegally, became his heir.

Soon thereafter the end was in sight for truly Gaelic High King candidates. Henry claimed that 'still extant letters attest that "all islands" belong to The Church of Rome (a la Constantine) and that Pope Adrian 1V had given him a golden ring, adorned by an emerald, in token of his appointment as **King of Ireland**.

The whole business was finally sealed up when Henry 11 himself paid an official state visit to the country, where he was reported shocked by the state of things.

2 - Extreme rejection pathology and outright denial greets any suggestion that Cork has ever been subject to Psychic Repression by a particular group or groups in the past (or present). 'We in Cork and Cork county are only accustomed to democracy and liberty in our expression of ourselves and our culture,' says Professor Timothy Roche in an affidavit sworn in connection with a libel case he was pursuing arising out of the majority report. 'To suggest that Cork people would allow themselves be made fools of by Totalitarian Nonsensists, Fascists, Neo-Empire Loyalists, Socialists, Librarians, Newspaper Columnists, a Tom, Dick Or Harry Fly-By-Night, People Who Write Books, Demented Grandmothers, Inquisitors, The Holy Roman Empire, Sex Education, The Culchie Party, the Church Party, is calumny.' None of these, Professor Roche was keen to remind us, has had any lasting influence in Cork. When it was pointed out that the Lasdiacs obviously had a baleful influence on the young Economy/Eamon, Roche responded that it went to prove that the author was not from Cork. 'What do you suppose this poor fellow, or any simple Barbarian tribe, thought as they watched, say, a column of cleaned up, very smart, rigidly organised Roman soldiers marching into their humble terrain? Economy's reaction could be in fact at the very least an ancient folk memory of the Roman Invasion of Ireland, its first documented mention in Irish history,' he said proudly. This is what opened up the subsequent rich vein in research on the Roman influence in Irish culture. It also proves, Cork says, the universality of the Cork experience.

chapter SEVEN

There were little children playing in a farmer's field next to the village and they were throwing bundles of the red mud at one another in some kind of game. It was clear that the changed soil was for them the best thing to have ever appeared on the scene. But the farmer, struggling with the same coagulated soil, would not have concurred with them in the same opinion. Economy stared at the youngsters, seeing in them his younger self. It was obvious that they did not attend any school, for their feet showed clear signs of never having worn shoes, the prerequisite for school and learning. He felt a kinship with the young children. He remembered that he had not been allowed to play with the other children in his own neighbourhood. There was a belief amongst the adults there that he was a danger to them. They would certainly see as something base and subversive his wish now to join in their harmless games, to run with them in the wild creeks and partake in their childish talk and irreverent ways. He felt sadness as he looked at the children, knowing that he dare not approach them.

At that hour the men would be out looking for the next day's meal (which is how they always liked to describe their daily forays), whilst the women would be inside the humble huts preparing whatever food there was available for the evening. He sensed that he could not approach these huts of the women whilst the men were absent. It was not clear why this was so; perhaps he was also a danger to them in the same inexplicable way he was to the children. He sat down on one of the village stones and waited to see if anyone would approach him. The children were taking a closer interest in his presence and some of them had stopped what they were doing and were looking at him. After a while they came a little nearer. He did not look up or speak but waited, pretending to be taken instead with watching the little insects making their living on the earth below him. At last a number of the women left the huts and approached him cautiously. They ordered the children to move back and they themselves did not come too near to him. Their brows were furrowed.

"Can we be of help to you?" the tallest woman asked. She was the wife of the tallest and hence most powerful man in the village, it being the custom (in the absence of any other obvious qualities) to marry and even rise in status according to one's height in that particular village.

"I have seen a terrible attack," said Economy in a voice that was high.

"Where are you from?" the tall woman asked.

He gave no reply. Instead he spoke again in a rasping voice.

"I saw the body of a man up there," he said and he pointed in the direction from which he had come.

"Are you from the Wither woods?" the spokeswoman demanded to know.

"If you had seen his wounds and the tearing of his guts you too would have been terrified."

"His answers make no sense to me. All I hear is a mumble," the woman said disapprovingly.

"They nearly killed me too," said Economy.

"You are not a former Balhopian or Inisbay trainee scholar are you, gone a bit astray after wandering a long time in the backwoods?"

"They came from the sky," Economy said.

"You are a wild man from the mountain top?" she asked now.

"The man was an earth tiller, and they were after his roden berries."

She looked at him now with some relief and amusement.

"When the men come back they will question you about where you have come from and where you are going to," she said sardonically, beginning to reason from his apparent inability to explain himself, that he was after all a harmless fellow, and her tone of voice made the other women giggle.

"You can wait there outside the trading centre until the men come back. They can amuse themselves trying to make sense of you," she said in a not-unfriendly manner.[1]

The women now seemed to lose interest in their visitor and they walked back with their children to the huts and cooking places, starting to sing about tans, sprats and mid-day naps. (A cultural tradition was that when they were bored or overworked, they sang). When Economy appeared at the entrance of the trading centre the controller reached out and struck him a blow on the head. This meant that he did not want him to enter the store. The man then proceeded to strike his own head with the palm of his hand. This apparently meant that he was confounded. It was a custom of the island that a person should receive a free gift of a sweet fist, a type of native ludge, each and every time he or she entered a trading centre, (some people spent all their time just going in and out of stores for this reason), prior to making any commercial, philosophic or moral contract, and this admirable custom was accompanied by the equally admirable custom of not allowing into a trading store any customer one did not wish to deal with on any commercial, philosophic or moral basis, or offer free ludge to, in the first place. In other words they were usually not allowed in if they looked poor or broke.

Economy peered inside through the aperture at the display of goods that the proprietor had put up for trade. He was surprised at the poor quality of the items on the shelf. He thought that there was nothing useful there and that the owner had only put them out to fill up space. Even his own poor village store had more than this! There were cracked plates of useless, inedible sauce seed, plain jars that were empty, except one that had apple seeds, and beside this was a fisherman's boot. He saw what he thought was a lump of white marble in one corner and an oblong stone of the Balhop rock, so precious to the Assalanders (but useless here), in another. There was a long stick of island-bread that looked so stale and hard that it was more like a walking stick or a cane for resisting burglars or Ebits with.

As he stood there he heard a commotion behind him. He turned around and saw that the women were greeting their men who had all come back from the day's outing. It was apparent that the men had not had a very successful time and that their pickings were not much to write home about. In fact the women seemed to be laughing at them behind their backs. They humoured the men, mollycoddled them with affectionate pats and made exaggerated attempts at praising their measly 'catch' (a few cabbage leaves). Economy listened intently to the words spoken between them.

"It is lucky that you men have us women to look after your comforts. Your dinners are in there on the fire all ready for you," said the tallest one.

"Ah, thank you women, but you still need we men to protect you from all sorts of things, don't you? Who keeps the oins away when they come rampaging in from the bush, and who keeps out all unwelcome strangers when they turn up on the village trackway?" the tallest woman's husband asked.

"Oh, ye are all great men, there is no doubt about that," the woman replied, humouring him and the others, not mentioning that wild oins hadn't been seen in the neighbourhood for a generation. It was always best to ensure that they were kept in good cheer and didn't sulk, for then they became tedious and refused to do anything or to go into their huts for the night.

This was the case, that the women grew and produced all the food in that community, while the men partook in games or went off to the fields and woods supposedly to capture wild animals for food, but they were afraid of the wild pigs and of the big hornets and even more so of the wild oins, so that their 'hunting' adventures always ended only with long, eloquently-delivered accounts of their bravado in the field, which was meant to compensate for their light hands and empty bags.

"There is a visitor in the village. He is quite harmless and he did not try to molest the children or us. He has a strange story to tell about flying oins or something that came out of the sky on the mountain top," the tall woman told them, hoping that in this visitor they would find another diversion to keep them occupied for a time, and out of their way, while they got on with the important tasks of the village.

The men looked over to where Economy was sitting and they could not decide whether to call out to him or go over to him. The tall chief eventually, after much heart-searching, made a decision.

"Hey, let's go over and have a look at him," he shouted with bravado and all the men shouted together with excitement and were filled with the hope of perhaps some amusement to compensate for another barren day in the bush. Yet nobody was willing to take the first step. Then they all got in a line and took one step forward and two steps back. Realising that a shameful facedown was about to take place in which not even his own great height would compensate for loss of face, the chief himself finally walked forward with apparently firm, steady and brave steps. Next minute the men had surrounded Economy and were asking him different questions all at once.

'Who are you, did you come by cart or by foot, what's the tale of the flying oins, was your dad with the floating-fleets, are you a great explorer, travelling the world, is your injury the mark of a great warrior?'

Economy was pleased that they were not angry with him, and he was thankful that the women had spoken well of him. He could not understand why they all appeared to be so friendly, their humility apparently an inborn trait. His own village had never treated him with such respect! He spoke slowly and carefully nevertheless, aware that perhaps a wrongly intoned word might be misconstrued by those listening.

"The birds of the air are not to be trusted, nor our walks upon the pathways of the earth.

Look out, for upon your heads next will fall the feathered flock."

As they heard these words the men thought that they saw another span of exigent-existence, a different rational-irrational dimension in the funny look of Economy, as well as in his whole, strange bodily shape.

Eamon had been ready for anything from these people of the remote mountain village he had fortuitously come across, a sound thrashing, loud verbal abuse, stoning-from-a-distance. What he did not expect, or even at first understand in their attitude, was a kind of soft welcome, an acceptance, a non-judgmental judgment, a live-and-let-live attitude, even just relief at having a new face about the place. It aroused a happy feeling in him, a tremble of joy such as he had never experienced before and which made him think that he might, after all, one day, come to be considered as just 'one of the lads'. He was not ever to forget this moment of self-recognition. Not memories of the Social Services, nor of physical and other abuse by his guardian et al, nor of his long, lonely youth exiled from the schoolhouse and community, or even the story of his abandonment at birth were ever to subvert completely the happy memory of this moment.

Eamon smiled in a silly sort of way now at those standing around him as he struggled for something to say.

"There is a body of a wild man in the bush who was scavenged by birds," said Economy, hoping that his words would increase the respect they obviously had for him.

Little did he know it now but he had hit upon a sensitive, long standing apprehension in the religion of that place – the Dread of the Return of The Wild Man of the Mountain, which had dominated their theological debates and their nightmares for generations. He was a fearful and unpredictable god who spoke through human representatives who always seemed to have some serious physical impediment or defect, especially of speech, which made the edicts and messages sound strange as well as hard to understand, and perhaps sometimes even worse than they really were. Now here was another fellow, also with a bodily impediment, who did not bring a new edict from the mountain, but claimed to have found the god dead!

"Wild man! The Wild man is dead? You have given us wonderful news by bringing this report to us, for that monster has been terrifying our village for generations. None of us would ever dare to go on an oin track before! Now we are free to wander where we like, thanks to you!"

"I don't know who he is," whispered another man to the chief, "but he speaks like a prophet."

"I will give him a test," said the chief quietly, "and then we will know if he is a prophet or not."

He spoke in a solemn tone to Economy.

"You speak in a mysterious but true way. Here is a question that you may be able to answer if you are really a prophet. What is the name of The Wild man of the Hills?"

At this the men huddled together in groups and started to mutter among themselves. The question obviously was of great significance for their religion. They were anxious and excited and they were soon carried away in fervour of anticipation, jumping up and down and turning in tight, agitated circles as they awaited an answer.

Economy now spoke loudly for the benefit of what he knew would most likely be a potentially scathing audience.

"Five hundred stone leaps up lies the old man in the bush,
whose mortal remains fill me with fear.
His mouth opens no more to cry out for his breakfast,
nor do his hands reach for berries.
Bedraggled in his torn-up clothes,
his face has been scavenged by birds.
Cursed earth tiller is his name!"

"Old man! The Forebear! Earth tiller! He who brought the original curse on us all by driving his spade into the ground! The Wild man is our ancestor! Now I understand," shouted the chief.

The others kept now repeating this newly established truth amongst themselves:

"The Wild man is our Ancestor."

"It is true!"

"Ancestor... Wild Man Old Man dead... killed... no more ... stranger... village a prophet," were the words being passed from mouth to mouth at that moment.

The men looked at each other, quietly and knowingly. The tall chief spoke to Economy.

"Come into my house-hut and we will have a very long chat, a chat to last as long as three hundred past generations and maybe even longer than that. Fold your clothes over your head and come inside like a good man."

They seemed to have an awe of him now. He could not understand why. (The instruction to 'fold your clothes over your head' was only given to holy men to protect them from seeing the sins of ordinary men.)

"Will you give me a drink of coleoil to cure the pain that is in me," he asked.

They seemed to consider it strange that a prophet should require so ordinary a sustenance. They went inside the dupple hut of the Big Head villager (his nickname and official title), and the room was soon overcrowded. There was a strong smell of drink, sawdust, odours from human bodies and a haze of smoke. After Economy had drunk his drink and was feeling better he settled back his feet and issued forth an altogether almighty belch. On the wall was a strange light coming from a large box and there were moving pictures of people's faces and other things being emitted from it, along with high-pitched sounds. The whole thing glowed like a magic lantern.[2] Economy did not know what it was. He had never seen anything like it before. He had heard of certain boxes in Balhop that made such noises and human talk, but he had never quite believed the story. Now here was something with pictures as well as words that was even more strange and wonderful.

"There is nothing like walking on two legs," he said philosophically to the large group of men crowded around him;

"and feeling two feet on the ground is something that you get used to. If any one of you knew what it is like to have just one leg, you would well understand my joy. Once I did not even know what every child knows, how to walk properly and play hop, step and jump. I now go easily where my legs lead me and I can get to where I am going in much quicker time. And have you heard the noise?"

"Noise? What noise?" asked the chief.

"It is a strange noise that is getting louder and nearer! It may be louder because it is nearer or louder because it is far away. I don't know. I can hear it from a tall tree, or from the rock summit on a mountain. If you strain your ears carefully you can hear it. It is a new sound behind every old sound. Have you heard it in your village yet?"

The chief looked at the other men and they all thought a while and then shook their heads.

"No, we haven't," was the chief's reply.

"Have you observed a change in the behaviour of the birds in the sky recently?" he asked.

Again the men looked at each other and shook their heads and muttered that they had not.

"I pray that your fowl are not taken by robbers," Economy said, his voice dropping to a whisper, a sadness coming over his face and his whole frame now suddenly convulsed by great sorrow.

Eamon had broken down in the company of his new friends. They could not stop him talking unceasingly and with much expression, in the street and public bar, during the day and during the night, as he told how he had been the cause of all the noted troubles of the island, going back to the time of his birth. He had committed crimes that were grave. They had been an affront to nature itself. Not even the Original Ancestor could have committed the crimes he had. So great was his evil it was possible that he would go on committing these crimes for as long as he lived. The villagers laughed at all this and tried to make him happy by feeding him more and more strong drink that, of course, only made him feel worse and confess to even more crimes. He continued to weep copious tears in front of these onlookers, who had to turn away in embarrassment, the chief saying urgently, out of earshot, that it was their duty to take care of this fellow for did not all the legends and fables point to the fact that one day the Great Ancestor would return, albeit in an unrecognisable form, so as to test them for their faithfulness and hospitality, and possibly to bring better times?

Excitement increased as the expensive drink was replaced by a cheaper and more potent vegetable ferment. A few of the men came close to Economy, to touch him or to pinch him.

A while later they and Economy all tumbled out of the hut and into the village square. It was getting towards dusk and the rain was falling heavily. There was a lively discussion and they stood still, waiting apparently to hear the strange sound that Economy had described. They waited some time and the rain became heavier. It was becoming so wet that they were about to go back inside when they thought they heard it.

It was a noise in the distance. It was a high-pitched noise, a low, thundering noise. It was unlike anything they had ever heard before. But it was only Captain Art's ship on its latest visit the island. It was threatening to go out of control in the storm and he was sounding its horn to warn other ships of its predicament. Later on, experts would claim that the only noise, all along, was the big ship.

They listened intently to this for a long period of time, in length amounting to a round of two complete echoes of an Ebit's curse, straining their ears. When it finally stopped they were at a loss for words. They all went inside without waiting for further developments, taking Economy with them.

The men finally heeded the women's calls and went sometime later in a subdued mood to their spouses' huts to get their evening meals, leaving Economy in the chief's hut where he was not offered even one doughnut or the bite of anything at all the whole evening; they did not believe that this unusual being could ever desire to eat ordinary food.

In the morning while Economy was still asleep the men went to the women's sector. They were very worried and most of them had slept very little during the night. The chief was at the front and with him were two slightly less tall individuals acting as 'agreement men', (the role of these was to back up everything a speaker said in discussions with women). Economy had been working on their imagination in a strange way. In addition to giving them nightmares about birds and noises from an unknown source, they were also beginning to wonder how such a weakling could have killed one so mighty as The Wild Man.

"Can I have a word with you, Helen?" the chief shouted outside his wife's hut.

There was the flutter of feet and a rustle of apparel inside and the sound of many women and children's voices. Eventually the tall lady's head appeared at the entrance. She spoke gently and with an obvious effort at being patient.

"What do you want? I thought you would be all off to the woods by now."

"All the men have come to a decision. Few of us slept well, if at all, you know. The whole village must collect up its roots and pack its bags and leave. We are in great danger. We must all go together, at once, in order to save our skins," said the chief, who was called Dan by the other men.

His wife looked at Dan and then at the other men and laughed loudly. They were always trying to get out of their responsibilities! This was a new ploy to escape all the jobs around the village that they had been given and that had been piling up over a very long period. "Go away and have a day's sport in the bush. It is foolishness. I suppose the visitor has put queer notions into your heads. Go away and do not be drinking all that bubble!"

This last instruction was spoken in a stern tone and the men were afraid to argue with her any further. They walked away slowly, beginning to feel a little foolish and now starting to wonder if Economy had been making fools of them all. To their surprise they found the wanderer under the cabbage tree in the middle of a large group of children. They were greatly surprised to see that he was showing them how to write the letters of the alphabet on the ground.

The children were overjoyed. They obviously thought that Economy was some great scholar! The adults were loath to interfere in that which they did not understand. They were glad for anything that kept the children occupied and out of their way. Not for them the unworthy suspicion of countryside art and learning that existed in higher Balhopian circles and amongst the more profoundly serious scholars in the towns. They held that it led to idle, wasted and sometimes-troublesome (and troublemaking) lives amongst those not suited to it. However, simple country folk believe that any, or all, learning is good in itself regardless of its source.[3]

They decided to put up with him for the rest of the day, having it in mind to 'deal' with him later. The children were so taken with Economy however, that he stayed on in the village and he became to that unschooled lot a harbinger and scholar of great note.

He stayed for one whole month. (Scholars who later came there to study the new, and scandalous phenomenon of the learning imparted by an ignorant, mad stick collector, reported that this was a length of time that exceeded any ever spent by a Soldier scholar in the region). It was there that Economy devised a new alphabet system on the ground in one night, instigated an era of hope in which no one any longer feared, or even believed in The Wild Man and, for shame at their own laziness when facing their newly educated children, caused the men to stay around the village doing their chores. And all this was caused simply by Economy's presence and his joining in the children's games.

By the end of that time all of his prophecies and revelations were seen to have come to pass. It all began in the third week, when Economy and his pupils were still struggling to produce their first-ever word, and feelings of doubt and despair were beginning to arise about their ability to learn or understand anything at all, that there came a sudden halt to Economy's lessons. It was an unexpected and welcome relief, due to a cessation in the rainfall that caught everybody by surprise and Economy's pupils ran from the shelter of the big cabbage tree

The Madness of Eamon Moriarty

and the whole village rushed out into the open and there were immediate outbursts of revelry and celebrations in the settlement. It was then remembered that Economy had been talking about a day when the rains would stop and the whole island would be dry again. So excited were people that, even though the rain had resumed its downfall shortly afterwards, nobody bothered to return to their normal activities for a number of days after this, and Economy's lessons remained suspended.

Early one morning at the end of the third week, when things seemed to have returned to normal and Economy and his pupils finally gave up the effort at word construction and turned their enthusiasm instead to some mud bashing exercises, which drew from out of them extremely unusual, primitive and precocious formations, another prophecy came true. The rain was being particularly heavy and the shadows of the night-time were being very slow to leave the earth when there came out early in the morning a woman who had been disturbed in her sleep by strange sounds and was worried that something might have happened to her fowl during the night. She it was who first reported the first ever case of chicken stealing in that village! For her bird was missing from its pen, the door having been prised open by hand or hands unknown. No sign of said bird was discovered in subsequent searches, and the woman had cried out in tribulation and wrung her hands and was driven to complete distraction by the great effrontery of what had happened. Eventually her face had to be covered by the other women for seven months to hide the affliction of her loss.

They asked Economy for his opinion. He spoke about the Curse of Predestination. This he had heard about from that scholar who had glass in front of his eyes in the days of his childhood. He began to regale them with stories for many long hours from memory, which seemed to have contained all that he had ever heard. It was all related in a strangely mixed up manner with no order or logical pattern. At times even he gave the impression of not understanding what he was saying, legend becoming mixed up with historical facts, superstition with religious beliefs, mythical heroes identified, or confused, with real people. But it was certainly this strange curse that had to be overcome by humankind that had caused the calamity of the bird loss. His listeners could only admire his wisdom. Economy had surprised even himself with his words, for he had never suspected before now that he had possessed these thoughts in his head.

Nothing was ever the same again after that. Economy's explanations made things apparently worse at first. Because of the Curse of Predestination, which now became implanted into their dreams and prayers, no longer could folk walk casually down lanes, climb a prominence or jump into familiar streams for a swim without feeling uneasy with an inescapable foreboding that something horrible might happen to them. They could not play a game against another village without worrying unduly over the repercussions of the result for their community. No longer, either, could culinary or other attractions such as communal meals, cockfighting or agricultural/cultural events based on the husbandry of poultry be mentioned without squeamishness and feelings of guilt and shame on the part of the villagers. The whole subject of 'fowl sin' was soon to become taboo, a topic to be avoided on every happy or sad occasion. It came to be established as the worst crime of all, overshadowing all other crimes and failings.

The third prophetic event was the apparent, unexpected return of the villagers' dreaded ancestor in the guise of the walking, crumbling mountain. It was the same old woman, distracted and blinded, who spotted the approach of the mountain as she was out on an early morning walk supposedly washing her feet but really keeping an eye out through her blindfold for the despicable bird thief. Her attention was drawn by some inexplicable power to the mountain where she saw a fierce and frightful storm lashing the summit amid an awful thunder. It appeared to her that the whole mountain edifice was crumbling and tumbling down in the direction of the village. Her cries of alarm brought out the whole population. The men, who had not gone into the bush that morning because of the great uncertainty caused by their thoughts about Predestination, also saw the mountain coming down towards them and they cried out in great panic. Economy could not see the mountain moving at all but, enforced to give an opinion, said that what they might be seeing could be their great chief ancestor returning in anger to punish them for their many misdeeds and their lazy way of life.

This encroachment of the mountain on the village and its environs had not been one of Economy's prophecies. This was the whole point. Everybody said that it was his greatest prophecy because he had not foretold it and it had happened nonetheless. Another change in their perception came now. Whereas before they had believed their village to be quite free of influences from the surrounding world, an independent entity aloof and isolated from the rest of mankind, unfettered by the interference of official or unofficial bodies and all those causes, effects or influences that so ensnared and enfeebled other communities and peoples, they now saw that they too were indeed a part of all that which was around them. They were subject to the entire manner of impositions from nature and of the universe the same as anybody else. It was a shock and an education for them. Even as they watched with relief the fall of the mountain petering out in the lower foot lands quite a few miles away, and the countryside return to its normal stability, they were never again the same people as they had been before. Economy was the first to notice now a weary, new worldly wisdom in their expressions. There was also some hatred, rage, disaffection in their eyes too when they looked at him.

They were glad to see Economy off the very next day. After he had gone (apparently quite happily and willingly), the men met together and appointed his brightest pupil as their first official scholar and opened their first-ever-village-school. The mountain was put back in its place, although it was now to them nothing more than a minor hill and they seemed to have completely overcome their laziness and lack of responsibility as they tidied up the surrounding countryside and made themselves busy about the village. Even the things that previously filled them with feelings of awe or terror did not do so any more. They did not bother to go back into the woods or to sport there after that, but they stayed at home and helped their women around the settlement and learned how to grow things and cook, and to make all manner of useful implements and items from wood and when that became scarce, the hard-baked red earth. Later on, as a result of a visit from some Tennits, they began to interest themselves in all kinds of metal things.

Eamon's time in the village, believed to have extended to the length of one complete journey of the largest moon around the village, saw for the first time in that region the emergence of something that could be called civic consciousness and sense of communal responsibility. The fortunate setting up of a structured educational establishment, (originating in the need to integrate into their society a single mad individual), mirrors how social developments often involve huge leaps in evolutionary and social dynamics that appear to be quite fortuitous. In the meantime, Eamon had the time of his life playing with the local children in the fields and rivers of the vicinity, partaking in their ventures and accepting with good humour their regular jibes and practical jokes. The adults learned to consider this unschooled lad, yet fearful prophet, this harmless fellow who had killed a feared ancestor, this stick gatherer who could perform mural forming, not only as worthy of fear and suspicion, but of laughter and pity as well.

"May your days be long and glad," said the old bird-keeping woman to him one day with a knowing wink, and he decided at that moment that it was time to go, for he knew that the old lady's strange affability and curious blessing were not to be taken at face value, but were probably a subtle hint that she knew more than he or anybody else realised. She had sussed out his 'evil ways', and was giving him a prior warning that she would expose him at the first possible opportunity. Perhaps only the Predestination Curse kept her from speaking out loudly and clearly at the moment.

He slipped out under the cover of darkness, before he would have to face anyone in the morning with the guilt written all over his face.

Notes

1 - It appears that Eamon/Economy had actually come across a remote mountain village where the people were not acquainted with any of the rules of society. It was soon to transpire that they did not believe in locking mad people up, or putting them away. They had a tradition of somehow tolerating them. There, apparently, misfits moved about freely, seemingly unnoticed and uncommented upon, allowed to carry on with what were obviously considered to be their unremarkable activities. There can be no simple interpretation as to why Eamon was given immediate hospitality and, if not an official, then at least an informal place in society there. Neither the fact that the community was without the proper facilities for dealing with such social deviants, or the fact that they were accustomed to thinking that all visitors to their humble village, however eccentric, must have originated from a higher level of civilization, as shown by their simply having arrived there from somewhere else, and even more especially by their not having originated in that village, were satisfactory answers. A possible light was

later to be shed on the issue by a Professor of Vivisection, who stated that during his term in this village Eamon/Economy probably was the recipient, for the first time in his life, of the gratis human emotion of pity. The feelings of philanthropy and charity that this created in the villagers raised their self-esteem and simultaneously made them feel empowered in some way.

2 - Great play has been made of the mention of a 'picture box' in this part of Economy's manuscript. Galway's contingent insists that this reference to what is obviously a television set, or at least the running of a film projector in a small village community hall, proves without doubt that he is a modern character and possibly even dates the manuscript to the 1960's at the earliest, or later. Cork rejoins that far from proving that he is a modern Corkman it only shows the prophetic and inspirational nature of the said character by his early, medieval or pre-medieval revelation of the conceptualisation of modern mass media inventions before their time had come (not much different from the technical visions of Leonardo da Vinci in fact). It shows not only the possible genius of this Economy character but also demonstrates that mankind's most valuable literary text (i.e. the text at hand) was found in Cork and, if it was indeed that it ever came to be proven that it was written in ancient Cork, it goes to point to the possibility that Cork was indeed the cradle of the world's brightest brain.

Dr Crane has a more down-to-earth theory. Referring to integrated models of auditory and visionary hallucinations in impaired integration of the cerebral hemispheres, he says that certain abnormalities not only constrain the effective integration of environmental input but increase the likelihood of internally generated stimuli competing with external events for responses. Such are 'voices' or 'noise' which follow a pattern not unlike a patient whispering to him/herself, whilst visualised hallucinations (such as the 'television set') have a different aetiology coming from the right cerebral hemisphere as primary delusions constituting an individual's attempt to rationalise and create order out of bizarre occurrences such as, in this instance, the excitement and melodrama and the chatter of the chaotic collection of excitable men in that Big Head villager's room allied to the incomplete inter-hemispherical communication between both sides of the brain.

Dr Crane goes so far as to accommodate both the Cork and the Galway schools when he suggests that the impractical drawings of helicopters, steam engines and spherical screw gadgets by the well-renowned medieval 'genius' Leonardo da Vinci constitute proof that the Italian artist was mentally ill and his 'prophecies' no more than the ruminations of a sick mind.

It was a Cork clergyman who brought up the relevance to this issue of the teachings of the great medieval Schoolmen, one of whom asserted that everything that was conceived on earth was in the first instance conceived in Heaven. In that case it would make sense that, with the likes of savants such as Economy, they might well be able to conceive of 'mad things' which would appear or materialize in reality later. An anecdote about a man who had been certified insane by the local health authorities due to his compulsive obsession with a great mirror put in space above the earth by the Japanese, which was able to reflect energy to the earth and intercept or deploy harmful incoming radiation was related by someone who also asked the question: in the light of Soviet and American efforts in space was he so mad after all?

3 - The myth of the Unqualified Teacher taking over in a learning establishment and making the community rue the day it ever set eyes on him/her is well-known throughout history and indeed in every culture and continent. For he usually ruined all that had gone before and instituted unnecessary, or at least certainly uncalled for revolution in society. It has also been said nevertheless, in answer to this, that the greatest teachers were those with no written or paper qualifications, e.g. Our Lord, Socrates, Mohammed and Gautama Buddha, to name just a few, and it should not be forgotten that they led by exposition and example rather than from highly technical tomes and degrees from this or that college or university.

chapter EIGHT

With just a little bag of personal possessions (it contained only some truths and half-truths), he went walking along the trail out of the village. In a corner of the sky where the cloud was less dense was the glow of a very weak sun. As he was watching this phenomenon above he misplaced his feet and slipped suddenly down to earth, landing in a heap much further on from where he had just been. He let out a loud shout of impatience, for if he had not been stargazing and thinking lofty thoughts this would not have happened. He wondered if his bad leg had been affected by the fall. He bent over to examine it; it was to all appearances in good order and it felt fine. Soon he was away again, trying to restore his spirits by giving an occasional skip and whistling his own version of the National Song.

He attempted to keep his thoughts on a more prosaic level, for his safe progress depended on his walking on an even keel. He started watching the normal, ordinary things around him, determined not to look either upwards or even ahead but to remain on the bodily, familiar plane. His newly acquired balance of mind was soon disturbed, however, when the blackness of the ever-wet herbage began to swirl around in his head and he felt he was becoming lost in the maze of some time-submerged primeval wilderness, bereft of civilised or even earthly conditions or landmarks. The muddy path was making his progress both difficult and slow. In fact after just a few minutes of this earthy-concentration he was ready to give it up and it was with relief that he looked up at the sky again;

but it was not with much recompense for the sun glow was gone and the heavens opened in a great fury and the rain tumbled down heavily like oil pitch from a black cauldron. He could no longer tell if it was day or night. He looked to each side of him to discern his pathway but his eye could not penetrate the darkness. He sat down and almost at once began to blend in with the surroundings so that later, in the dawn, his huddled shape was barely distinguishable from the adjoining rocks and tree shapes. The isolation of Economy became in this spot so absolute that his 'persona' was no longer apparent. Of his physical and moral presence there was no evidence. His transient existence entered into and become one with the banal, onerous world of the island as it moved with the stars under the unspoken guilt of the dark universe. It was like some epic without meaning.[1]

The reports of Economy's mural forming on a piece of parchment had already reached as far as the capital by means of a circuitous route that included his own region, Inisbay, the hilltop observatory above Inisbay, the lower regions of Baylat and Logjam, being passed around by farmers, Tennits, unemployed fishermen and even by the poor, subject river labourer; by the hermits known as bagbushmen, and then by the migratory Ebits, who of course had their own debased version of what had been written. The story was eventually carried by the respectable sort of scholar and the monks. Finally it came to be heard in the parlours of the political leaders in Balhop, who were in admiration of the rural endeavour it portrayed, and especially of the peculiar innocence of the real world it revealed.[2]

They asked to see samples of the inscriptions, whose reputation by now far exceeded both the quantity and perhaps the quality of what actually existed until eventually, in some mouths, it bore no relation at all to the actual reality of what Economy had put on the parchment. It was only very much later that it came to be questioned whether Economy had actually written anything down at all, and there were plenty of rival candidates for the authorship of the three or four documents that were by then going the rounds, all claiming to be the genuine article. As is so often the case when dealing with historical subjects and remote, obscure people the actual accomplishments of Economy had a very different reality to the reputation that became attached to them. In this case the piece of parchment that the vengeful visitors had found in Na's hut had quite an adventure in the barns and gossip spots of the locality, with not a few additions being put on it by funny men here and there. The total destruction of the said item, (the wooden murals had unfortunately already been broken up), was prevented by a last minute change of heart on the part of the Relapsed Monk. He was an inadvertent hero, who by his sheer bad temper saved the manuscript for posterity. He said that he thought that the people were making fools of themselves by putting puerile graffiti on the original script, showing themselves to be cretins; that they obviously did not understand what they were reading; that he himself had had a good look at what Economy had done before it became near-unintelligible owing to the messing about. He thought that although no sentence had actually been completed, there was some sense in what Economy had written, or at least in what he appeared to have been trying to say. The whole point was the astonishing vision, or 'cheek' depending on your point of view, of an untutored peasant putting his thoughts down on parchment. These thoughts must be the most undefiled thoughts ever written for they had not have been corrupted by 'culture'. The proper and respected authority, Top Carrot, would wish to see the writings in their original form when he returned, said the monk, and would give an official, definitive version of them. He himself might also wish to give a personal opinion about them to Top. It would be very hard for Top Carrot to read them as they now were. It was his own opinion that there really was a word decipherable in the text but he would keep his theory to himself until Top returned. He would not now say any more about what he really thought, but he did believe that Economy had all the hallmarks of a prophetic, doomed nature.

Old Gobhook went into a sweat and rubbed his brow with his hand.

"Top Carrot will not be returning. His mental and critical powers are not what they were, and would not be in any state to examine this scroll," he said somewhat desperately; "if he does return he will no longer be treated like the great man he believes himself to be, holding sway over this region and receiving the plaudits of every peasant and ignoramus in the land. I am sure that he does not wish for a confrontation with me! I am the chief leader now! I agree it would be a good idea to save the parchment, most eminent Relapsed Monk, and send it to Balhop as evidence of the appalling state of affairs that Top Carrot has left behind him. I also suspect he may be trying to get a permanent position over there. Well, this piece of tripe should put an end to his ambitions. I don't see how you can read so much into a few scribbles; I expect the literary experts will dress it all up in order to make us impressed with their expertise and inside knowledge. Give me the parchment, lads, let's use it to our advantage and make of it a curse and retribution on all who practice Assaland-style politics or step out of the official line."

Gobhook took the parchment and rolled it up and put it into his pipe and not for one second did he suspect another reason for the Relapsed Monk's intervention. It did not occur to him that the same monk had put something else on the sheet while nobody was paying attention. This was a slander

The Madness of Eamon Moriarty

against Gobhook, accusing him of falsehoods and pretence, insinuating also a concocted piece of scandal about a rumour the farmers had supposedly spread about the Tennits and Fishermen. All in all, it was adding up to a right scandal sheet and the monk said a prayer that all their reputations would be entirely ruined by it in the end, just like his was long ago! Gobhook, meanwhile, sent the piece on its way to Balhop and it did eventually arrive there, but not before the poor river labourer had been stopped, quite roughly, by the Tennits, who took the paper and had then managed to get a despicable crab hermit to read it for them. The Tennits were so incensed by what they heard read out that they there and then declared war on all farmers in that region, insisting that this was the only way to avenge their honour. Meanwhile, they forced the crab hermit to write down their own choice insults on the parchment.

Notes

1 - This reference to the island being 'banal' and 'onerous' has led to insinuations that the whole piece is just meant as a denigration of Cork, which imputation has led to warnings that have not discounted the use of physical force. That Cork was conceived of by the author as a banal and boring place, one where it was banal and onerous to have to live, is of course a serious accusation in the eyes of a people so proud. An answer has been provided by a member of the Cork steering committee, Reverend O'Driscoll who as a Philosopher, as well as having qualifications in Moral Theology, brought up (not for the first time) the subject of Existentialism. He says that Eamon had obviously reached the stage of utter darkness, devoid of belief in anything – the classic existentialist situation – and that if only he had spoken to the right person at the right time, namely a member of the clergy, he would have been guided in the proper direction and enabled to make that 'leap of faith' that is called for in this very situation. Everything that happens after this point is a direct result of his not having found the faith, according to Reverend O'Driscoll. Eamon had plunged straight into a post-Existentialist

syndrome variously described as Free Thinking, Rational Subjectivism or Madness. Asked to elaborate further on this existentialism, Reverend O'Driscoll said that it was interesting that the author should try to conceal his real name, as this is exactly what Soren Kierkegaard, the Founder of Existentialism, did when he appeared as a writer(s) in various guises such as Johannes Climacus, Johanned de Silentio, Anti-Climacus and so on, and only occasionally as himself. It was also significant that one never quite knew how to take the Danish philosopher and his writings, and whether the latter were to be deemed as satire, fiction or non-fiction, religious rhapsodies or philosophical treatises. Now this is exactly the state of affairs in the case of 'The History of the World'. It is, said O'Driscoll, the work of a guilt-laden personality, who is of the mistaken belief that he is a useless and insignificant individual. The upshot of Reverend O'Driscoll's analysis is that the author is not saying that Cork, or any other place, is boring but that he is simply experiencing the 'nausea of existence' (see Jean Paul Sartre) at that very moment.

2 - Before the actual decipherment of the script was made, (an account of which occurs later in the book), ideas on what this much hyped-up writing really consists of abounded. You name it and it was suggested in one journal or other. From the theory that it was part of a plot instigated by the Monks to outdo the Scholars in the race to find the truth by enlisting the help of the Proletariat, whose Consciousness had come to be rated higher than that of the Bourgeois, by giving a fortuitously indecipherable text the imprimatur of the Peasant Primitive, to the theory that it was some sort of backwood's juju, consisting of the prehistoric codes of early mankind in which hunting and gathering, stick collecting and berry picking activities meant calling upon the dubious help of obscure muses and idle gods, there was no shortage of argument or discourse. If Economy were the author of those 'fatal insults' (as they turned out to be), it leads us directly into the question of Inspiration. There is of course Divine Inspiration, as Reverend O'Driscoll pointed out. It is not without significance that great works of Divine Authorship such as the Bible, Joseph Smith's Book of Mormon and the Secret Writings of Ras Tafari have also had a very close link to the soil of this earth. We may begin with the human form, itself made of dust; The Ten Commandments carved in two tablets of stone, the clay tablets that Joseph Smith found under the ground, the secrets of the soil contained in Ras Tafari-ism and so forth. Economy (who also wrote on the ground) and his rude materials were not unlike those other books of clay. Inspiration of course was for long laid at the feet of the Nine Sister Goddesses and their chosen categories, Calliope (epic poetry), Clio (history), Euterpe (lyric poetry), Melpomene (tragedy), Terpsichore (choral songs), Erato (love poetry), Polyhymnia (sacred poetry), Urania (astronomy) and Thalia (comedy) -the Muses. While there has always been the belief that genius is a pure gift of the gods rather than the result of hard work or acquired human skill yet, as the new Lord Mayor of Cork (an amateur violinist himself) points out in the published version of the report, there is no known muse for Economy's writing – for what might be considered less as being in the category of literature, and more as that of defamation and insult.

chapter NINE

Some time later, actually probably very early in the morning but it was hard to tell due to the cloud-ridden conditions, the hungry Economy was disturbed by a passing oin. It was at that moment that a thought came to him. It was like the appearance of a light in a dark forest, of the finding of crystal stone in a heap of rubble, a thought and yet a revelation from above. Even though it came from on high it had a resonance in his bodily appetites, a gnawing in the stomach, a moistening of glands, even a smacking of lips. Was it an idea from the ether or was it simply a realisation of a previously unknown appetite hidden deep within? Such a question has often been asked down the ages whenever man has made, or inadvertently stumbled across, a great discovery that for some unknown reason had never previously occurred to his very wise ancestors.

It was the idea that it might be possible to eat oins. Despite the gloom, he felt now as he had in his younger days when, after sipping the drop of the scented, chimerical jungle-juice (known in Balhop as just plain, old fashioned black tea), he used to sit back with the anticipation of an imaginary, heaped-up, glorious breakfast and look out through his toes at the light of the rays of the old sun and the waking-up of nature played on renascent chords in his spirit; and he would hum that tune that had no words.[1]

All of nature entered into him now and spoke in a symphony of joy. The most unspeakable, unheard-of idea was coming from the secret knowledge and wisdom that emanated from all the ordinary, simple things around him, celebrating the abundance and fruitfulness of nature. He heard with fascination now the dumb earth speak, sensed that the deaf world could hear and out of the rocks came potent, wonderful words, like a boast, or speech – 'we stones build up men's walls, strengthen their castles, at corners stand watch, strong weapons make and to us monarch, monk and poor men are beholden.' The vegetation joined in the joyful chorus, shadowy yet wistfully – 'patient and rooted, we plants go a-falling, into the greedy fire, gold turned to mud; yet look at us, still growing and blowing in the breeze, for as man cuts us down, we sprout up again!'

The whole earth had come alive! Economy for a moment was able to look through both his eyes.[2]

It was the quietly grazing oin and its gentle foal in front of him that had prompted and sustained this flow of exhilarated thoughts. They stood there quietly, not bothered by his presence. Their tameness was no doubt due to their changed situation in the island. Paradoxically their diminished numbers, which had never been properly explained but which scholars linked to the more humid weather conditions which also may not have been conducive to a fertile, procreative sort of behaviour amongst what was essentially a dry savanna animal, had led to a decline in the awe in which they were held in a non-oin meat eating society. Their previous fear of the creatures had lately changed to amusement and indifference, considering them now to be objects almost of quaint nobility. The reduction in oin numbers and possible demise of the species also led paradoxically to an increased freedom for these animals so that they no longer hid themselves in the bush. As the adult oin gazed at Economy he heard it now say to him, in a song-like voice –

'You see me here, with my foal, as I see you there, with your hunger. Smell, touch, come and taste my milk, my meat.'

Looking at this harmless creature (their aggression must have been only been an old wives' tale) Economy made the first, tentative move, in all of that island's history, at subduing an oin and attempting to domesticate it for man's own use.[3]

There, in front of him, was a bountiful source not just of the common dead oin's hair but of meat and milk and inner and outer parts which could be garnered for man's use if only he could get that oin to go with him and stay with him. He foresaw a mighty increase of oins, a great herd, that would multiply and grow and bring to the island great prosperity! What a wonderful thought it was, of fields full of chewing, contented oins, baby foals, sprightly yearlings, mature, stolid bulls no longer fearful creatures, or objects of superstition and ridicule, but the subject of proud contemplation by farmers and the cause of self-congratulatory handshakes and warm, honest opinions and appraisals amongst the steadily progressing husbandmen and women. No more would there be complaints from the farmers of oin-chewed hedges as henceforth all the creatures would be safely contained within their own enclosures. There would be a boon for the island and peace and prosperity would come to the whole hungry populace. He himself would become an immensely wealthy farmer, perhaps the richest in the whole wide world!

He stood up and held out a grass-filled hand to the curious oin. The foal, which was not indeed of the mother's own natural issue but was a fosterling, ran to join them. To Economy's surprise the mother oin did not turn to protect her foal or to flee. It just stayed where it was and ate the grass out of his hand! It was a wonderful sight! It was then that Economy noticed for the first time that, contrary to all the legends, oins only had one layer of teeth. Very quickly he tied a grab worth rope around the calf's head and then led it and the compliant mother down the track that he was now able to see quite clearly in the white shadow of the rainy day. He wasn't too concerned about which direction he took for he was intent now only on finding an unclaimed field for 'his animals'.

Not far away Economy saw ahead of him the damp spirit-and-smoke of a settlement and on the far side of the settlement lay what appeared to be an unused field of grass. Because of the ancestral curse which had obliged them – and all past and future generations – to partake in the condemned occupation of ground cultivation, and due to a superstition that all fields of best quality grass were to be left for the exclusive use of 'the fairies', there was the ancient tradition upheld by strict island law that all peasants and landless folk were to restrict themselves only on those fields that were incapable, due to paucity of soil or some other natural condition, of supporting any type of worthwhile grass, and leave the large, fertile fields to the farmers who knew best what to do with them. This was why Economy stopped at the next village he came to, walking through the street with two oins at his side – it was in order to obtain pasturage for his animals on the unused fields of grass.

There was a general amusement in the village at the sight of Economy and his two oins. The villagers, wanting to know why he had stopped there on his journey, questioned him.

"Why are you holding on to those two oins?" they asked laughing at him at the same time.

The children gathered around and pulled on the oins's tails and one of them took a soft blob of clay from the ground and threw it at the larger oin.

"I am taking my two animals to that empty field over there that nobody uses. That will give my oins food for a time. Firstly we will need to fatten them up," said Economy in a matter-of-fact voice.

"You are going to become Lord of the Manor then?" laughed one man in a mocking voice.

The Madness of Eamon Moriarty

Economy was in the habit of taking mockery as a compliment, for it seemed that it was only fools that people took seriously enough to bother to laugh at. Yet there seemed to be an air of change in this village, caused by a new sort of sophistication and sarcasm, which in turn was the result of a cultural change that had started in a village higher up where Economy had spent some time and was already passing down through the valleys at an unprecedented speed, causing disruption of the old ways and new inter-village rivalry and jealousy. Indeed, it had reached this village even before Economy.

Loud laughter spread in ripples through the bystanders. More wisecracks were made at his expense. A small piece of earth was flung at his back by one of the more forward children, but Economy did not seem to notice this playful but dangerous incident, which might have led to his stoning to death, the frequent fate of unwanted visitors to the villages.

"Food and drink from oins?" wondered the chief's sidekick, looking serious.

"What will the other villagers say? They will think we have gone mad."

Economy pointed at his two animals that were now lying down on the track in a peaceful, tired manner;

"The other leaders and people can eat and drink from the oins too! Everybody can eat and drink from oins! Give me the field for my oins, and the villagers can help me to look after them. Collect in more oins! I will soon go down to the town to find out how it was that I came into the world. And when I return here there will be prosperity and I will live in peace and friendship amongst you. Oin-dung will be a plentiful, treasured wealth, the rains will stop and the birds will cease in their attacks on the crops as there will be a plenitude of food for all."

Although they were not looking at him as he spoke (this was a peculiar habit of folk that he had first noticed in the previous village) he knew that his words were being listened to. But he sensed a distrust and dislike of him as well, such as that people have of those who make them think about things. The men looked troubled and perplexed, for the eating of oins had always been taboo, and the use of unused land unheard of. A very small young man now stepped forward and fortuitously saved the day. This non-descript fellow now became an inadvertent collaborator of Economy and an unsung hero of mankind simply by being a know-it-all. He was in himself, a narrow minded, self-opinionated and self-overrated thinker, for he was given to thinking and speculating rationally. He spoke pompously, for he thought he was the only person there who knew what was going on. "I went to visit a friend I have in another village and with whom I always discuss every matter under the sky. In his village there has been a great hustle and bustle lately and they have been doing a lot of things. They are much more sophisticated up there, and they have even opened an educational establishment for the useless, mad and ignorant members of the community. Their whole village is very tidy and they have planted a few bushes at the gates! The women no longer make jokes about the men and they allow them to stay overnight. Now I see, too, that if we do as you say we will have all we need in our own back yard! Our whole standard of living and quality of life will be improved. It is a very good idea."

The others looked at this intellectual and then at Economy with wonder. It meant that they would not be a backward village anymore. They would be better again than that other backward village higher up the valley!

"Collect up all the oins you can," said the chief loudly; "it will be every man's task to set up his own oin farm and direct its husbandry. You shall all become wealthy farmers just like those fat men down in the lower valleys. For what have we to lose, only the friendship of our neighbours, and that is worse than their enmity. In the meanwhile, watch out for the farmers and don't let them get to hear what we are up to."

When they looked around Economy had gone. He was over the way, reciting to the bystanders a song he had heard from Na about how the Early People Had First Discovered The Ancient Wisdom By Eating The Forbidden Food In The Days Of The Legends. He sang about how they were all going to become very wise and happy people now. His listeners thought he was just singing a scurrilous ditty.

In order to facilitate Economy's departure from the neighbourhood – there was a fear that he might cast some powerful spell over them – they took away his oins, telling him that they would be giving them a better home than he ever could. They quickly had prepared for him a free, but tasteless snack of gin buns and cow seed made from little known weeds collected by Ebits which had to be cooked continuously for two moons; (it was the food that was left outside doors in case the fairies and witches called). A little while later Economy, after a short talk to anyone who would listen about dreams and the practice of walking properly, went to give the local village idiot help with putting the oins in the field. He wept quietly for the loss of his two four-legged companions. Instead of returning to have a final ritual wash in the washing barn, as would normally have been the custom, he set off instead down the path leaving the puzzled village idiot wondering where he was going. So he managed to make off without having to go through any of the farewell formalities that would have necessarily been greatly complicated for having come uninvited to this poor, but proud village.

As quick as word-lightning the news spread through the valleys that some villagers were keeping oins and everybody made a great joke of it at first whilst making sure that they too went out and got some oins and put them in empty or unused fields.

So also it was that a spate of a new type of crime started, the stealing of neighbouring villagers' oins, and this vice soon spread to other parts of the island encouraging, as if through a process of osmosis, the feverish uptake of oin farming by all manner of people, rough rogues, indifferent sorts and even quiet, gentle, thoughtful people as a permanent, and eventually, after a long process, a respectable activity. Within a matter of days, while Economy was still making his way through the herbage along the ever-winding trail, the practice of oin keeping (and oin rustling) became well established in all the hill and plain areas.

Specially chosen individuals in each community were appointed to care for the animals, some to do all the hard, dirty work involved (it took them a long time to get used to the smell), and some to arrange the financial dealings which fortunately involved no smelly work. Indeed it was seen initially as a disreputable, incredibly dishonest and spiritually dubious, though undoubtedly profitable, sort of enterprise. These 'oinkers' were looked down upon as nearly always being crooked types who were accustomed to cheating on their families, friends and community and who took to oin dealing like fish to water.

And within a short period of time much the largest stock of domesticated oins were to be seen confined and grazing happily in the rich farmers' fields. Later, in the small villages, it was to become the Great Controversy as to which village intellectual had come up with the idea of oin farming first, for these poor villagers were left with nothing else to do but devise new pastimes such as arguing about the progress they saw all around them but of which they were not a part. All the business, and all the profits, of the oin industry were continuously it seemed going into the pockets of somebody else, especially those of the big farmers and Balhop businessmen.

The Madness of Eamon Moriarty

Later on it was to be claimed that it was a speech by a leader who was responsible for agrarian activities in the island, banning oin-keeping forthwith pending a government enquiry, which actually hastened the upsurge in oin-collectivisation and confirmed its permanent place in the life of the country. And certainly declaring anything to be an illegal activity in the island was a plus point for it, for such speeches always have the reverse desired effect on recalcitrant people, proving once again the only fact ever shown to be undoubtedly true in the whole history of time and space – that governments and rulers never learn from past experience. Village intellectuals, accustomed to the machinations of rulers, came to believe somewhat cynically that the Agricultural minister knew all along what the result of his speech would be, which was why he made it.

Note – this same speech was found on a loose sheet inside Economy's text.

"I address you, farmers and peasants of the hills, you who are the backbone of the country, whose brawn so welcomingly complements the brains of our lowland town classes. Therefore it has come as a disappointment to us in government circles that rumours are about concerning a non-approved activity involving oins. As you know, our wealth and spiritual salvation is based on exporting lots of the Balhop stone to Assaland, and without the ludge and rice they give us in return we would all be in the poorhouse by now. What can we do with oins? Will Assalanders eat them? Where would economic production be if everybody started breeding oins? Might they not be bad for the health? What is worst of all – neither the Government nor the Inland Revenue were informed when unpatriotic individuals started out on this caper, making big bucks and going off abroad to enjoy their ill gotten gains. Bad luck to them!"

However, the irony was that Economy himself, being without oins of his own, did not ever get to taste oin meat.

And later he did not attempt to capture, kill, eat or milk any of the oins he came across, for he felt that they were his friends and he even gave up his dream of being a great oin rancher, reverting to foraging in the ground for whatever weeds or edible plants were available.[4]

The legend later grew up that Economy had appeared in the second village accompanied not by oins but by a somewhat flap-eared, shaggy-tailed dog and her pup. The local oins, which became the basis of one of the most prosperous industries in the country, had always been the inviolable inheritance of the local big farmer, Mr O'Flatter, and had never been wild creatures or part and parcel of the local terrain as some local folklore would have it. This story, contrived to cover the guilt of the people at the theft of Economy's two beasts, immediately developed and spread, especially amongst the children, into the myth that the two canines were wild wolf types hitherto unheard of in the region, and that Economy had lived with them in the bush and had eaten of their flesh and drank of their blood in order to keep alive. This tale then became fact and appeared in all the written accounts, as also the tale which explained that following a strange, short-lived local outbreak of an unprecedented preying on a traditional farm livestock viz. poultry that occurred in the area around this time, the tradition of frenetic 'wild beast-hunting' expeditions was launched in times thereafter by anxious shooting parties in search of 'the beast that was never seen'. And yet a revolutionary change took place at that moment in the village, as the market price of oins rocketed and the economically depressed people began to specialise in oin meat-production, and every other kind of meat-enjoyment, without any ceremony and forgoing the normally required blessing of any new project by the Hierarchical Monks. It is not easy to disentangle the sequence of events but it appears the changeover of the local farmers from sinful tillage to pastoral farming happened when a sympathetic, charitable farmer, Mr O'Flatter, took pity on Economy and his dogs

The Madness of Eamon Moriarty

and employed him in the back fields for the keeping of some oins he, Mr O'Flatter, had recently mysteriously acquired in a certain legendary way, which was to become one of the 'great stories' that were passed down by word of mouth from generation to generation. From that time onwards there was no looking back with regards to any other kind of farming, due perhaps originally to the availability of cheap labour in the form of 'Economy and his dogs'. Even the continual downpour of rain was welcomed as it encouraged the growth of pasturage. The Monks and scholars were soon to express outrage at the ceasing of their annual tithes of crops and there were many calls amongst the conservative elements in society for a return to Friday fish-eating. There was concern, even consternation, at the employing of an outsider in a local farming job, for there was more than one young, habitually idle person in the village now who felt that he had been done out of a living by a stranger; even if it was a form of work that would never have been carried out by anyone else. This in turn caused the whole lot of them to develop, for the first time in their lives, a proprietorial attitude towards the wilderness and nature itself. There was now a jealous possessiveness of the whole universe in general, and of oins in particular.

Notes

1 - What is the difference between waking up in the countryside and waking up in the city? This question, seemingly harmless and even trite in itself, addresses one of the main changes in modern social history. Whereas before, the majority of mankind lived and worked in the rural milieu and awoke to a beautiful sunrise or a healthy rain-filled land full of birds and animals, now most people lived in towns where the apparatus and phenomena of nature is not so evident and you are more likely to see buildings and hear busy traffic on first coming to daily consciousness, with the rising sun invisible behind those mammoth towers created by (errant?) human knowledge, endeavour and aspiration. It means that waking up, and hence our first impressions of the world, are no longer what they once were. Man, as he goes about his toiletries and adjusts to a newly-awake existence, does so in the context of an

environment where the land itself and all that it represents no longer exists. It is significant, for example, that all the Irish writers of note have written in an urban rather than a rural context. The reason is simple. Living in the countryside drives you mad, as commented a number of the academics from Cork City, due to the lack of any order. Dr Crane, also, accepted the possibility, when it was mooted by Professor Roche, that the lonely and disorderly rural background of Eamon explained to an extent his early descent into insanity. Whereas if he had lived in say, Cork city, the situation would have been very different. The tidy and neat streets, the organised arrangements of everyday life in home, shop and workplace, the proper, civilised courtesies of human contacts and the management of more or less straight thoroughfares in a logical pattern explained why so few of the blessed denizens there have a mental health problem, (according to these experts). Note – Dr Crane's agreement (for once) with the rest of the panel on this occasion was the savoir-faire move that gained for him a place on the University Governing Body.

2 - Later on it was suggested by Professor Roche that Eamon must have felt at that moment like God on the Sixth Day of creation, when He looked at His handiwork, 'saw that it was good', and handed over governance of it to Man. There was shock and horror expressed at this by the Galway and religious representatives. To suggest that God would 'hand over' responsibility for the universe to a backward ruffian and ignoramus was outrageous. It is not for the first time that a dangerous glamour has come to be attached to the lad's random musings, and near blasphemous interpretations put on his imaginary 'powers'. Fr O'Driscoll said that the part of the bible which says that man has governance over earth and lower creatures was not meant to be interpreted as referring to the ordinary, common-as-muck lower class of human, but to the more astute, clear-headed, responsible sort of person who would know exactly how to use his powers in a moral way. 'You mean the vegetarians?" asked Roche sarcastically. Dr Crane said that what they were talking about was not whether Economy had put himself on a par with God or even philosophy at all, but were the normal delusions of a sick mind full of 'the jumble of bizarre ideas' and they were not to take offence at anything that Eamon thought, said or even did, as he was 'not responsible' for his own ruminations or actions.

3 - The famous paper 'The transformation from tillage to pastoral farming for reasons due to Economy', has had to be completely reappraised in the light of this text. That article was written by an assiduous cleric of the Church of Ireland who thought no more of what he had described and explained than he might have of an indifferent sermon and the paper only eventually came to light after a dust-up by members of the academic staff, having lain forgotten under layers of documents in the Trinity College library where, it is said, all of Irish history lies. It is now asserted that it influenced Marx (who read everything that was around at the time) in the depressed years when he was beginning to think that what he was writing was a 'load of horse manure' – words he used in a fit of pique, according to a contemporary from his local King's Cross pub days – and reinforced his perceived opinion that all socio-economic change is caused by large groups of blind, stupid, mindless people obeying the irresistible forces of nature. Now here in The History it is suggested that such revolutionary change is actually initiated by a single, semi-clear eyed, somewhat mad but inspired individual who might feel a bit hungry and then go on to eat something which is considered non-kosher and after that, once the so-called 'permanent taboo' has been broken, everyone else proceeds to eat it. It leads some to suggest that it is absolutely necessary for such an 'individual' (a word hated by the Determinists) to exist in society for most people won't eat or touch anything unless somebody else tries it first. A very fat, gourmet-obsessed member of the panel, Professor Roche, today insists, as a result of reading The History and the C. of I. pamphlet, that all of human history lies in the belly of the hungry man, especially the Cork hungry man.

4 - For an appreciation, or at least an understanding, of Economy's fastidiousness about putting into effect what he was preaching see 'Asceticism as Madness-Madness as Asceticism' by Cesare Borgia, where the author attempts to justify his rather full life by lampooning the rest of the Church for its teaching on sin and penance, using not just rigorous intellectual argument but also satire and irony to show that an aversion from this world's goods is a true sign of insanity. Who has ever seen a rich man who was at the same time a lunatic – he somewhat rhetorically asks in his introduction. He goes on to show in a very finely argued piece that while the worldly Romans and his contemporary Renaissance 'fat cats', were the cruellest, basest persons who had ever lived yet they were also the sanest. He cited their many worldly 'achievements', an empire with all its sanitary and public facilities, and of course the Renaissance itself, as the fruit of their common sense. Correspondingly, says Galway, it would certainly have been seen as proof of a total cognisance with reality as well as a healthy balance of mind if Economy had gone on to enjoy oin meat himself.

chapter ten

The petty insult of the forgery on the much-handed-around manuscript was the final straw. The Tennits' patience gave way to a new and increased anger that convulsed also the somewhat easily led, demoralised fishermen. That was how the war began. There had been many such wars over thousands of years between different tribes in the area but on this occasion there was, for the first time ever, at least a definite 'cause' of the war. (The fact that no scholar could agree on what this was did not disprove that there was a cause). The other reason it became romanticised later in the new Lasdiac school textbooks was that it was the first war in which all the right was on the one side only – the farmers.

At first there was an inter-ally war between the allies over what name and banner they should fight under. This was only settled by Firk Woodlander standing on his traditions and pride and, waving a large standing stick saying that as he, Firk, was titular proprietor of all their property and wealth now, they should all go together under the name of Firk's Men and have as their banner his long-kept shirt of a rare, foreign cotton which had been given to him as a National Day present by the Greatest Leader Ever To Have Ruled On The Island, whose name he could not remember right then.

"Let me go to my hut and get it to show you," he said excitedly, and without waiting for any further opinion ran off with that loping stride so typical of Tennits.

The rest of them had no choice but to await his return. He came back, grinning and holding up one tattered, unpleasant smelling waistcoat.

"I thoughts that you Tennits never wores those," said Jal, stretching out an arm for Val to hand him a smeer drink and girding himself up for a test of proud mind-arm twisting wills with Firk.

"It is an old tradition," said Firk haughtily, of Tennits in their secrets of the day, to wear coats round their waists, and hold up their faces to the glory of the sky, and not succumb in weakness to smeer drink."

"It is all very well for you to talks like that," said Jal, "but I have never heards of a Tennit wores a waistcoat and I haves certainly never seens one in them. We fisherfolk haves secret things too, but we don'ts talks about them."

"Well, there is no need to make such a big thing of it! Today a Tennit should not wear a coat if a fisherman does not have one as well. Indeed we should all wear the same coats, so that Tennits and Fishermen will from now on always look alike! So, I make a presentation of this ancient, grand shirt to you, Jal my pal, hoping that you will accept it on behalf of all fisherfolk, even if you no longer go fishing, and let it be 'the banner that we fight under', giving it a name that will make us proud."

He looked in vain for a sign of enthusiasm from the fishermen.

"What will we call it then?" he finally asked.

"I don't knows what you woulds calls it," said Jal, "as it's only a useless rag that won'ts do any good or harm to anybody. I supposes we coulds calls it the Coat of the Fisherfolk. Nobody woulds objects to that."

"Since I have come to live with you, having made Dar's daughter my wife, and since all my own relatives and friends live here now too, I think it is time that we forgot that some of us are Fisherfolk and some are Tennits. Instead, let us name ourselves 'Firk's Men' and fight under this banner which we shall call Firk's Coat," he said loudly.

"Aye," agreed the other Tennits there, who unlike the fisherfolk were stimulated rather than depressed by the new, overcrowded living conditions.

The rest of the fishermen were too befuddled by the effects of their smeer drinks, (this beer, unlike coleoil, had the unusual effect of accentuating rather than diminishing consciousness so that they became extremely confused by having to think clear thoughts, what with loud whistles coming out of their noses, tons of spit out of their mouths and puffs of smoke pouring out of their ears whenever they tried to talk), to continue to put up much of an opposition and Jal could see that his case was lost, so they flunked their sleeves and doffed their felt-cap hoods (recent gifts of the Tennits) in a show of acceptance. Agreement and accord were reached when the Tennits gave a push to the arms of the drinking fishermen forcing them to down their cups more quickly – and therefore more pleasurably – thus producing an even greater indulgence in drink and all in a much more jolly atmosphere, even if still with an embarrassing over-conscious effort at clear thinking and talking on the part of the fisherfolk, leading to even greater nausea and expulsion of bodily matter.

So, as Firk's Men planned where to assert and defend their rights, the altered parchment itself arrived in Balhop sometime after the reports of its existence had reached there. Needless to say, with all the interest being shown by folk, not to mention innumerable versions of its contents, the earlier enthusiasm that the urban potentates had held for the rural mural was quickly dimmed. They now saw the whole affair as something that was getting out of hand; as the beginnings of a backwood's questioning of their own, assiduously gained monopoly of knowledge, wisdom and votes. To them there was the spark of heresy of rural heterodoxy in all this skulduggery; indeed the very absence of solid information and of precise content or statement of policy made the whole thing more threatening. With the possibility of even more of the country yokels migrating to the city in the harsh economic times with their unclean, dissolute and schismatic ways, the Balhopians too now showed their alarm and concern by standing up for their own rights on their neighbours' toes and displaying the whites of their teeth in deep, thoughtful looks and grimaces.

Economy felt a new glow at the base of his heart's imagination and he sat down on a light, quirky frog that unexpectedly began to carry him forward on a journey down the grass-feathered slope to the bottom of the hill. There he found himself squatting in a happy pile after an unforeseen trip of sheer pleasure and delight. As he dreamed now, everyday things were a new sensory experience to him and the most common of sights and objects brought the wonder of a new revelation. He was a millionaire a hundred times over now, a great oin dealer, with the stump end of a small stick becoming the rich man's cigarella in his puffing mouth. Every non-noteworthy thing lying about, or any commonplace constituent of the environment became fabulous wealth; leaves became gold, a bush a treasure chest, a tree a glittering palace; even the dark, heavy rain took on a numinous appearance. There was complete, autonomous governance over what his eye could see. Nothing came into view that he did not consciously approve of and allow. He was able to bring into unity the incompatible separateness of all natural things, of all measurements such as right and left, backwards and forwards, downwards and upwards, bad and good, dry and wet, earth and sky. They became a single reality in that of the strange phenomenon of his own thinking and dreaming.[1]

The Madness of Eamon Moriarty

As he awoke he knew that the frog-like creature had left him. He rolled his hand in the earth and with his free finger made clay markings of red letters on his face and all over his body. This gave him release and comfort. He enjoyed being free to do this now, as Na had made a hell of a fuss when he had painted himself in the past, and had always made him wash immediately. To his disappointment, however, the marks did not stay very long as the rain almost immediately and unceremoniously washed them off.

He talked to himself, listening to the echoes of his words where they ran into each other, small, ignorant, incomplete, or even silly words becoming joined and transformed into big, unified, more remarkable words of his own –

'When I was born my father and my mother tried to kill me. I woke up in a box to find I had been robbed of my own body. A strange woman took me in; she claimed to be my mother. From the rain and mountain top I came to visit the plains, with a message written on my flesh.'

Eamon was feeling a bit distracted with 'thoughts' at the moment, as he washed himself in a gripe. It was as if a power above had attached long strings to his head and the parts of his body were being pulled in different directions. He wondered where was the mighty puppet master controlling him and ordering events around him? Lines of reasoning had become entangled with each other and there was an ache in his head, and more especially now in his ears, which caused him increased trepidation. He could not do anything to stop the thoughts pouring out all connected together in an unending mass and, at the same time, other thoughts pouring into his head in long lines like columns of soldier ants each ingoing and outgoing line wobbling and getting in the way of the other lines while his ears ached with the hiss or hum of some primitive warning. Up till now he had been carrying his dreams along on the back of his imagination as his most prized possessions, picturing himself as many things – a rich lord of a forest patch where he could gather sticks unmolested; the owner of the fine palace of a single-room hut where he could live alone and unmolested; a world traveller moving about by means of the fastest, most efficient means of transport possible, his own fully functional feet. When they would see his wealth, rivalling that of the greatest Pharaoh or emperor, they would not laugh at him anymore! So it was he had taken into his possession a stray dog and her pup and gone to another village in the hope of a new respectability, hoping to establish himself in employment with the aid of his new 'helpers'; and even perhaps one day be a person of property and prestige equal to that of at least the humblest villager. They had laughed at him and belittled his dogs but he did not show his disappointment. Just because it was said he was a mad one was no reason to assert that he could not be someone of influence in the world. He had hoped for work in a peasant's field, but when his dogs had disappeared he went away from the village a poorer, but a still unvanquished man.

He walked along without his dreams, having found them to be a burden on the spirit. He noticed that he was no longer feeling any strangeness in his other leg. It seemed to be behaving just like the first one and he thought to himself that his walking was as normal now as that of other folk. As he went along he heard a terrible rumpus coming from behind a mass of grabworth bushes which were growing on the side of the trackway – people were always dropping partly-eaten nuts there which later grew into the ugly grabworth bushes. The noise seemed so disjointed from the natural sounds of the neighbourhood that Economy didn't hear it properly at first. At least he ignored the disturbing cacophony for a time. Eventually he decided to have a look and see what was making the commotion. The sounds to him were like the roar of an outsized, enraged wasp.[2]

He had come across the bush war that was taking place between the Tennits and Fishermen on the one hand, and the Farmers. At that particular moment the conflict seemed to hinge on a battle between one very angry farmer and a tall Tennit, Firk Woodlander. The other combatants were standing and watching the fight between these two gladiators. They swung big cabbage tree branches at one another, swishing at each other's legs and faces with the strong, abrasive leaves. It was a fight of utter viciousness, being pursued to the death, the two of them desperately leaping about and into the air to avoid each other's blows, and ducking sideways and this and that way as well as contorting themselves, heedless of dignity, so as to launch more death-dealing blows at the enemy. Economy had never seen anything like it before. Certainly he had often witnessed much bloodletting between folk, but he had never before seen such ferocity as in this battle. He felt a strange sense of unreality about the scene, such was its violence. He saw with surprise that the farmer who was wielding the big branch was Mr McCrachan, who had reared all those big plump birds. It was a big surprise to see such a successful, conservative farmer as Mr McCrachan acting the blackguard like that and taking part in such an unseemly spectacle. Firk struck him across the face with the branch and Mr McCrachan let out a loud cry and the Tennit hit him again and the farmer fell on the ground. Other Tennits ran forward and stamped with their flat feet on Mr McCrachan, while the fishermen, recovering now from their own prolonged state of fright when they had been doing nothing but watch the Tennits do all the work, and seeing the farmer floored, now joined in the fray and laid into the enemy with their own long, pointed sticks.

Economy wept to see the mayhem, for he knew that what he was seeing enacted before him was the consequence of all his crimes.

The Madness of Eamon Moriarty

The fight increased until it sounded like a thousand wasps now, all mad at each other. Branches and bits of twigs were flying everywhere and mud and dirt was flung up into the air and the surrounding vegetation quivered in a kind of fright at the racket.

Economy camouflaged himself in the grabworths and was on the verge of leaving this distressful place when a new and more terrible sight held him back. There was something going on now that made him disbelieve at first what he was seeing through his eye. He even had to take a quick look through his right eye. The men had stopped fighting and had been joined by the women who up to this had been standing to one side of the fray, encouraging the men in their fighting and shouting that no quarter be given. What he saw now made his heart jump. A woman, who stood out from all the others there because she was young and beautiful, was being led to a tree to which she was tied. The women, the Tennits, the fisherfolk and the Farmers all began to strike her with sticks. With a shout Economy rushed forward;

"Spare her."

The appearance of the agitated, irate Economy stopped the whipping. As it was to be described later, he tried to protect the woman by 'affronting her' with his own body, pressing himself up against her. He then turned and confronted the crowd, who were all looking befuddled and quite shocked.

He spotted two people he recognised as Old Gobhook and the Water Clerk, and there were other familiar faces in the crowd too.

As they gazed at him with baffled, even somewhat fearful eyes, he realised that they did not recognise him, for they were indeed not staring at him at all but at something or someone else behind him. He did not understand why they couldn't see him properly.

Firk Woodlander, Jal and Gobhook himself came to the front of the crowd and Gobhook spoke with curiosity:

"Who are you, why is there red paint all over you and why do you call out to Dar's daughter?"

Some said that he had nothing on at all, others that he wore a small girdle around his lower middle. He glistened like a spectre before them. He spoke with a great upheaval of emotion.

"O dearest mother, how long it is that I have been searching for you, and how far into the deep bowels of earth I have looked for you. There is a thunder in my heart at finding you at last, and great sorrow at finding you in such trouble. Woe to those who have taken you from me and have bound you up! I have dreamed about you in the long realms of the night and the vast reaches of the sky. I have sought your hidden face in the clouds of the days. O mother, I am the son you left behind."

He fell on his knees and stared up at her. He burst into tears with a croaking groan.

A look of perplexity appeared on the girl's face, but also a sudden and new pride. It was now that she for the first time became conscious of her married status. A newly-monogamous, puritanical, upright society, one in total contrast to the earlier, non-chivalrous, irresponsible, polygamous society that had pertained of old was instigated at that moment.[3] For Firk himself, unscathed from the scuffle, walked over to his wife and put his arm around the grievously-bemused, affronted and much-assaulted woman in a gesture that, for the first time in history, was seen as not simply an old pride in the existence of the male protective capacity, but actually one of jealous possessiveness. He had been previously willing that his community, and even those who were to some extent strangers and not his kith and kin, beat the hell out of his 'chosen spouse', on this occasion for the two very good reasons of having cooked a large and sumptuous meal in the fisherfolk style which had offended his Woodland palate; and then for having unquestioningly been the cause of the tilt in the hemispherical location of certain crucial stars and planets by conceiving on the wrong date in the month, which in turn, he believed, explained his tripping up earlier in the week into a ditch when a stone had come inexplicably out of the sky and hit him on the head.

Indifferent as most islanders had been in the past to the possession of a wife, since Firk's marriage to Dar's daughter the relationship of man and woman had begun to take on a new significance in that region. It was becoming everyman's desire to have a wife, and so they had instituted a custom of beating up a woman on any pretext in order to gain control over her so as to be better able to incorporate them into their houses, as distinct from the women's houses. Economy's coming across what was essentially a domestic dispute (accentuated by local community tensions; there was something about what a Tennit's wife had said about what a farmer's wife said about what a fisher wife said about what the farmers said about what the Tennits said about what the farmers said about what the fisherfolk had said to the Tennits about what the farmers had said about what the Tennits had said about what the fisherfolk had said to the Tennits who said to the farmer's wife who said to the fisher wife who said to the Tennit's wife who said it back again about the farmer's wife) had the effect of bringing to a psychological and cultural apogee a number of underlying, immutable currents in the neighbourhood.

There was, henceforth, the immediate and radical new emphasis on gaining individual possessions such as a wife, that was contemporaneous and simultaneous with the rise in fortunes of many seemingly unprepossessing individuals, who now managed to better their own world simply by intermarrying into a prominent clan. There was soon to develop the wise if cynical tradition that the father of any daughter who was about to 'get hitched' to any man (i.e. become married to him) had to provide a certain number of the once-loathed oins (the actual number depended on the wealth and status of the father which came eventually, and perhaps inevitably, to be measured in numbers of oins), and this was regardless of whether the husband-to-be was a Tennit, fisherman, farmer or even a scholar. So as they all were affected and worried by the sight of Economy weeping at the feet of Dar's daughter, whom they all realised now was really, indeed, the wife of Firk and a very beautiful young woman into the bargain, they felt a new sense of individual responsibility and remorse. This made them all suddenly very emotional, but even jealous all the more, and such strong feelings as they were certainly unaccustomed to experiencing went straight to their heads and they all became unaccountably chivalrous.

"She is not your mother. She is my wife," Firk shouted at Eamon.

"How can she be your mother when she is as young as yourself?"

There was a mixture of scornful laughter and subdued giggles from those looking on. This jealousy was, indeed, a confusing new emotion. They did not know what to think, or even to feel about things. They looked now at Dar's daughter as at someone with a colourful past such that they could only guess at. The observers did not know which was the more inexplicable sight, Economy's strange words or Firk's embarrassing display of an emotion (and their own as well) over something as unimportant as a wife!

Economy did not respond to the question.

"Why do you think she is your mother?" Firk asked in a more sympathetic way as though he was speaking to an Ebit, thinking that Economy indeed might be of mixed Ebit parentage, an outcast who had inadvertently strayed into normal society. Firk told himself now that he was addressing an unfortunate inferior; he liked to think that he was a genial, tolerant person, not prejudiced against anybody in the world (except the Farmers, who were a rich and bigoted lot). At last Economy ceased his crying and looked up at the tall Tennit who stood above him as stern as any irate monk over a fallen scholar.

"When I saw her in need at the hands of the crowd, a deep thought rent me and my blood lit up with fire. My heart said then that she could only be my mother, to be so innocent and beautiful. I will ask her, for she will know the answer."

Economy looked at her and spoke with the hesitation of one who was perhaps building up for a big disappointment:

"Are you my mother? Did you not have me, and then leave me due to unforeseeable and unavoidable circumstances?"

Dar's daughter answered.

"How can I be your mother, when I am not even more of an age than you yourself. How can I have given birth to you, when I was but an infant myself when you were born? Is it possible, that I could have been a mother to you, indulging your every whim and sham, when I was also but a fretting child cajoled as you were? What strange upturn of nature is this, when a mother is an infant and an infant a mother? O tell me, for I am greatly troubled by you, my punishment will be all the greater for the imposition by you of an unsought motherhood."

She looked towards her husband with perplexity and a plea for understanding. Only unhealthy, prurient minds would fail to sympathise.

"I do not know," replied Economy, "the matter of these things called dates and time and numbers of years. All I know is that I thought you were my mother and I felt a great ache at

The Madness of Eamon Moriarty 151

seeing you being made to bear such punishment with such a lack of joy in your face. It is the same to me if you are my mother or if you are not my mother".

Firk took his wife off the punishment stick and with a revolutionary and never-before-seen-fervour and forgiveness, took her possessively and consolingly into his hands and led her protectively and proudly away under the eyes of a multitude which had temporarily forgotten its previous vindictiveness and which became filled with even more unfamiliar emotions such as eros and a fierce cupidity yet also of hidden pride and an even stronger determination for each to possess a wife of his own, and her property, and to have at least as much as Firk's wealth and good fortune in having such a marvellous wife.

An emergency meeting was held in secret by the match stewards and the other officials representing the powers-that-be in the community after the premature ending of the camogie game. It was agreed that word of Eamony's infraction and of the severe fright the poor girl (and all the ladies) had been subject to, and of the disruption of the game (they concocted a score of a draw) must not go out into the wider public domain, as it would not only disturb the very young but would be a public relations disaster as far as the reputation of the whole valley was concerned. Everybody in their villages, including those long dead, alive now and still to come would be tarred by the same brush and be suspected of being related to the mad youth. It was very important to stress to everybody publicly that Eamon was not only a 'harmless' chap for whom the Social Services had proven a distinct failure such as should have brought forth an outcry that would have moved, if not earth and high heaven, at least local public opinion, but also that he was not from their district. The people of Ballyhilty and neighbourhood had done their bit in looking after the outcast, and pending the proper authorities taking the situation in hand, it would be only fair for

The Madness of Eamon Moriarty

another district to take Eamon under its wings for a while. There were other worries. A dead body had turned up recently in the camogie field. At the moment it was believed hopefully that a natural explanation such as a wild animal run amuck was the most likely cause of death. Indeed the corpse had been found with severe wounds, caused by the imposition of a sharp, strong object. A scald crow's beak was still the likely contender. Nobody wanted to believe that the young fellow was capable of harming anybody, even though he had his own alarming ways and there were reports, for instance, of his being heard shouting out total nonsense (questions such as where, how, why) in the dead of night in the far distant woods. It should be remembered that they had a happy record in the community for they had never had, in history or in pre-history, a single murder reported in all that time. Despite the fact that innumerable dismembered bodies in various stages of disarray and decomposition turned up at regular intervals there had never been any suggestion of foul play. Indeed there were two words that did not exist in that country, as an instance of either one of them had never been recorded, and both would never be allowed to enter the lingua franca of the place; murder and insanity!

They were proud of their peaceful way-of-life. Meanwhile the people of Ballyvogue further down the valley should not be concerned but be glad to take their part in caring for this one unfortunate member of their community as an act of neighbourly cooperation and charity and at the same time representation would be made as high up as the county capital, Inisbay, and to no lesser a personage than the Lord Chief Justice leader there, to have the problem properly dealt with.

The next person to speak was Valentine McCarthy, who was quite a smart aleck and the strange thing was that nobody had ever remembered anything he had ever said or, if they did try to concentrate on what he was saying, could never understand any of it. They would not listen now either, or try to understand or remember.

The Madness of Eamon Moriarty

"We should all remember", said Val, who was also a prominent member of the Ballyvogue Rotary Club, "that lunacy is no longer the stigma that it once was. There has for too long been a conspiracy of silence around this infliction that reflects no credit on society. It is time that we acknowledged that we all have someone in our family, or at least know someone in our immediate circle, who has had to be – for want of a better phrase – 'put away'. There is no shame in this, really."

As usual, nobody appeared to hear what he had said, or even notice that he had said anything.

Another committee member spoke, not having listened to Val but with a similar propensity not to panic.

"It would be a better idea altogether if we hid this Eamon fellow somewhere in our village out of sight of the authorities. We do not want Ballyvogue or Ballyhilty getting any bad reputation in the towns. A curtain of silence should fall down on all the events of today and no more should ever be heard about it," said Finbar Woods, a more canny person than Val McCarthy and one who had made his money without having to join any Rotary Club.

Notes

1 - There may be a word for this 'reality' in more civilised languages, and here scholars of French or German can retire to their dictionaries because the author apparently has not got the knowledge or even the inclination to pepper his piece with unpronounceable, untranslatable exotic words that appear so often in scholarly masterpieces to the frustration and vexation of the non-polyglot man or woman. Take for instance 'sangfroid', a particular offender that occurs to one here that appears frequently in writers' repertoires, and ask oneself does one ever know what it means exactly? Or does it necessitate effort and waste of precious time to try and find out in heavy, cumbersome dictionaries the exact connotation of such words, a task that is nearly always fruitless in these cases? At the same time it must be admitted that there are many things in human experience for which there are no words in the Monarch's English.

2 - This is reckoned by the Galwegians to refer to the time that Eamon suddenly came across a camogie match between two local teams in the Regional McCarthy Championships, almost devoid of decent clothing and after having 'dropped out of sight for a period of some time'. He caused an immediate halt to the proceedings that had been going at full vent. It is believed by Galway that what ensued was a sexual exhibition, an affront if not of an actual attack on one young camogie player who became it seemed the subject of his particular attention. The suggestion of illegitimacy and the previous history of a young, now-married lady also came up.

This explanation of course was not acceptable to the Cork panel. Quite apart from the fact that nowhere in the text are 'sexual' matters referred to or even hinted at, (of course there are always those who love to inspire much debate and controversy about matters of sex, due to obsession with the subject), they also claim it is not likely that such an important innovator, or catalyst, of social, political and commercial change as Economy was proving himself to be in society would at the same time have been bothered by such things as personal sexual problems. It is quite obvious that his irruption into what was a very real, historical battle and its premature foreclosure (a great feat in itself, as the contest was being carried on with the great devil-may-care gusto of the savage Godless Ancients who were blind to the realities of death and destruction), was an example of the fellow's charisma and unspoken influence. It was only comparable say, to that of Moses when he called back the Red Sea and it obeyed, or when Noah said it would rain and it did. Economy, they said, by a similar apparent challenge to all the forces of reason and nature, had saved the region from further, pointless bloodshed. Dr Crane took his usual tack, speaking ominously about an Oedipus Complex in referring to the obsession with the young maid and discussing such matters as libidinous fantasies, obsessions and lewd transferences which were above the heads of most of his listeners. It was decided, out of respect for both Dr Crane and the public, to put his words in the report as Dr Crane's 'biological theorem'.

3 - The inhabitants of the region were for long known for their negative attitude to the institution of marriage. A very large number of the male population, especially the farmers, were most reluctant to leave the sides of

their mothers and fathers and go to live with women who were completely unrelated to them. In some ways this might have seemed like a loyal or patriotic attitude, as some of them claimed, saving the community from much unnecessary expense and from too many children who only represented more mouths to feed. It ensured that there was not any illegal passing of property from its rightful owners and heirs to snotty-nosed outsiders. It also ensured that elderly Farmers, fisherfolk and Tennits were not just 'kicked out into the street' by their in-laws but were able to remain in the comfortable circumstances to which they were accustomed. This led to an unspoken conspiracy against the family into which the scholars and monks were most willingly and easily drawn. Many of these had originally gone into their chosen profession with the aim of escaping the institution of marriage, as the best monks do not marry in any case, and scholars attained more respect if they kept to themselves and lived in 'ivory towers'. It was not long before there were theories and scholarly if not even religious doctrines and books not so much outlawing marriage as gravely discouraging it in society and elevating the non-married state to a higher level of physical and moral being. Other theories or books against marriage often used the latest philosophical and political fads to decry the usefulness of sexual relations, allowing only that sufficient children might be produced to replace the aging population as the only justification of them within a legal framework. Consequently marriage often became a sort of underground activity instead, often involving the usual features of the Black Market such as commodities (spouses) being passed around from hand to hand surreptitiously, spectacularly high 'bride prices' and even an overseas or foreign market and trade in the condemned business. There arose a special class of 'marriage-dealers' who did well out of the whole thing. Their job was to fix or 'arrange' marriage between couples who had never even seen one another previously and this had to be done secretly so as not to embarrass the authorities. Many was the ship or other vehicle of transport that saw the tainted 'goods' quietly slipping out of town, village or farm with all the appearances of going on a fine holiday.

This also explains why the island often witnessed marriages taking place at a very elderly age, as then it would be seen as a necessary legal remedy for certain property ills and at that age it didn't matter much anyway.

chapter ELEVEN

The farmers went off home in a quiet mood, relieved at least to have been spared an outright bashing. They retired to reconsider their whole war strategy. The fighting with the fisherfolk and Tennits could never again be the same, healthy, respectable sport it once was. Their Fisherfolk and Tennit foes also stayed off battle for a while, indulging their new sense of communal responsibility.[1] Economy was taken back with them to the village and a sustained, corporate interest was taken in his case by the villagers who seemed determined to take his mind off his obsession with his lost mother. He remained under their watchful eyes while they strove earnestly to prove to themselves and to the whole world that he was not mad at all, as he had now come to live with them in their community. After the debacle of the latest battle, their reputation now depended on affirming that Economy was in fact quite sane, even if sometimes giving the appearance of being insane. Or, as one or two argued, even if he had been a bit insane, he should now be taught how to behave, speak and act in the manner of a completely normal and balanced resident of the community. This belief in Economy's sanity had some of the attributes of that very strong supposition such as may be found in the most advanced, technological societies that only judges, powerful politicians, professors, scientists and saints can ever be safely declared insane.

He was dressed up in the new fisherman/Tennit's suit (flap jacket with wool lining and a Tennit's cap), and made to feel at home and part of their society, although he had to live alone in his own hut. They did not refer to his affliction, and pretended that he was as normal as they, telling themselves that he did not look ridiculous in the new outfit that even most fisherfolk and Tennits had not deigned to wear publicly (at least not yet) for fear of ridicule. He was given the same fisherman's breakfast and Tennit tea and was spoken to as though he had always been one of them. Economy went along with all this as best he could, ignoring the hypocrisy (for he knew that much of their acceptance depended on his continuing to wear the fisherfolk/Tennit clothes). There were many signs of unease observable in even the most sophisticated village resident as he passed by and the former was enforced to give a greeting or time of day. Yet he had always preferred Tennits and fisherfolk to the Farmers, finding that they were less attached to private property and were quite spiritual in their religious lives. He was feeling strangely tranquil after what was now being called his 'nervous breakdown'. He had entered that placid time/space continuum where the world goes very quiet and every feeling is anaesthetized. Yet it was a fact that he found this keeping up of appearances a great strain. Inside him there was something threatening at any moment to break out and throw off those fisherfolk/Tennit clothes.[2]

As a thoughtful, even soulful spirit settled over the area due to the euphoria caused by feelings of moral worthiness, there was not much sign of outward change in Economy himself. He did not seem much consoled by their sympathy or brought to any sort of communicative disposition by their thoughtful considerations. He did not eat willingly of the food he was offered. He sat morosely under one of the settlement's paving stones and did not think. He fell into a sombre mood; he closed his eye hoping he might find comfort in the darkness of sleep, thinking no more the grey thoughts of each cloud-filled, silent, immovable day. He sat back and saw in the eye's dark, universal cupboard his own ghostly being and looked at the bones of his existence and felt the long, skeletal fingers of fate instil in him both a knowledge of his ignorance and a wish to possess the world. He was awoken by the shaking hand of Firk pulling and tugging at him and withdrawing him out of his deep slumber. He was shouting at Economy, saying something about a gift and an eye-opener that he had brought for him and would he be pulling himself together and out of that rut he was in and wake up and take his place among the living. Economy, who heard these calls in his sleep, answered in a hollow voice that seemed to be that of a ghost:

"Go away, there is nothing I can see anymore. My dreams are of no further use, for they are your dreams. For what should I wake up, for what dreams, what troubles?"

"You are wandering in a fit of your mind. Come out of it, lad, and tell us what your name is, and then you can greet Halola here," said Firk with an element of arm bullying.

A heavy shower of rain came down from the sky and Firk, Jal and the other bystanders directed its flow so that it fell on Economy and woke him up from his slumber. Halola was eagerly presented to him, for everyone believed that they had found the answer to the village's problem. The fact was that many of them wanted to see Economy settle down and happily married to one of the girls. Such forced 'marriages' were a device that had worked in many similar, extreme situations in the past – a centuries' old business that never wanted for new, extreme experiments. The lad looked at Halola and there was relief for the fact that at last he eventually spoke.

"She isn't my mother," he said.

"Of course she isn't," said Firk, smiling, "she is a lady who would make a very suitable wife for you."

He proceeded to speak in high praise of the matronly lady who, he said, had looked after countless generations of the recusant, iconoclastic or stranded individuals who had made their way to the village. He went on to exaggerate somewhat the description of her 'positive' qualities.

"Halola may be embarrassed and even angry to hear me say this, but she is the most nifty woman around. She can be ten heads tall at the best of her, and her body stretches out as long and deep as the River Sip. She is known to be able to kiss with her boots on any tree twenty middle island stone throw lengths distant. Her heart and hands are as strong as two worlds crashing together in a very sweet song. Her looks are as varied as the changing face of a wind-disturbed lake, swelling and shifting with the passage of its own nature-reflecting tide. Look at her arms! At rest they are; but they can be like the comforting coming together of friendly ships at sea. Listen to her singsong, young man, and you will be lulled to bliss on its soft shore, or awoken sweetly by its great winds. Her breath will blow you off the mountain trackways, and she will turn you from your old, wasteful ways and troublesome words and make you busy with the feeding of her, and her many children and more besides! Let her take you into her home, lad, and she will see to it that you no longer go about disturbing the peace of the neighbourhood as a poor wanderer. Become like us, and not have stories of your troubled doings make our neighbours speak contemptuously of us. Live with Halola here, and you will forget all about your mother and your woes."

Halola, to many there a despised if kind village mother who had originated from many long lines of families involved in the disreputable multiple-generational fostering and kin-bonding of unwanted children, who was treated with great respect by those exiles with fond memories of having being fostered by her and who had long since migrated far away and made their fortunes, yet also with extreme disrespect by everyone still living in the village who knew what a rude, even foolish lady she was, and whose family origins were not known to be clearly of either Tennit, fisherfolk or Farmer stock but she sometimes called herself Ten Fish as everybody these days had to have some surname, and yet was said by many to be a sister of Jal though she claimed to be his mother, while some said she was his daughter, had a good look at Economy and said that it was a bad day when she would have to take a lad as poor as that into her care! She was getting too old for impossible tasks, but she might still have one good nurturing session left in her.

Later on Jal said sourly – for he had been making no progress in his chats with Economy, when he had been trying to get the lad to listen to him, to his views and opinions, and to take his advice –

"You mights at least explains the facts of life to him."

"What do you mean?" asked Halola.

"I hads a talk with him. Do not lets word of this comes out to the children, Halola, whatever you do, but he has mad beliefs. He does not knows even what human beings are! He does not accepts that we, this present generation, are immortal beings, made to lives here by our Ancestor for ever and ever. No, he believes that we are mades of ordinary flesh and blood, just like the animals and Ebits, that we haves been borns too, and not been here all the time, and that we dies just like all those other generations! And where does the person go when the body dies then, I asks him! He says he knows for sure as that we goes to the Land of the Supernatural, or the Land of Far Beyond. Where you learns this, I asks him. I heard it in school one day, he says. Don't looks at me as if I am mad, I'm just telling you what this fellow says. Listen, he does not knows even where children comes from. He thinks that what we sees when women as undergoes their trials is really happenings! He says we shoulds believes what we sees before our eyes! If you says to him true

The Madness of Eamon Moriarty

fact that they appears miraculously in the garden patch under the cabbage trees, such as some says as puts there by the fairies, he just looks at you. When I asks him, how do you thinks babies gets to be inside their mothers, he says that the men puts them in there! Did you ever hears? Listens, don't laughs, listens, I asks him how does the man puts the young babe there – with his hands – and he says 'no', with what folks calls his didgeridoo! And then I asks how does the baby gets out, escapes from its mother's belly or whats, and you'd thinks it was a silly question from the look he gives you! Oh yes, I saids jokingly to him, one minute the babe is inside and the next minute is outside in the wide world! Just like that! Well he has a most wonderful story on that and if you, as a lady, do not takes umbrage, I will relates it to you here and now, so long you do nots repeats it, the lad's theory on how babies appears – they *comes out of their mothers!* Then of course the question follows, where do they comes out of, and the answer is, according to this fellow is . . . well, I can't brings myself to say it but it is one of those parts of the body where . . . ."

Jal caught his breath.

"And what's more, so I asks him again, what is this world? He says a scholar once tolds him all about it and he thinks we is livings on a lump of rock hangings in the sky! Well, his brains is scarce as a farmer's handshake! And the rock gots there by fallings off another bigger lump of rock in the sky which gots there from fallings off an even bigger lump of rock in the sky, and so on and so on and so on! And what holds we up is invisible strings like forces that we can't sees and that if these ropes gets broken we woulds falls down forever! And he says there are such things in the sky that we can't even sees, and yet that we can't counts because they are too many! Even though Astronomical Monks haves counts them all! Astronomical Monks teaches us that there are two thousand and fifty four stars, five hundred and twenty seven planets, sixty nine moons, and that they are all puts there for one reason, so that they all holds us in place around us and gives us protection because we is the cleverest beings. We do not to asks what stars are because we do not needs to knows, only the Chief Monk knows. But he says he knows what stars are and are no more remarkable than the sand in the sea! And then he laughs! I am so sorry I speaks to him at all. I am upsets and confused about many things now."

Indeed from then on Jal and the villagers were to become unsettled in all their beliefs, not because a wise and learned person had contradicted them, but because an ignorant, mad person without any social status had done so.

"It is not a woman's duty to teach him the truth," said Halola cagily.

"The poor fellow never had a father to beat the facts of life into him," said Firk joining in. He too had been talking privately to Economy. He was looking anxiously around him now to see if anybody else was listening, for he did not want too many people to know that he also had been engaging in informal discussions with the village 'madman', trying to persuade him to become like them. Firk had lately to assume many public duties. He was already thinking of the next election and of standing for the seat of Putuporshutup, a poor outlying suburb of the village that was already complaining about the appearance of oin markets and Ebits in their vicinity, and would not look well on the further toleration by officialdom of such a person as Economy in the area.

"He is better off with his own beliefs. We should not try to make him see the truth, for it would do a lot of harm," said Halola wisely.

"The children and young people are distracted from their work by him, so that they do not wish to go about their chores but stay around staring at him all day. And does not every man ask himself deeper questions now? He makes us believe that all we know is useless and our own talk is gobbledygook. Are you really happy to see grown men inquiring about the value of human life, the meaningless of war, seeking after their mothers and brothers, or fathers, sisters or girlfriends, or grandmothers even, sons, daughters or cousins, even if only for fear that he might go and claim them too? What a condition this will lead us into, with family relationships, friendship, kinship, who we are and where we are going to becoming our central concern, leaving no time for bubble drinking, sports, fighting and defending our reputations against the farmers and outsiders. Take him, Halola and smother him with kisses, for then they will see that he has no need of a mother, a father, a friend or even a troublesome, systematic philosophy."

Halola was worried. All her previous fostering had been of the distraught, bereft, disappointed, embittered, traumatised and dysfunctional, the dregs of society who, even if they always did try to destroy her home and furnishings or beat her up when they felt like it, were at least normal. But now she faced a real challenge, for just when her much abused body was beginning to feel the full effects of a long and exhaustive working life that she had hoped was nearly over, she was being given the worst client of all – that of an innocent.

"He doesn't cause fear in me, yet I am nervous of having him in the house. Who knows what he might do? He is scarcely more than a boy; yet there is something primitive about him. I find a bittersweet taste that is not unpleasant in the air around him. He is not handsome yet there is something in him that draws my eyes unwillingly to him. He is not talkative, yet he makes me think about things I do not want to think about. He does not make me laugh the way Jed the Village Clown does, and yet there is something in him that makes me want to laugh. I will take him into my household and see if there is any use to which he can be put."[3]

The complicated machinations and well-oiled wheels of the Social Services Department eventually caught up with the boy again in the neighbouring village where he was discovered to be in the care of a local widow, who was accustomed to taking in young orphans and runaways and which activity, even if it was with the connivance of the village authorities, broke all official government guidelines. They felt anger at not having been officially informed of the existence of this unregistered community home (house of ill repute as some called it) and of the lad's presence in the village. They had learnt of it in quite an embarrassing manner, when a visiting inspector from Head Office was informed casually by a river labourer who had ferried him across the flooded Sip that there was a mad boy in a village who had been going around killing lots of people. The inspector brought the information to them with the relish of any guardian of morals who has discovered clear evidence that people were not doing their job. Once word got to the departmental HQ in the town the paperwork was immediately set in motion. This time the case workers were much less willing to go back to the countryside, as 'what are the likely dangers?' seemed to be their main attitude. These villages resented any outsiders coming in to tell them their business, they said. The fact was they knew that Eamon would have grown much bigger and stronger by now, and had possibly become even more violent. He should be left where he was. The general attitude was that he was probably quite happy there. But the inspector wanted a report so it was agreed that the next visit should again include the services of the strong, no-nonsense official, local dignitary Tom Curran, recently appointed to the new, highly paid post of Head of Social Services, who had a grassroots knowledge of the area. He was out of the office at the moment (as usual). It would take some time to find him as he always seemed to be in two places at the same time these days. But when Mr Curran wanted to 'play it heavy' there was no one to beat him. So they set off for different spots around Inisbay, Balhop and the island at large to try to find Tom Curran.

On the promise of a solid meal and plenty of sleep Halola made Economy follow her into her compound. The lad settled into the large kitchen and commenced to eat her out of every empty cupboard, pantry, pot and pan in the place. After he had his fill of emptiness he noticed a few things about the room he was in. It was very hot in there, stifling in fact, but he could not get out. There was a plain, locked door with a pair of magnificent hinges on each side. The hinges were in fact the swarthy arms of two idle, glowering giants. The interior of the room consisted of bare shelves and around the floor was the debris of countless generations of that island's 'low' culture. Looking out of place was a long couch in the corner.[4]

Economy believed that he would have peace in that particular part of the house where the men were usually loath to gather. He still feared the possibility of Gobhook and the others coming to the village. However he concentrated on changing his physical appearance as much as possible, contorting himself so that he did not look like himself at all. He was constantly changing his facial expressions, making sure that they were never the same from one moment to the next. Happy or sad, glad or angry, sometimes both angry and glad, or happy and sad, it made no difference. This way there was even less chance that, by catching his precise mood, they might recognise him.

And he would set out on his journey again one day. As soon as his presence had become so accepted and commonplace a sight in the village that he would not be missed, or his going away noticed, he would be off.

When the hinges were drawn back the door vanished and Halola and a child appeared. Halola had an amused, yet serious and inquiring look in her eyes and a swaggering gait in her walk. She demanded that he let her be his mother as he had never had one. Economy became extremely nervous, and was even a bit shocked by her forwardness.[5]

She ordered the timid, obedient child to hand over the big plate of food he was carrying to the first of the giants, the one standing nearest to them. The child, after what seemed an awfully long time walking over to where the giant was, even though he had at first seemed to be standing next to the giant, carefully held up the plate to the giant's face. The giant bent down and lifted the plate away extravagantly, as if he had spirited it out of nowhere, whereupon the door, which had suddenly reappeared in view, fell off its hinges. The giant came over in a single stride to where Economy was sitting on the couch and towered over him with an adamant, overpowering glare from his scorching blue eyes. Economy did not feel threatened, as in a funny kind of way it seemed as if the giant only wanted him to do something that was easy and quite harmless. The second giant, he observed, was still standing in the entranceway holding up his end of the fallen door. Economy was forced to lie back on the couch and await whatever it was that was in store for him. Before he could even think of anything to say or do he was grabbed by the giant and the food was forcibly poured down his throat. It was evidently important to the giant that none of the food was spilled or wasted and that it stayed down inside him, and with one hand restraining Economy, his other arm went out of the room and returned with an instrument or weapon, of a lethal appearance that might have been a rod, or even a spear. He fixed the plate over Economy's mouth and with the implement, pressed it down very hard. The suffocation Economy felt was total – though not dreadful – and when the giant left him he experienced a strange calm and no pain.

After the experience Economy was never again afraid of giants.

"I am sorry that it had to be done like this," said Halola, sitting beside him and holding him by the ears, "but sometimes it is for the best if we have to make you suffer first, and then patch you up later." "It didn't hurt too much, "Economy said, not really knowing what to think.

Halola spoke softly.

"I see who you are now. But I don't want the men to realise who you are. You don't have to tell them and you don't even have to tell me."

Economy did not know what to make of these words either. Maybe it would be best to assume duplicity on her part, (for she had already started giving him chores). It was some scheme perhaps to keep him there to do all the hard work in the kitchen; the standing over a hot stove, the scrubbing and polishing and mucking out that even the women wouldn't do. He could see that Halola somehow saw through him, that she now knew how to deal with him.

He had an urge to talk.

"Why does everybody fight?"

"They are fighting over horrible words in a mural which was found recently. It is said to be the work of an illiterate troublemaker who by using witchcraft, obtained the power to write and who has caused nothing but ceaseless headaches and misery for the community. After he and the witch were burnt at the stake, they found the murals in their hut.[6] They say that he is to blame for all the bad books that have ever been written in this island. He has since gone over, with the witch herself, to the Land of Ne'er-Do-Well that lies between the borders of the Living World and the Land of the Supernatural And Far Beyond which is inhabited by people such as grave robbers, useless witch doctors, artists, writers and rogue astronomers."

"That is terrible indeed. Did he cause a great deal of trouble then?" asked Economy.

"Oh yes. They say he was the son of a low caste stick gatherer. Together they caused whole regions to become barren of woods, plants and soil, causing them to be washed away when their stick gathering and scavenging exposed the land to the great rains. They have caused, as well, the eruption of those volcanoes which we have been hearing about, but which nobody seems to know where they are. They have caused as well, the destruction of the mountains, the imminent fall of huge rocks from outer space and the unending fighting which has long been giving our country a bad name. They have caused the . . . ."

"The rain?" interrupted Economy.

"Yes, the blasted rain, that fills our days with wetness and darkness and makes it impossible to dry clothes, and which you can't drink or eat or do anything useful with."

Economy felt the marks on his flesh glowing and melting with shame and the heat of anguish running down his body.

"The war will continue until the end of time, they say.[7] Neither Firk's men or the Farmers are very good fighters compared to say the Assaland Knights, but the fisherfolk are the worst and they are always sending envoys to make peace treaties whenever the going gets tough. The Farmers' appointed political representative is Mr Gobhook, who always starts it going again if the war seems to be running out of steam. One day, all the people were very tired of fighting and they were discussing becoming friends, when Gobhook stood up and said that if he were a Tennit he would not have stood by while one of his own people was butchered by the farmers, referring to an incident that had been completely forgotten by everyone up till then. And – he said – he would not have let one of his women be taken to become the wife of an ugly Tennit either! So it all started off again. Sometimes it is

The Madness of Eamon Moriarty

difficult to know whose side he is on. He does not join in the battles but watches the fray from a safe position and counts the victories and losses, and hands the victory sticks over for safe keeping to his big friend, the Water Clerk from Inisbay. The Water Clerk has the reputation of being the Greatest Interfering Busybody whose good deeds are known everywhere. He is spoken of as a future Minister For Good Works. Firk tries hard to be friends with Mr Gobhook in private, and he laughs at the farmer Leader's jokes and he plays crackerjack with him in the Party Rooms sometimes.[8] They have been seen to swop shirts. But ... Mr Gobhook makes fun of him behind his back," said Halola.

It was plain to see that she was feeling somewhat cynical about the whole business of local affairs.

"I know Mr Gobhook. He is a crook who speaks falsehoods," said Economy angrily. For the first time in his life he was actually expressing a coherent, comprehensible, political opinion, and also showing an uncharacteristic appreciation of local politics.

"A usurper and Big Farmers' Party political hireling who has turned his back on his own people and on the Small Farmers' Party in a lean time. He should not be considered as a leader at all, for the real leader is a man who has had to go away on important business. He is Top Carrot and I hope that he will return soon and deal with this Gobhook. The interloper tries to blame everything on the absent leader, Top Carrot. Well, the day Top comes back will be a great day, and it is my hope to see it."

"Why should you care about such things as long as you are happy and content with me? I know you," said Halola gently.

"You know who I am?"

There was curiosity in his voice, as well as dread.

"Every mother knows her child. You are a child, not a man. Each woman knows her man and sees inside him, but men do not know what is beyond their own faces. They are too busy out sporting or warring, but they only fight the loud, braggardly giants. They pretend that they are doing something great and brave, but they know all the time that the giants are cowardly. And now they make their women fight for them as well. They would not spot a dragon even if it entered the compound for they would say, how can an invisible thing exist? They would not know how to curse away a sneaky old ogre even if it presented its debased face in their own faces."

"I know now that there is a great fear of words in the island, if not in the world, and nobody who makes murals is ever safe from troubles and curses. That is why the scholars and the monks, who write much, go to such extreme lengths to protect themselves by hiding in inaccessible places and covering their works with diplomas and certificates and even strange magic symbols that they put on each mural to stop anybody else from copying or even reading it . . . ."

"Who told you all this?" asked Halola, surprised at Economy's knowledge.

"The scholar who once taught me."

"He must have been a very good teacher. You remember everything he told you."

"He was a great teacher. He seemed to talk more when I was looking at him. Then he would smile and stare into the sky and talk away and not let anything deflect him from his words, not a storm or an outburst of slate throwing or a Scholar Inspector coming into the room. It was as if he knew that I was listening. Because I was at the school for such a little time I can remember everything that he said to me."

"I have never heard that said about a scholar's words before."

Economy held his breath for he was on the verge of making a great confession. He spoke heavily yet with relief, as if a great weight was beginning to be lifted from him.

"That stick gatherer who made his marks on the murals in the same way that rulers give way to their imaginings when they stick a wild oin with a sharp pole, or Farmers feed their mouths with bubble drink, or Ebits suck roden berries, or monks sing happapalujahs and hallupalalahs, or Tennits jump on matching sticks over a hot-cold fire on National Day, was me. Halola, which is more sinful, to make a mural or to steal foul from a Farmer?"

"The question," laughed Halola, "is worse than the answer. But I will keep your secrets and not tell anyone, if you do what I tell you. I will not let you out of my sight, and you will polish my pots and pans and look after the washbasins. If you go away, the men will learn of your past deeds and will chase you. Do not go near any other woman in the village, for the men have become very jealous of late, and they will exact retribution if you approach their wives. This is a very necessary warning. I will be angry and jealous to see you near them too!"

She lifted the heavy hem of her skirt where it had been resting on Economy holding him down, and he felt relieved to be free of its great, cumbersome weight.

As Halola kissed his nose and left him he was glad. He got out of the cupboard as quickly as he could, feeling a sense of immense relief and he entered the back kitchen. He could not remember now how he had got from the couch to the cupboard, but dismissed his confusion as the product of that unusual and embarrassing experience that seemed now, already, to be long in the past. The pots and pans were hanging up all around the room, shining. They were very massive utensils and occupied their places more for decorative purposes than practical use, for all the supplies of food in the world would not have been sufficient to fill them. With a nervous anticipation and a certain amount of satisfaction at actually having a job to do (it would not be long before he realised that he was in fact being exploited for his labour) he proceeded to take down the receptacles with great care and went about washing them and polishing them, using the best island nail grease and making a great din so that the loud noises coming from the room gave an impression to those on the outside of a great, busied activity.

Within a fairly short period of time Economy had become such a fixed figure in that kitchen that Halola and the other women were coming in and going out willy-nilly saying embarrassing and controversial things they wouldn't normally say openly in front of anyone. In the meantime he went on washing and filling containers with water and eventually his skills reached a state of such note that there were put at his disposal more important ingredients such as remains of food scraps, raw oin meat, throwaway curry and cooking liquids (which he had to transfer from pot to pot). Then he became in fact, as well as in reputation, the established worker in that busy kitchen.

Little children came in to see him and he threw bits and pieces of food at their feet holding on to his scrubbing hat with much laughter and roguish satisfaction, enjoying his new position as kitchen lad. There was a shine on each pot and a washed appearance to every wall and corner that made Halola exclaim happily. No more moans now about the damaged utensils and broken pottery. She was filled with wonder at how much her life had changed! Some women were jealous of the new order and they spitefully suggested that the kitchen was too old and should be taken down and changed for a new one; that there was a strange smell in the place and that the kitchen lad should be fired.

Then one day a scrap between the folk who lived nearby took place at the doorstep of the hearth and Economy had to rush out and stop it, separating the factions who were all arguing about the walls of the kitchen and whether they should be changed or not, and about the cleanliness and kitchen skills and qualifications of their relatives, and even about the drunkenness of their grandmothers. The range of his work increased. He was put in charge of all the freedoms of the house and then of the neighbourhood. He was given control of the workings of the unspoilt air; the guardianship of the atmospheres of the perimeters was his responsibility, as was the undisputed governorship of the upper sky. The multitudes of the sequences of the time's hour-watch hands were at his disposal, and he became the emperor of dust.

It was a fact that, for the first time in his life, Eamon felt a little more secure in his existence and there was a semblance of normality and acceptance about his situation during the months he was in that village. Even though he still saw the world through an eye that was accustomed to interpreting things a little differently than the rest of society, and it would have been not incorrect to apply the term unusual to many of his observations as manifested in this text, yet he was able with the co-operation of everyone there to live a life that was without major or observable disasters. At a time when his symptoms were stable and his mood quiescent he had been given a role in society that allowed him a little space of his own and even some utilitarian purpose in the world. That is, until the 'experts' came in with their notes and tomfoolery which was to see the end of Eamon's short life of normality, and the beginning of his downslide into the abyss of regulated certification.

Nor was it the 'certification' of the kind so often extolled by scholars to generations of truculent and unwilling schoolchildren.

It was a certification of a kind that society concocts for those who do not register for its exams. It was true, as Lead Social Worker (Tom Curran had, by reason of his political position in the community, become obliged to take a leading role in removing Eamon's case from the cul de sac of a mere social problem into the open freeway of a political issue) maintained that the lad had been 'used' by those in the community who should have known better; that he had been exposed to vice in a 'man-woman' relationship with the well-known 'Madame' of the neighbourhood, and which outrageous scandal drew raised eyebrows in the whole Social Services' team. This latter matter indeed began to grow out of all proportion in significance, with the team curiously eager to research out more, viz. spending many long hours in seminars debating how 'far' the relationship had proceeded, what were its exact physical details, discussions peppered with toilet/bathroom jokes, bawdry bedroom anecdotes and seemingly unending, salacious denigration in the schoolboy style of the bodily parts and human biology in general, with loud peals of uncontrollable laughter being emitted from behind the closed doors of the committee room to the wonder of passers-by; what effect it had on Eamon and did it leave him with any sense of morality afterwards. It was also true that this unfortunate victim of life was sometimes a subject of laughter, even mirth and of buffoonery, (for instance whenever he was seen in the company of the said lady, who had only ever afforded him protective, motherly affection). In an unspoken kind of way the 'normality' of the community's acceptance was seen as a threat by the team to their own conceptions of immorality and their expertise in solving perplexing human dilemmas. They could not understand why he hadn't been made, instead, a scapegoat for all the village ills and punished unmercifully and continuously or at the very least, totally ostracised or sent into exile. Then they would have felt a bit better about it for they could at least have understood the situation and instigated a rescue mission. Instead he was actually given a job there and allowed to live his own life! They began to wonder about that village.

Even the sight of Gobhook coming in one day to pick at the crab blossoms when he thought nobody of importance was looking, did not put Economy off and he had a bit of a laugh to himself. Of course when he laughed it was a prolonged, uncontrollable laughter that would have caused consternation in anyone who heard it, but this laughter was not audible or perceptible to most people. He told Halola about it when she was in a less hectic and tiresome mood and had come to him with a strange physical aggressiveness to give him a surprisingly painful pinch.

"They were having another one of their battles," she laughed, "and he must have sneaked in when he thought nobody was about."

"He didn't see me when I opened the door for him, thinking it might have been you. He must have thought I was one of the giants for he paid no attention to me whatsoever. I tried to let the door fall on him as he went out, but he thought it was just jammed," said Economy.

"Good for you," said Halola, and thereupon she made him honorary overseer of all past and future kitchen habits, so that eventually the nature of the villagers' tastes and dietary habits came to be unconsciously affected in new and strange ways by the presence of the wanderer in their eating places, such as a predilection for the previously distasteful oin meat, and an abhorrence of the old staple, once-popular chicken and fish.

Notes

1 - Tennits are a group of people who perhaps need a degree of further explanation, as they are a rather mysterious lot especially as they appear in the text. It is held by historians that they represent a people who came more lately to the island, and who practiced that anti-establishmentarian, anti-Monks and Anti-Astronomical religion that so clashed with the beliefs and practices of the fisherfolk and Farmers. It would seem that the religion of the Tennits was as follows: (a) that the Monks were the instruments of a vast, cosmic plot by a secret power in Assaland to take over their settlements and turn them into mushroom plots, (b) that the Astronomical Monks' and Scholars' claimed-ownership of the stars and planets was illegal, and discouraged ordinary people from talking about them, or even looking at

them, and (c) that they themselves should be the rulers of the island as their religion was the only true one. In Cork these days, (said a Professor of Particle Physics, who was noteworthy for his ecumenical efforts at improving co-operation between all the contradictory elements on the committees he served on), there have been attempts by members of the community to live together that were very admirable, setting an example that could be followed elsewhere.

The Cork Majority Official Report also says that the fisherfolk, Farmers and Tennits represent the three different stages in socio-economic evolution – and in that 'order of development' – so that the Tennits were really the top of the pile, the crafts people of the world, who lived off the labour and produce of the other two, who were a more down-to-earth, folksy sort happy to leave the Tennits to their own pernickety, secretive industrial devices. But late economic decline meant that the Tennits had to go and make a living by partaking in normal food collection and production just like everybody else.

2 - Definitions of insanity took up part Section 12ADGbA(a) of the Report. It was amazing how each of the participants had his or her own favourite theory on the subject, opinions of which they were inanely and disproportionately possessive and proud. According to one Jansenism-leaning reverend gentleman there is no such thing as insanity or 'being out of one's mind', but only sinful states which are only too well-documented in the great paintings, all high art and sculpture, in classical books, theatre, music and in the annals of human political and social history. This chap, Eamon or whatever his name is, is the quintessential sinner, or the sinner par excellence, and he shows unmistakable signs of having much remorse for his sins. These must have been something terrible in the first place to cause such a torment of conscience! He had his own private theory on what one of those sins was. Eamon's alienation from society was the temporal and due punishment for the same sin.

Professor Roche, blarneying somewhat, said that there was a peculiar touch of genius in the population of their famed county which sometimes took the form of a kind of creative madness, as evidenced for example in the poetically rapid rate of talk in Cork along with its colourful nature, and also in the books that have been produced there over the years. It was 'being touched' that

The Madness of Eamon Moriarty

produced works of peasant genius such as they were investigating and should it ever be proven that it was the work of a Corkman then they only had reason to be proud. Needless to say, Professor Roche proved to be the most open-minded of the Cork panel, for the others were very wary of discussing topics of literacy and art, asserting that it was a Dublin preserve.

Another theory suggested that it was irrelevant where 'the chap came from', as the pathological state that was being described was transnational and transcultural. It was to do with the idea of 'control' over one's surroundings and over one's activities, and/or the lack of it. When one's emotions or mental 'energy' loses its synchronicity with the 'real' world there follows the state that results from this: 'cracked', 'round the bend', 'unhinged' and so on, always referring to a very specific feature – that of somehow being 'off the rails'. Staying on track is very dodgy in a world that is lopsided anyway. So it is when you don't know that you are a little bit mad that the trouble arises. Most people generally would accept that they are at the best of times barely 'staying on the rails' or 'keeping to the left side of the road', and at the very least are a little bit questionable upstairs. It was only time to worry whenever someone in this world claims that they are definitely, seriously, and totally sane! Most people, Corkonians no exception, are only too willing to admit that it's a mad world, if only because of the people who inhabit it, as the report said in one of its more philosophical asides.

Another way, continued the commentator, to look at all this is as follows: this world is mainly one of parallels; if it was a world of convergences everything would eventually collide and explode or implode. If it was a world of diverging forces by now everything would have gone on its own merry way and there would be nothing around us. It is when the brain fails to stick to this strict parallelism that trouble occurs. And not only do we live in a world of parallel forces but also one of reciprocity and symmetry in just about everything; insanity happens when the brain stops thinking symmetrically, was the final verdict.

3 - Jed, the Village Clown was unlike Economy in some noteworthy ways: firstly for being the only person in the village able to, literally, stand on his head. Jed could also faultlessly sing the National Song backwards (while Economy had never even learnt the words at all) and solemnly recite poetry where not one word made sense. He could mimic Jalosp, the Chief Monk, by making long, scatological speeches about Astronomical ceremonies, ancient island Headdresses and Dietary traditions in the Land of the Supernatural, which always brought forth peals of laughter from his listeners. He would dress up as a young woman and then speak in the voice of an elderly scholar about the hardships of life for young women in the village, (this especially brought paroxysms of hilarity out in the watching men, for it was their way of getting back at the ladies for the embarrassment of having to live and put up with them); dress up as an old woman and speak in the voice of a young village lad about her/his hunting achievements, athletic feats and war trophies, which always went down well with the ladies. Finally, there was his 'grande achievement', which was to take off his village idiot's clothes and put on the respectable village dress, daub his nose red and his cheeks white with red spots and lambaste everyone in the village by name and occupation for all their trifling misdeeds and mistakes, sparing no one in a dressing down that did not skirt the truth about any person or thing in a tirade worthy of any irate senior monk overseer.

4 - It would seem that Economy might have been constantly hallucinating by this time. There is no other way to explain his strange observations of a quite normal household. Indeed by the time of their second visit the Welfare officers had reported what they considered to be deterioration in his mental state and this 'improvement' was highlighted later in the bitter debate over the issue of his compulsory commitment to a public institution, at the ratepayers' expense.

5 - Here we have what experts claim is another hallucination. Some contend however that it is far from being a hallucination, that it is Economy/Eamon's account of a real physical experience of some kind at the hands of Halola. Dr Crane concurs in this opinion, and goes on to say that the act, whatever it was, would have seemed just like a dream, or a nightmare to him depending on whether he enjoyed it or not. He would have no understanding of the experience whatsoever as people with his condition would be unable to relate to any of the personal or moral aspects involved. Whether the experience helped him or led to further troubles, depends on how one interprets events afterwards.

6 - Burning at 'The Hot Gossip' stake was a cruel way to go. It was a ritual in the island that every so often some childless spinster, lady with a deformed child, or widow setting about doing good works be subjected to the ceremony of being burnt in a public place in the 'smoke with fire' of derogatory comment, scandal and all sorts of tittle-tattle.

Meanwhile, the departmental debacle over the Eamon case had been 'smoke-screened' by the creation of rather scarifying anecdotes concerning the lad's activities.

7 - Every second generation in the island, for as far back as you can go, always had to have a war break out. These intra-communal and fratricidal bloodlettings were never referred to as killings or massacres but only as 'hosting' and 'raids' – hence the tradition that there had never been a criminal murder in the island, only political assassinations.

8 - Cracker-jack in the Party Room – believed to refer to electoral campaign planning sessions on behalf of the well-known Big Farmer Party, as distinct from the Small Farmer Party, which tended to align with the Peasants' Party. Before the Days of Emancipation of Wives it was always carried out through the exclusively male game of Cracker-jack.

Chapter Twelve

A Great meeting, without the attendance of Mouth Merrick who had failed to turn up, (some said he had been held up by an eclipse of a planet which he noticed whilst on his toilet box, others that he felt there would be a diminution of his authority in consenting to attend a seminar on the subject of some mere earthly manifestation), was held in the Giants' Hall of Island House castle in Balhop, having been convened by the Chief monk with the compliance of Professor Sammy, who said he possessed some interesting information and a theory of the utmost importance he wished to elucidate. There was such an array of bemedalled, significant personages crowded outside the castle door at the island-equivalent of six o'clock in the evening that Halo, watching from the distance of his outer body's odour limit, was forced to remark that it must be the end of the world, for what he was seeing before him were the sure signs of the Day of Judgement. If the truth be known, some of the nobles there were not far removed from a comparable appreciation to Halo's, as more than one of them thought that such an admixture of official labels, medals and honours put a meaningless value on each individual distinction, for there were none that clearly outshone the others. It made each one feel, privately, that somehow the whole works (the pursuit of island honours) was not worth it. This strangely humble thought in some members of the establishment was accompanied by a belief that it should not be taken with more than a grain of island salt that this meeting of busied officialdom was going to solve anything at all.

The Madness of Eamon Moriarty

That entrenched general attitude to meetings explained their lack of concern when they found that the door of the hall wouldn't open and nothing the chief doorkeeper did would open it.

They stood around making meaningless time-of-day comments to one another and thought the lockout might herald a premature and somewhat appropriate end to the proposed debate. The professor alone showed distress, while the Chief monk (whom they realised now was the Priest-official Jalosp who, suspecting heresy, had taken on the functions of Chief monk himself) mustered a look of irritation and gave a whining groan which seemed to have an etiology evolving from some other, quite different problem he had on his mind. "Will somebody open the door, or do you think I don't have anything better to do than stand around here while that brand new moon that was reported to us recently may yet make an appearance and not been seen by me, the chief astronomer of the universe? What is holding the door closed?" he said with annoyance.

"One minute your excellency," shouted the panicking doorkeeper, demanding of the sub-doorkeeper that he get the door open at once. The assistant suggested they give a strong heave with all the assembled people pushing together.

"That is not a sensible proposal," the Chief monk snapped back.

Then an argument on the physics and chemistry of breaking into locked rooms broke out amongst the officials.

"Let me have a try at it," said one of the bemedalled fellows, rubbing his gloved hands together as if he was about to perform some spell on the door handle.

They stood aside, not in awe but in resigned boredom to let him get at the wooden doorknob that was shaped in the form of a soldier-scholar's ear. As he twisted, pushed and pulled at the knob the others indulged in little bits of idle conversation to pass the time.

"It is typical of the way our island affairs are run that we can't have meetings in comfortable barns instead of these cold castles, where the doors don't open properly."

"Well, that would not be in Jalosp's style," sniggered one official, looking over his shoulder at the Chief monk whose mind was elsewhere, knowing that what he said would be well received by his cynical listeners.

"Whoever arranged this meeting couldn't organise a smeer party in a bubble mill."

"Obviously they intended that nobody should ever get in there."

"Well, it looks completely locked to me," said the custodian of impounded rural dances, looking self-satisfied.

When the men finally got down to trying to force the door, it was the unanimous opinion that direct physical action was the only way. Even the Chief monk did not object to this. But it was all unnecessary, for after the third and apparently futile push the door was opened from within by the hands of some mysterious inside man. They flocked haphazardly into the hall, their mood now tinged with an air of gratuitous excitement and anticipation.

The Chief monk opened the meeting after everybody had seated themselves on boxes, the monk himself having his own high box.

"Mouth Merrick sends apologies for his absence, which is due to unforeseen circumstances. The meeting has been called because Professor Sammy has come up with a new idea. The professor is a man who you are all aware wracks his brains on our behalf and is up all night working on the latest things in science and politics so that the rest of us can take it easy. He it is who carries on the tedious business of finding solutions for all the island's problems while the rest of us, who can't keep up with his thoughts and formulations, just prefer to sit around all day doing nothing; or maybe we have been forcibly retired due to ill health or malpractice, or for the lack of any real interest in our jobs, or are otherwise engaged in the pursuit of personal hobbies down by the seashore, facing up to the vicissitudes of an idle life which has been imposed on us by our lack of scholarly ability. Well, this great professor has an idea. He has something to say that may save us from the impending ruin that we see overtaking our country."

After this characteristically tongue-in-cheek, if sarcastic opening, he paused, suddenly stuck for words. He now unexpectedly found himself having a crisis of conscience. He knew now that he was a spiritual failure. He should have encouraged people rather than mocked them. He should be a positive person who gave great speeches that people would remember for ages and ages. And this unprecedented lapse in confidence was all because he had suddenly found himself stuck for words! He wished, now, for someone to save him from any further embarrassment.

"You can speak, Professor," he said grandly, and sat down.

"As ye are aware," said the professor, "I have been conducting experiments on our island affairs for many years. I have always been watchful of things that I suspect may be the very phenomena that I am researching. Well now, at this moment the fulfilment of all my predictions is at hand. A few days ago a ship ran aground on the coast not far from Balhop. It was an Assaland boat. The captain himself, known to us as Captain Art and a useful benefactor to the island in the past, was sadly drowned at sea. Most of the crew and passengers were washed up on shore. There were also Lasdiacs on the ship, and ever since they have been wandering around, apparently at loggerheads amongst themselves over what to do.[1] However, there seems to be no way to prevent these people from coming here with their equipment and clever boxes.

The last time a sizable group of them came over they persuaded some of our scholars to go back to Assaland with them, so dazzled were our people by their talk and by what they heard said about that foreign land. If any more had gone the island would have been bereft of any intellectual life. Indeed that was probably the chief aim of their mission! They said everything in Assaland is bigger. The ludge factory is bigger than our whole island; it takes two weeks to walk from one end of it to the other. But the ludge factory is nothing compared to the Statue Of The Supreme Knight, Ramrod the Second, known colloquially as The Metal Warrior, which is made of our very own island stone and stands higher than the clouds.[2] Then there is the grass, the Assaland grass which is greener and grows higher than all the grasses found anywhere else in the world. These are, according to the Lasdiacs, sights to be seen.

It is my theory that they have returned for this same purpose of indoctrination. I believe it is their design to persuade all our intelligent leaders to go over to Assaland, where they will become mere clerks and low-grade technicians, and replace them here with their puppets. But a great opportunity has come to us. Making use of the temporary dislodgment of their minds caused by the ship's sinking, one leader in our midst has done what no man before him has ever achieved. He has not only met the Lasdiacs, he has actually spoken to them."

There was murmuring in the room.

"At the same time as the Lasdiac ship was approaching our coast word came to me that this same leader had come into town. He has not made his presence publicly known, and has not shown himself prominently in high places. He has instead been humbly occupying himself with cleaning up the litter in the market places. That is the very reason this man is well thought of in the highest circles – he is so *humble*. He has left his hard-won status in his own region to come here to serve us. There is no one else like him for common sense. He is at the moment the doughty employee of our public corporation, having been taken on by one Mr Galsworthy, his own brother's brother-in-law, the same a lifelong servant of the council. This humble man has lately been seen chatting amiably to the Lasdiacs in the downtown park and, more significantly, they have been talking to him! He tells them about the time he escorted their predecessors through the rural terrain that was then, as now, devoid of road signs. He had put them on the correct highway back to Balhop when they got lost, and they remembered that incident from so long ago! This is a breakthrough. We will hear more from the very man himself. He and I both agree that the end of our civilisation as it is now constituted is foreshadowed in the arrival of this latest batch of 'experts'."

There were loud gasps from the listeners. They studied his face to see if perhaps he was only indulging in that type of island rhetoric that causes the speaker to have on his face the expectation that people are listening to him.

As no alteration took place in his bland expression, or in the tenor of his voice, it had to be assumed that he was being serious in what he was saying, a rare thing in speech making.

"I happen to believe, however, that the island will be a better place for that!"

This made them all whistle and mutter all the more.

"I don't know why you are all putting the cudgels in my ears. You had better listen to the man himself. For he came along with me and he is here in the middle of ye."

Everybody looked around to see the man of whom Sammy had such a high opinion, their fidgeting ceasing at the prospect of some new revelation.

A man shuffled embarrassedly on his box. It was then that they noticed he was the only person in the room who did not have any medals pinned to his clothing. He appeared confused. He looked up quizzically at Professor Sammy and he didn't seem to know what to do.

"Step forward, Mr Top Carrot, and take a seat right up here at the front of the hall," shouted down the professor in a hearty voice. Top Carrot appeared afraid to leave his seat and he stared glumly down at all the feet around him, unwilling to look anybody in the face.

"Come on, Mr Carrot," said Sammy, his grey beard flowing, "your views are no less important or relevant than those of people here. Your village is no less an important place than Balhop or Inisbay. Indeed many of our wisest failures, or most foolish successes, have come from the villages. The Founder of that obscure sect whose members love their neighbours, and who are so difficult to locate, once said when He had overcome the impediments of His narrow upbringing in a remote village and become Someone in the world, that it didn't matter if you were of no account in men's eyes. They poked fun at Him and His country cousins through rude comments and mock trials. He went back to educate His fellow villagers, and He showed His true class, as they were finally stringing Him up for getting ideas above His station, by forgiving them all. Come up here and tell them about the great old days in the hinterland."

Top Carrot went slowly up to the front and turned and faced the audience, embarrassed and swaying uneasily.

"Ah, I don't want to bore these city folk with my useless anecdotes and opinions," he said in a very quiet voice.

"Tell me, what do you make of these Lasdiacs?" asked Professor Sammy.

"They have some good ideas, especially Charles," said Carrot, finding his full voice.

"Is it true that they have no hair on their heads?" asked a member of the audience, who was somewhat jealous of Top's breakthrough and whose career had been in the island diplomatic service, which was the only such service in the world whose members never went overseas, and whose chief role was to preserve the island population from any contact with foreigners. He had won his medal for his huge success in this policy.[3]

Top made a disclosure that shocked the audience and caused them to collectively lose their breath.

"They shave it off deliberately."

"I am proposing," said Sammy loudly, waving his hand to change the subject, "that we make this humble citizen king of our island."

There was silence.

"After numerous experiments, I have made a discovery. It is due to our way of thinking that things have not been going right. The only cure will be a ruler who will dispense with any necessity for thought, to whom we can direct all our aspirations and devotion without any need for criticism. You see, for far too long we have depended on the O-Nut when making decisions of public and private policy."

They all looked at one another.

"But let me tell you of one experiment I carried out lately, and I will show you how I came to my conclusion. I obtained an extra-large O-Nut that I cut and placed on the venerable chamber seat in the castle museum that, as you all know, was at one time the infamous throne of the Cruel Ruler who gave our ancestors such a rueful time in the Days of the Ruffled Feathers. Let me remind you. There was a competition every year to select an occupant for this seat, who received a mock crown and was elevated in a big box up to the sky for everyone to laugh at. This was done no matter how important, or respected the occupant may have been previously. The function of the ceremonial seat was to release all the accumulated tensions in society of the previous year. The mock king was not allowed down until he had said, or done, something beyond the bounds of decency or common sense. The accomplishment of this task would release the 'victor' and give him a mystical respect in the community after that for as long as he lived. This would not be for very long, as he had usually poisoned himself with coleoil while he was up there.

I weighed the value of the O-Nut against the sum total of our present island leaders. I came up with a remarkable result. The O-Nut weighed the more, for when I had come back into the laboratory after a snack and a nap on the kitchen stove, for thinking makes me hungry, I found that the chair had not upheld the weight of the nut as balanced by the collective weight of our leaders and the whole structure had collapsed in a shambles. This clearly demonstrates the lack of substance to our collective decision-making!

Top Carrot fits the bill. He brought the rule of politics to the rural districts. He has told me all about the people who live in his part of the country. He describes the smiling, courteous looks on their faces as strangers somewhat cagily go through what was once hostile territory, on foot or drive past on carts, expecting rocks and verbal onslaughts to come hurtling out at them. And all you get nowadays is a casual wave and even an occasional 'good day'. He said that if you experience the warmth of their gracious nods and hearty handshakes, or bask in the glow of their friendly, courteous eyes and hear their unique words for plain, ordinary, common things that normally go by cruder names in the towns, it would make you laugh and warm your soul. And when you hear them sing in their lilting brogues your heart is thrilled. Who else could have brought these wild, poetic people to heel? And he can do the same for all our cynical city folk too, the malcontents, the footpads and the unemployed, by diverting their attention from their present harmful, dangerous preoccupation with harping on their legal and social rights to a safer target. I mean the legally appointed, constitutionally enshrined, traditional monarchy of King Top Carrot! No longer will important, respectable members of society have to put up with abuse from the common, uneducated population on the lookout for easy butts for their venom. For in future all disdain, mockery and blame will be laid on our monarch. Great blessings and curses will pile up on him as he sits resplendent in the abstruse costumes and royal nonsensical sayings and concocted heritage, glowing with regal disdain for the mob as he walks along what were once common paths but now are the exclusive preserve of the royal entourage. As he and his scrumptiously attired courtiers go in procession singing the old, staid songs the whole population of the island can have a good laugh and make their ridiculous jokes and sing their silly songs to their hearts' content and no harm done. We have been missing out in this land by relying on those staid old politicians from the island tribes, The Clever Dicks, Silly Billys and Smart Alecs to be our Chief rulers. They indeed know all about business, agriculture, industry, finance, commerce, diplomacy, defence, sports and public discussions, but nothing at all about the tedious and tricky business of turning the tables on the clever city cynics and ignorant country clucks who think they know it all, with their continual challenges and baiting and trying to impress everyone with their independent views and their critical minds and wisecracks. And also, the Chief ruler has told me that he wouldn't mind giving up his job; 'I have to attend too many meetings as it is', were his words".

"Do we really need rulers, or systems of government at all?" asked an anarchist member of the audience, who was a senior partner in Balhop's biggest legal firm, Asrmguugely and Company.

"It is apparent that none of you have opened your eyes lately. I myself had not noticed what's been going on in the country until Mr Carrot opened my eyes for me. We have all indeed studied public policies, attended stroppleblossom parties, heard many speeches, seen the building works in Balhop and all the other much commented on events of daily life. But we have failed to notice what has been taking place behind our backs. Indeed it is the same Top Carrot who has brought many of these things to my attention, when we spent some evenings chatting together recently (he necessarily incognito) in a scholars' drinking barn, where I discovered that all the learning of us scholars counts for nothing. Not, anyway, against the eye and ear-sharp observations of this canny rustic sage! You know he made me see things I had never even imagined were happening before? For instance, there are terrible disturbances taking place over much of the island that I had never even noticed. He gives causes for these. He points out that the never-ending rain, which we all accept as inevitable, is in fact preventable. He said that they don't have the problem in other countries, and of course this is quite true. He told me about the conflicts and deteriorating situation on the playing fields of our once-peaceful parishes where what were once sporting matches between neighbours have turned into major bloodletting wars. The camogie stick is being used as a weapon of death and destruction in a ruthless pursuit of the ambition of every minor club in every minor village to come out top in the competitions and to be hailed as overall island victors. This, he says, is to compensate for other, deeper frustrations in society that he did not explain to me. I only wish I had brought him out more on that matter. He says that the other day he came across evidence that our extremely valuable mountains are disappearing not, as the scholars explain, slowly and piece by piece over millions of years without us being aware of it, but much more quickly and with the imminent possibility of the whole island disappearing. Complete mountains have collapsed on villages in some rural districts. He has not only observed this; he showed me the scar on his arm obtained when he tried to hold back these gigantic mountainous inundations. The brave man! And we worry here in Balhop about such 'drastic' things as a small fall in house prices, or a miniscule rise in the price of ludge! He described to me, in such heartbreaking detail that I was crying at the end of it, the poor quality and high prices in recent years of basic food items in the countryside. There, he says, they have to subsist on wild berries and, listen to this, oin meat! They have such a deprived, put-upon existence that I am ashamed to be a Balhopian. I, who enjoy all sorts of imported niceties that are always on display aplenty in the stores, have until now ignored the fate of my less well-off island brethren. I have to admit that today I am contemptuous of the name Balhopian, and the least I can do, that we can all do, is to make him king."

A Balhopian resident of many generations spoke.

"I have a warning to pass on to you all. There is now intermarrying between Tennits and fisherfolk that is producing a hybrid type of offspring who in the future will be a major social problem. They will become a calculating, lawless, crude but ruthless species of person, working all-hours accruing to themselves the wealth of Balhop yet at the same time turning out to be a lazy, unpatriotic lot who will live off the charity of the rest of us in dirty slums full of their countless children. A strong king will know how to deal with these people."

The Chief monk spoke.

"Do not panic, my people. The professor is entitled to his opinion, but he has been made a complete fool of by the country fellow. Sure we monks are accustomed to dealing with this type of charlatan in the confessional box. Yet at the same time he sounds like a smart fellow who knows how to deal with the Lasdiacs who, after all, only want to replace us monks."

"Of course he can deal with them," stated the professor boldly, relishing the fact that at long last people were listening to what he had to say, his beard now taking on an animated life of its own as the mesmerised audience's eyes followed its dancing movements and perturbations;

192 The Madness of Eamon Moriarty

"no matter what we think, or how long and how deeply we think, we can do nothing to change the world. It is a time, dear people, for leaving it all for the king to decide."

An irate literature scholar spoke next:[4]

"Things couldn't be much worse under a monarchy. Why is it that uneducated peasants can make a mockery of centuries of our learning by coming here with their crude, self-sculptured anecdotes, which not even our wisest scribes, with the aid of numerous fellow-scribes and using the longest, heaviest tomes and dictionaries in the island have been able to transcribe or decipher. This state of affairs is a direct result of the incompetence of our present educational system"

"There is another question you have been leaving out," said Sammy.

"May I sit down?" asked Top Carrot suddenly.

"Most certainly you may," replied Sammy. The Chief monk nodded at Top Carrot to confirm his permission, glaring at Sammy at the same time for having taken upon himself the authority of chairman.

"What is the question we have been leaving out?" asked the Chief monk.

"It concerns the self-same scroll."

"Where is it?"

"In actual fact I have it here in my pocket," said Sammy.

Notes

[1] - 'How we turned Disaster into Triumph' or To The men Of Fifty Eight became a popular Lasdiac hymn after this event. The Lasdiacs, in hindsight, considered the sinking of the ship to be a good omen as it meant that the slack-hearted among them became more committed to the mission, as there was no going back. Also, the destruction of vessels had, in history, a good advertisement in those brilliant, previous conquerors, the Newly Appointed Tribe and the Sweepers With A New Brush, who had never considered a landing auspicious without a ceremony called 'burning your boats'.

The Madness of Eamon Moriarty

To The Men Of 'Fifty Eight
Glory O, Glory O
to that great day,
our ship sank, our captain fell
and we were on our way!
Glory O, O Glory O
to the Bold Lasdiac Men.

2 - Ramrod II, The Metal Warrior, was the scourge of Assaland's only ever worthy enemy, Lacus, chief of the gods, who had become jealous of Assaland's power, wealth and beauty. Lacus was the god of the invading blonde-haired Achaians who ruled over the black-haired natives with an iron fist and who soon got into trouble themselves with Lacus for getting too big for their boots. The Achaians, who even today form the dominant ruling class in Assaland, had imposed their own rigid religious Order of the Patriarchal Sugar Loaf (the tallest mountain in Assaland) Sky Gods, in preference to the earth and ocean goddesses of the native matriarchal culture, suppressing all the local heart-centred, sentimental (if erstwhile cannibalistic) cults and ascribing all wisdom to Lacus. For a time they had few problems, their palace being really a fortress, standing firm against all unwanted intrusion, the centre of a system of strategic roads giving easy access to all of Assaland and their iron weapons proving superior to the cheap, softer bronze of the natives. (The Ancient Egyptians too had problems with their restless ambitions, recording that 'the islands of the sea' were being disturbed and the coasts of 'good old Egypt' raided constantly by the Akhaiwashi – another name they went under). But the Achaians were not content with their worldly power alone and attempted to take some of Lacus's power for themselves. Along comes Ramrod II, who declares that all priests must be men, that the children of the gods are born out of Lacus's head rather than the womb of a woman, and that henceforth he was the ultimate Leader Of The Fates and The Boss Of Necessity. In that war which Ramrod won was the final victory of the Achaians, making them masters of all and mighty enemies of others who claimed that their gods were above the now-deified Achaian rulers. Nobody dared point out that Ramrod was really only a legend and that there was no historical evidence for such a warrior ever having existed, or for such an auspicious military campaign ever

having taken place. Indeed nobody in Assaland had ever even wanted to go to those local, insignificant islands or spend time away from stolid and, let it be said, comfortable Assaland in the first place. The Lasdiacs who had come were members of a theologically discredited minor order (i.e. there were no jobs for them back home) and the island was in fact only their fifth choice of mission field after Egypt, The Pillars of Penzance, the Greek islands and the wide open, endless plain of Utter Pradesh! (Note of the Classics Department).

3 - The story of the first ever and only diplomatic mission abroad is quickly told and explains the philosophy of that department. A Chief Ruler Of The Island had wanted this mission because he had had read to him, on his long-dying deathbed, a well-known book on politics by a medieval Italian intellectual, which gave him grand ideas about the possibilities of enjoying the amazing illusions of power to be discovered in ruling an even smaller, insignificant place than that of his own island. This ruler had been up to that point a very shy, retiring individual who always avoided having to make decisions that interfered with his main preoccupations, which was how to avoid his pet hates, such as going out in the rain, or to indulge his hobbies, such as watching the chariot races from the comfort of a rain-proof box, or especially interfered with his lifelong neurotic habit of convincing the population that he was on the verge of dying whilst-remaining-in-power. In fact he was better known for the celebrity of his younger days as a top player in a male camogie team than for mere politics. He had been elected to the post of Chief Ruler for his adeptness on the camogie field alone as well as his gentlemanly niceness, his personality having been impressed on the populace through a novel means never used before in political history, a campaign of passing his 'image cards' around the countryside by means of the magic picture boxes seen by Eamon in the village centre. Everything had gone all right until he read the book. Then this formerly pipe smoking, placid, easygoing chap decided to take his job more seriously, quit the pipe, got out of bed and sent ex-fishermen delegates (accustomed to sea travel) to the nearest, smallest island with a view to incorporating it in some kind of 'empire'. The fishing boat carrying the diplomatic duo (Fill and Lip) headed for the island of Upper Handia with the initial aim of discussing a defence pact in an alliance to impress the Lower Handians. They made a big mistake by

dressing up, thinking that they were 'above' the Upper Handians and not simply ordinary fishermen themselves. Fill wore green linen underwear (visible around the knees), a tight-fitting, red cotton trousers with gold braids finishing at the knees (a type of knickerbockers) which showed his backside to great effect (and Upper Handians hated large backsides), a white silk shirt with a very high collar and golden (not real gold) buttons, a purple dyed woollen jacket with colourful flashes which represented nothing at all, leather pointed shoes and a black, very tall hat. He carried a white walking cane with a black 'ivory' knob and walked slowly and purposely two steps behind Lip. Lip dressed up as a prophet, wearing a simple white gown with a hood hanging down at the back and simple leather slippers. He let his beard grow very long. He put on an ascetic face and walked with his head down. He carried a heavy book that had been lent to him by the monks. A further problem was that they did not know the slightest thing about politics locally and underrated the belligerence and sullenness of the Upper Handians who, for instance, were not even on speaking terms with their nearest neighbours in Lower Handia. The people on Lower Handia were descended from the Tennits; this was the probable reason for the friction between them and their neighbours, for the Upper Handians were an off-cut from the ancestors of the fishermen and Farmers. This 'small island' self-consciousness ensured without a doubt that their arrival would be met by suspicion. Later it was argued that if they had gone as plain fishermen with a gift of some fish things might have turned out differently. The first reaction on their arrival was astonishment, followed by hilarity and then hostility. They were beaten up and sent back, ingloriously.

4 - 'A History of Island Literature' was the seminal work of this academic, who finally resolved the conflict between the Obscurants and the Practicals, the two great schools of literature. Not for them the staid modes of Classical Antiquity, the Passionate and Lively school of the Middle Ages, Neoclassicism, Romanticism, Naturalism or Modern Criticism, textbooks of which abounded in Assaland bookshops but which were not available even for loan on the island, and in any case they would not have made much sense to a people who were more into the oral rather than the written tradition. The Obscurants believed that Literature should only 'take place' in an unknown or at least unintelligible-to-the-majority language to save it from the corruptions of

everyday life. For this reason the scholars and to a lesser extent the monks kept a few thick, old, unopened books on their shelves and referred to these as The Literature. Everything else was just the Practicals. Island vernacular poets, singers and gossip mongers who spoke in a cultured, artistic sort of way were the chief outlets for 'the word' and the population paid great attention to their sayings and satirising, ignoring the great classical, standard works. It is in the light of this tradition that the controversy surrounding Eamon's/ Economy's writing may be interpreted. Here was someone who should, at the very least, have remained on the Practical side, but had ventured without qualification or license into Obscure Literature itself! All the theories on language, psychology, mythical ideas and the 'sublime' were under threat from what appeared to be local, banal popular verse that made nonsense of any criticism. The professor's book solved this problem for those who would understand it. He claimed that the taciturn words and banal songs of the peasantry were in fact the product of a fecund genesis within an archetypal glottis that reflected the most primitive in human expression. He said that this 'real' art could only be understood if the population was made to learn a language they could never read, write or even speak. This was the real reason for scholars and monks insisting on the introduction of Classical Assalandish in the schools, even if they themselves didn't have full mastery of it – and not just to keep the pupil numbers down. The professor produced a written version of a now-famous poem he claimed had been transcribed in the backwoods, though his critics said he had written it himself, which resolved all further disputes and showed the need for the New Criticism.

"Glottis"
Dishabille faff falderal
in holt, yore isomorphism-
inchmeal inchoation goliard-feoffee
crick –
esurient gyps orchitis conation,
compurgation yah.
Amative febrile palingenesis
temerarious half-seas-over –

The Madness of Eamon Moriarty

dehisce maecenas yaps.
Xenoglossia waggery
whilom rhapsodic rhymester-
litotes majuscules facetiae
hebdomadal optative taradiddle-
vamose
abeam –

chapter THIRTEEN

*H*e produced it from a pocket which lay somewhere within his immense gown. This man, who in the privacy of his home and without his gown looked quite meagre, a totally insignificant individual without charisma or 'presence' in any sense of the word, was in fact a shy, retiring type of man, nevertheless drove his family to distraction every morning by insisting on ceremoniously donning this garment at the breakfast table. For the task he enlisted the wife and children's concentration and aid in a great commotion and charade. The performance would be ongoing both during and even after the meal with this perfectionist always insisting that either it was incorrectly buttoned, unsatisfactorily secured or some other how not quite properly in place. Nevertheless outside his house and in his garb he always managed to show a calm, supremely confident air to the world.

"Hold it up in front of you where we can see it," said the monk.

Professor Sammy held the parchment aloft, and they all scrutinised the lettering that had been crudely inscribed there.

"Now do you see anything?" he asked.

"I see some words on it."

"Read them."

"I see written, 'monks and scholars stink to high heaven.'"[1]

There was a gasp from the audience.

"Good heavens! Well, the document is a more disgraceful thing than we ever even thought!"

"Read the rest," suggested Sammy.

"I hardly wish to."

"Go on," said the professor in an uncharacteristically jolly voice. He seemed to be enjoying the fact that his peers and fellow professionals were taken aback by those words.[2]

"Read it all out," shouted the others, "we cannot be shocked any more than we are now! Let us hear the rest of it."

"It says, 'our leaders are stupid'" read the monk.

Another stunned silence followed.

"There is something else here," said the monk in a hesitant voice;

"it says 'Top Carrot is wise.'"

They looked hard at Top Carrot, who seemed just as surprised as anyone else that his name also should appear in that obscure document.

Professor Sammy spoke out.

"What I believe," he said, "is that this fellow, who comes from a part of the country where I once taught – and I can assure you there are sages out there – is expressing an extremely enlightened analysis of the underlying causes of the malaise in our culture and society. He has expressed long-needed-to-be-said thoughts that have for many centuries been circulating unacknowledged and suppressed in our heads. He has brought into daylight once-unspeakable truths. For the very first time, we can say what we think and feel about our leaders, scholars and monks. And society will all be the better for it!"

"It's just the worst sort of graffiti," shouted an angry member of the audience, "I'll bet there are even more disgusting things written on it."

The man was so upset because if it was accepted that the scroll was legible and even worse, had some meaning, there would be a policy review at all levels and he would be liable to lose his post as the Custodian of Rural Dances and

Unsympathetic Countryside Art. It would probably mean for him the worst fate of all, which is reserved for failed government advisors, that is, a summons to serve on the only body in the island whose ordinances were sometimes, and annoyingly, followed, the Fenceside Sitters Of The Public Places. These were renowned for the sharpness of the insight of their observations of all new things and for their trenchant and erudite comments, but were held in disgust by all reputable folk because they sometimes went out of character and took matters into their own hands. They actually went about doing things like picking up litter, closing open gates, putting out chimney fires, blocking the wind off from sight-seeing groups of visitors or widows and orphans queuing for ludge. They were good at spotting unusual or eccentric behaviour in the common people, especially the denizens of the central plazas and downtown areas of Balhop. New appointees were sometimes dressed up and sent unwillingly on soul-destroying missions to schools, villages and public platforms to explain to present and future generations all about Unsympathetic Art and how, despite all the failure of island culture and learning, in whatever guise, to improve their drab lives in the past, it might still be possible to make their existence less poverty stricken and more acceptable in the future if somehow an improvement could be brought about in their own mental capacity. (And all of this for just a few bob).

"True," said the Chief monk looking closely at the document, "I see some that are unrepeatable, things that should never be heard by the ear or seen by the eye, either now or forevermore. This parchment should be placed in the lowest dungeon of the Public Prison Library where all banned information is kept out of harm's way, for the benefit of those future specialist scholars who, one day, hopefully will be immunized enough against the truth to be able to face, in the privacy of those same dungeon cells, the words exactly as they appear on the scroll."

Jalosp screwed his eyes and stared hard at the scroll, as if pretending that it was the first time he was seeing it. The others stood up and strained their necks or bent over at odd angles to look at the piece. A silence reigned in the hall and the only movements consisted of their heavy breathing, the puffing of hairy chests and restless, fidgety toes and fingers. It was the most historic moment ever in that country's history, the precise instant that they all experienced a cultureangst, but as it passed there was no one immediately aware that anything unusual had happened, or that any transformation in the island's culture had taken place at all! Such is the apparent banality of the moment of truly great revolutions.

At long last an expression came over Jalosp's face that bespoke the gradual coming-to-light of a new awareness.

"Let me see now," he said slowly, opening his hands wide in a gesture which seemed to embrace eternally all the accepted facts and experiences of mankind, then joining them together in a gesture that symbolised the coming together of all truth:

"we have heard what the words on this scroll say. But is the scroll telling the truth?"

Professor Sammy jumped to his feet.

"I was wondering if you were ever going to ask it," he shouted jubilantly.

"You will now see conducted by me my latest truth-finding experiment which has never been done in public before. You have only to make the right choice."

He lifted the scroll in the air and waved it around. Every eye followed his hand. Then he produced a number of small and very strange instruments from his pocket. The purpose of only one of these, a piece of flame-raising firestone, was immediately clear to everybody. Sammy asked Top Carrot to vacate the box he was sitting on and he placed his equipment down with rather too much deliberation and unnecessary ceremony that was perhaps just a normal scholar's typical concealment of his ignorance.

"Briefly," he said, "there is the reading proof and the burning proof. In either, the principle is the same – that the truth be manifested. If we read it more than once and arrive at the same sense, we will know it to be untrue, for in life we never know the same thing twice. We might expect to describe it as gibberish. Or would you prefer that I perform the burning proof? If I set this scroll on fire, and it burns fiercely and nothing remains after that but ashes, then there will be no doubt as to its truth. For nothing untrue can ever exist, so it cannot be destroyed! Which shall I do?"

"The burning proof. Burn it," was the unanimous demand.

"Do you agree, Chief monk?" asked Sammy.

"Whatever they want," replied the monk, "let that be your guide;" for he was never one to be interested in or impressed by any sort of proof. He, like the other astronomical monks, read only from extra-terrestrial events, falling meteors, flare-up stars, there-now-and-gone-tomorrow lights, wandering galaxies, even moonlight, the meaning of things, the proof of ideas, the value of fantasies and the truth of dreams.

"The Chief monk agrees," said Sammy. He prepared his burning instruments. There was a little goblet for holding ashes, a tweezers for holding the parchment (the purposes of both implements were now becoming clearer to the still somewhat bemused audience), and finally the firestone from which sparks are obtained. The paper was held aloft in the tweezers in a hand that trembled, whether from fear or excitement was unclear from the wide-eyed expression of the professor. He struck the stone producing a blue spark whose brightness and purity produced an involuntary awe in that sophisticated assemblage. Well, he told them, they would now see whether it would burn or not, and he struck a second blue spark at the paper's edge. The paper caught light and soon it became a ball of flame. The black remains crumbled and fell out of the tweezers into the goblet.

"There," said Professor Sammy, "it was, after all, no figment of the imagination. It was true, as true as its very essence which we saw burning to ashes just a moment ago." "True," repeated the crowd.

"What has been said cannot be unsaid," said Jalosp in a resigned voice;

"so the words on that parchment must forever remain in our heads."

So what the Chief monk had read out and what Professor Sammy had interpreted and then tested became the accepted official version of Economy's words in the island. There was great relief that the offending document had now been destroyed.

Many emotions and thoughts coursed through the audience, rivers like flotsam suddenly released through a dam, and their ideas on leaders and scholars and their role in society were revised and altered and destroyed until they found that even their fundamental opinions and beliefs were no longer what they were. They found it difficult to adjust to the discomfiture of this new cynicism and they sat there and scratched themselves uneasily on their heads and under their armpits and each shoved his box uneasily against that of his neighbour in petty jostling and quibbling over not-so-particular personal body habits in a sort of unconscious release of the unsettled condition that had now begun to reign in their minds. They even now found themselves liking the idea of a king whom the people could hate, despise and insult gratuitously in their own minds and hearts. The monk addressed them now, though with a bit less of the authority than would previously have been his.

"I would like to hear your views now. I wonder if you are thinking the same strange ideas that are coming into my head?"

A man spoke, his voice hoarse.

"How can we ever respect any authority after hearing what was in that scroll? We must have a king."

Sammy spoke triumphantly for being in sight of a great victory.

"If we make a crown of precious island stones for Top Carrot, and place it on his head, authority will be secured against its foes in the island, for he will be seen to be established and forever enthroned in a position above all authority. He will overlook us all with the power of a god. No dishonour or rudeness to monks, scholars or leaders will ever have any consequence again. For there will be someone higher than they, who will have a royal charter to be as stupid, or as smelly, as he wishes, with no reflection whatsoever on his status or influence. The king alone will have true honour, for he alone is praised in the scroll! He and his courtiers (and some of you will be those) will be irreproachable for their very smelliness and stupidity. No islander will ever dare to question his word. You people here will never be contradicted or insulted again for you will all have a royal charter to be what you are. The king alone will be respected, and detested, by everybody."

Jalosp spoke again.

"Now, Mr Carrot," he said, thinking very deeply, "how is it that your name is inscribed in that scroll?"

"I knew the fellow," said Top Carrot proudly, finding the confidence at last to speak out loudly, "and I agree with Professor Sammy, he was blessed with special insight."

"I would not be surprised if it was you who put him up to his tricks," shouted the Grand Master of the Businessmen-To-The-Shore-Region Fraternity.

He was suspicious of all peasantry-cunning, such as trying to put one of their own in as king and outwitting the rich and powerful establishment. He actually had a dream of being king himself (a fantasy that he could never admit even to himself), if only to gain more of the monopolies and charters that would surely follow from such an appointment. He was a gentleman whose main surrogate-profession had been to pass the illicit, valueless stones to simple shoreline folk as a secondary source of income for himself and to prevent them ever becoming involved in idea-smuggling, that detested and long-outlawed occupation of the underclass; while of course simultaneously the Balhop businessmen arranged for the legal, precious stones which were the product of sound financial policy to go unnoticed and untaxed through the official channels; and who despite his great wealth still maintained an interest in the loss-making, underground rock quarrying activities throughout the island. Perhaps he had mistaken this present controversy as representing another dreaded instance of idea smuggling, which was a periodically recurring activity amongst the un-banked classes, especially at times of crisis. (At least this is what he, as a trained accountant, thought. None of these thoughts occurred to anybody else).

"He was a stick gatherer who lived with an old woman who was not his real mother outside my village. They were the scourges of their community and of the surrounding farming district for years. I had to deal with many a complaint about them. It is only after I left that things got out of hand."

"Perhaps," said the monk, not satisfied with Carrot's 'virtuous' stance, "you can tell us if he was your political hireling?"

"Good gracious. He was a poor, simple sort of fellow whom not even the minor gods would notice, or be bothered by. He rarely ventured into the community centre. He was always off collecting sticks. I maintained he did a good job by clearing up storm-damaged fields and I always ensured that he kept away from saplings and healthy trees. The old woman, I have good reason to believe was a very fulsome, handsome girl in her youth. She was indeed often the subject of 'chatting up' by many a young man long ago. She even had a reputation for being a 'tease'. I had a bit of a graw for her myself, I must admit.[3] There is a great mystery about how she ever came to have such an odd child. Despite following up every theory and looking into every likely suspect, there is no one in the neighbourhood whom he resembles. He was not born from any known antecedents."

Top had been becoming angry as he spoke because of this attempt to denigrate him by-association. He demonstrated his impatience by showing the full width of his black-white teeth and stamping his foot on the floor, thereby crushing the unsuspecting toes of Sammy. The professor protested this injury with a stoical shake of his head and he succoured his toes with both hands to relieve the pain.

"Tell us, why did you talk to the Lasdiacs?" asked Jalosp.

"I went to them simply to ask if I could get a lift on their boat in order to make a short visit to Assaland. I wanted to go for the good of the island, for I was interested in bringing back information about the place. I thought I would broaden my mind and widen my horizons by seeing what it was like over there, and return to the island full of new ideas. What is wrong in wanting to see if my particular skills could not be improved upon? I might have come back with a greater knowledge of the type of people there, and of what makes them tick."

"And what did they say?" asked the monk.

"They were very chatty and agreed that there were very few of our islanders living over in Assaland. They said they looked forward to the day when there would be free travel and flow of goods and labour between both lands, and trust and friendship between our peoples. They took me into a private house, one that belongs to a Unapproachable and gave me much lovely food and drink.[4] They told me that they would show me over a ship when the next one arrived from Assaland."

"They don't sound like a such an unfriendly lot then," said the Chief monk quizzically, raising his eyebrows.

"They said they have it in mind to solve all our problems with their plan for telling us about their philosophy. Their philosophy, they said, will be enough to both feed and clothe us, set us on the path to wisdom and make the island a better place."

"Perhaps the era of mutual misunderstanding is over," said Jalosp, somewhat less than hopefully; (there was an unbridgeable gulf between the world of the monks and of the Lasdiacs. Pride and self-respect were upheld in both camps by the simple expedient of a deliberate total lack of contact between them over thirty centuries and the great, welcome abyss in cosmological doctrines that lay between them).

He continued:

"There is no getting away from them anyway, for they bring progress with them. And this thing called 'philosophy' I am interested in. It sounds like something we should look into and see about getting for ourselves. For too long we have been looking for meaning in the stars. I keep telling our novices to look down on the ground and they will see things there that will surprise them, (it also makes them work harder). And who is not to say that it will be the Lasdiacs, rather than us, who are changed? Many times in the past it has happened that the small, supposedly weak religion has taken over the world. I admire Mr Carrot for his enterprise, and even his idea of going to visit Assaland is a good one that I think, some of our other leaders might do well to consider. Mr Carrot shows initiative. There is no doubt that he is a beloved leader in his own village, and I think that he would make a very good king." (He would explain his promotion of Top Carrot to Mouth Merrick later by saying it was a good idea to have someone like him to take all the opprobrium of dealing with the Lasdiacs, for there must never be direct contact between monk and Lasdiac).

"I wonder," he said turning to Professor Sammy, "how you go about appointing a king?"

"Easy," said Sammy; "we just agree on the man, and place a crown on his head! Then he will be king. The only qualification needed for a king is that he is acceptable to those important people in the room who appoint him."

"I thought it would be a bit more complicated than that. Would not Mouth Merrick need to be informed?" the anarchist solicitor wanted to know.

"Look," said Sammy, with the confidence of someone who had prepared all the answers beforehand, "a king is a king and he has nothing to do with priest-officials, scholars, astronomers, the state of the country or the weather. He is afforded Divine protection once he has been appointed. If Mouth Merrick or others have any problems or queries about our actions today they can bring them up with the king afterwards. I am sure that they will find a very sympathetic listener in Top Carrot. I have an emergency crown in my possession, one that was used long ago in a forgotten period of experimental kings, and all we need is the agreement of the noble folk here present. For we are all nobles now by the mere fact of our presence at this meeting. And then we have a king!"

"Do you want to be king of the island then?" asked Jalosp.

"It would be a bit better job than what I am doing at the moment, and I feel I could offer my services as a leader to more people than I have been able to in the past. My family back home will be very pleased too, I think," said Top.

He had, in fact, been lured to the castle hall by the promise of a better job by Professor Sammy earlier in the day. But he had never expected anything as big as this.

"It would be nice to have our own king," said a woodcarver, who was already thinking up different designs for a brand new throne; "it will give jobs to many of us skilled Balhop people."

"Do you agree, gentlemen?" asked Sammy flipping his garment out with great gusto, and as the thoughts of the audience were already turning (in fact they had turned much earlier in the proceedings) to the prospect of relief in a great, sustained indulgence in strong liquor, especially as Sammy had promised plenty of celebratory drink back at his place, a stocking up which somehow had not been curtailed by the island-wide famine of stocks of roots and berries, and as there was a great, overwhelming impatience to get the meeting over with they all or most of them said they agreed, although few if any could say that they remembered saying it afterwards. Indeed not one could be found later who could repeat, rephrase, or even agree as to what they had assented to, or of what had been discussed at the meeting. Some were to deny totally that they had ever agreed to any of the decisions taken there.

There was an uneasy shifting in the room, with feet and bodies bobbing up, down and sideways and if it were not for the decorum demanded on such occasions there would have been a massive, unstoppable stampede for the door.

When Sammy produced a gold tinted, temporary crown from his bag they all quietened down a little and strained forward to have a look at it. There was some chatter and praise, and a very good-natured, accepting sort of atmosphere when Jalosp placed the crown on Top's head. Top smiled.

"You are now our king, King Top Carrot," said the monk cheerfully, and he worried now how he should properly address him.

Then there came a disturbance at the back of the hall that caused shock and horror. As everybody was clapping the door opened and Halo appeared, shouting at the top of his voice.

He pointed at Top Carrot, while at the same time not looking at him but staring with profound emotion at the ceiling.

"Don't listen to my brother. What has he been saying to you? It is he, I know him. He it was who drove me to this forsaken place and who placed me with the unfit and unkempt. He goes by many names. He is in league with the evil ones. He is very wicked himself. O Assalander, the end has come." With that Halo produced, as if from nowhere, bundles of the island red mud and flung it in all directions around the hall, hitting many of the guests on their faces. Then, with equal drama, he tore the cover of threadspin web off his head and for the first time exposed his face, which nobody in Balhop had ever seen before. His eyes and features, however, had a shocking intimacy. It was a face that somehow was familiar to them all.

Notes

1 - The most recent textual criticism theory, modelled around the theories of De Paris and MacFein, was devised as a counter theory to Neo-Obscuricism, the favoured school of recent times. Neo-Obscurant criticism concentrates on small stylistic details, asserting that languages are determined by immutable basic structures. It dismisses the importance of the author. The counter theory, Anti-Neo-Obscuricism, asserts that written texts appear to refer more to other texts than to some central, fixed reality, with essential ambiguities of meaning. Writers try to overcome the influence exerted by their predecessors by a process described by MacFein as a creative misreading of texts. The Lasdiacs, later, insisted that the Neo-Obscurant school had been vindicated by Economy's writing.

2 - Professor Sammy of late had been losing any sense of allegiance to his old profession of scholasticism. Previously he had been noted for his long, detailed, elaborate statistical analyses which he would present to the much put upon Balhop community in whatever form or forms he could, orally, visually, by the power of transference and even by means of a flamboyant body language. These synopses in the past were characterised by their clear,

The Madness of Eamon Moriarty

intricate, often elaborate lack of meaning. He had even for a period been elected Chief Ruler of the island for the very reason of this lack of any sort of dogmatic awkwardness. The fact was however, that unknown to his colleagues and close acquaintances, Professor Sammy had long since lost faith in his own analysing and descriptive skills, and he was only continuing to practise them in order to conceal the nature of his real work, which was to try and find out the meaning of life.

The Meaning Of Life according to Cork and Galway:

To some more sensitive observers of this controversy it can be deduced from inconsistencies in the Official Report that Cork and Galway have different understandings of the meaning of life. Galway, it seems, does not believe in the autonomous, independent existence of life in either a singular or multiple form, that is, until it has been discovered, pin-pointed, investigated and judged by them. This is seen for example in their refusal to consider that there was anything autonomous, exotic or non-local in 'Eamon's' document. As far as they are concerned, it is an entirely unremarkable bit of poesy the likes of which can be heard in any after-hours' pub conversation in the well-known southern county at any time of the year. It has no more uniqueness or individuality than, say, the singing of a thrush in a bush on a wet, cold spring morning. Cork's attempts to insert some kind of individuality and import into it is the equivalent, they say, of suggesting that the same thrush is speaking theological metaphysics from that unremarkable bush.

Cork, on the other hand, accepts life as a pre-existing, running stream over that great plain of dust and rock called the world. There are no boundaries to this life, so that many kinds of life overlap, joining together to form 'life' as such. So that thrush is, after all, a competent, if not a gifted, theologian and metaphysician and Economy's written works are the unconscious or semi-conscious images of the universal human soul or mind.

An interesting side debate (not documented) took place between a Galway professor and one from Cork. They dredged up that hoary old chestnut, Was there Meaning in the Days of the Dinosaurs? Imagine, one said, the time of the dinosaurs before extinction. The issue of Meaning without a human observer does not get beyond the fact of blind, natural force. Now place a

Corkman and a Galwayman in that scene. Meaning becomes a philosophical question. What does the Corkman say? There is meaning in the sight of a dinosaur grazing the tops of trees, the gift of beauty and life. On the other hand there is evil in the sight of a tyrannosaur offshoot chewing up a child. The meaning of life can only be found in the master plan of a creator who will bring all things right in the end. The Galwayman answers that this is an emotional view, and emotion determines too much in Cork. He answers that 'meaning' is a nonsensical issue (he does not tone down his language for the sake of human sensibility) and can only be satisfactorily answered at the end of time when full scientific knowledge will be available. Then 'meaning' will mean 'how'. Otherwise, he said, you might as well ask a dinosaur.

Umbrage was taken and the two men started to fight; foul language was used and they finished up not speaking to one another.

3 - Graw – love.

4 - Unapproachables – a small social group in Balhop who held everything in the island in disdain and who dreamed of living abroad.

chapter FOURTEEN

Firk's men were gathered outside during a lull in the rain. It was round about the time when the sun, long ago, would have been at its highest point in the sky. They had just come back from the woods after a bout of the much disapproved game of taking off their outside trousers, placing them over some misfortunate, runaway idols and then dancing in circles around them. There were no permanently residing monks, scholars or astronomers in that community to remind them of the existence of morals and spiritual matters, and they had not the faintest idea that a king had been appointed in Balhop whose authority now extended over the whole island, and who had now banned the 'sport' forthwith. So, unaware that they were breaching any legal or moral code, they had enjoyed the whole thing with much shouting and gusto.

The game had been organised at the last minute to relieve tensions, for they were in an angry mood as they stood there. They had visited a distant farming village on a mission selling a few prized apple tans, a handful of roden berries and some dead fish, hoping to receive excellent prices for their wares, only to find that the people were no longer interested in their goods and were in fact subsisting quite happily on oin meat. The farmers had appropriated for themselves vast herds of these creatures, and Firk's men were also surprised to discover that the finding of a wild oin was now an extremely rare occurrence indeed, as the creatures had become more valuable in the market place than in the bush. A single oin was more valuable now than all the stocks of tans and berries that a person could lay hands on. They were disgusted to find themselves being offered instead of local valuables just one decrepit, aged oin in exchange for all the apples, berries and fish they had brought. When they shook their heads and said that the proffered oin was almost dead from old age, the farmers shrugged their shoulders and walked away. It seemed to Firk's men that the farmers were deliberately devaluing any produce not produced on their own farms, taking it upon themselves to monopolise the island's wealth and attempting to exclude the Tennits and fishermen from any prosperity. The new oin enterprise had started spontaneously in the hillside villages near the top of the mountain, and the story of its success was spread by the latest graffiti which appeared on fences and posts on public track ways up and down the valleys; 'Do not harm the oin – eat him instead' and 'Oin meat beats starvation'. All these were ditties now on everybody's lips. Soon no village was being lax in its efforts to round up oins and the strange, unfamiliar smell of oin steak cooking pots filled the neighbourhoods. Firk's men returned through the valleys hungry and perplexed. They wondered what they would henceforth get their families to eat, since they had nothing valuable left to trade with. They would be more hungry and poorer now than ever. They sent a spy to have a peek at Gobhook's village and their anger was made more unbearable by what was observed. There was the man himself, Gobhook, instead of being in his office, standing at a corral, counting out the ignominious oins with a number of his friends, sharing what was obviously some dishonestly obtained booty. Firk heard all this in a paroxysm of speechlessness as he stood there with his men.

They realised that this was a got-up, foolish war that was only keeping them from partaking in the new wealth of the land. They understood now why the farmers were happy to continue with the war, for it was in their interests to keep

Firk's men preoccupied, scrambling after the honours of the field while they themselves carried on surreptitiously with their new lucrative business and monopolising the oin trade. This time, Firk resolved, they would not be put off by any slights or personal insults from their enemies. So great was their determination to end the war once and for all and get down to work that they immediately made a plan to invite Gobhook to their village on his own. They would beat him up if he didn't agree to make peace. So, an invitation was sent over the talking-waves by a single slingshot that landed a heavily coded rock in the garden of the Widow McDone. She immediately took it to be a personal message from one of those distant planets high above the world where her husband now resided, and called on the first figure of authority that she happened to meet, who was the Water Clerk out on a spying stroll to see what had caused the thump, to explain to her what it was he might want.

Gobhook, on seeing the rock and noting that it was of a common, local type, surmised that it had been sent there from a not-too-distant source, most likely from Firk's village and that, being too cowardly to come there, it was just another one of Firk's invitations to go and parley over some new, so-called 'concession'. (The last one had been over allowing under-age warriors in Firk's senior team). Who could ever trust a Tennit? So Gobhook put on his prize-cap and stock boots and set out, encouraged by the prospect of seeing Firk grovel again. He went alone, enjoying the dignity and pride of his own belligerent importance, walking, feeling, enthusing like a powerful ruler, and indeed thinking quite regal thoughts. By the time he got there he had imaginatively crowned himself with the great, priceless crown of power and victory, with all his enemies and friends crowding forward to beg at his feet.

Meanwhile Firk's men felt Gobhook's approach as that of an earthquake and great storm combined into one. The ground shook and the clouds flew about overhead with a great agitation. It seemed that fire and smoke were billowing up to the heavens in the far distance, and the noise of his footsteps was louder than the loudest thunder they had ever heard. He would surely destroy the whole village, they thought. When he came into view they saw that he was taller than the mountains, his arms were like trees swinging in the wind and his advancing boots were so huge they could not even see his legs. They could not look directly into his face; it was more glaring and more powerful than a noonday sun. Firk and his men just stood absolutely still as Gobhook arrived under the cover of his aloof arrogance and a gently falling shower of rain. The angry look increased on Gobhook's face when, on seeing that he was undoubtedly alone, they had produced their sternest scowls and waved their tightly clenched fists. Gobhook was smiling grimly now even as the small men bent down, picked up stones and raised them in the air to throw at him. Firk put into his own face the fiercest outrage, hoping for some effect. But it was to no avail.

Economy himself saw everything from the top wall he was cleaning. He hoped that justice would finally be done in the scene below him, for Top Carrot's usurper was surrounded by a large gang of unruly men. Economy too was feeling very angry and murderous. He would do the job himself if he could find a suitable implement. How he hated that man, his great enemy Gobhook. And of late life had become a great deal harder. The number, extent and tedium of tasks given to him had increased, such as the removing of valueless stones from the village track way and then having to put them back again into their original positions; drying the river-beds in lulls in the rain storms, and then repeating the operation after each succeeding downpour; and the major time-consuming chore of flinging projectiles at the hidden sky above the village, a task that would not cease until the sun shone once more.

He had also re-commenced talking loudly to himself and the idiosyncrasy of his walk had become pronounced again. He had stopped in his rambling internal discourse (his way of coping with the tedious work) when he saw the gathering in the square. Economy lifted his apron above his head and peered through the grill into the enclosure, clinging to the wall like some human insect. Gobhook was surrounded by an even larger crowd now, and it appeared as though the old master was indeed about to receive his comeuppance. But, with a leer on his upper lip, Gobhook turned the tables at once, and just laughed derisively at the people around him.

"You call yourselves men, but I call you something lower than cowards. Women! It is time that you all left here. For you are all only a nuisance in the neighbourhood! Pack up your stuff and leave the district at once. My men are hiding behind the bushes over there. I took the precaution of bringing them along with me just in case. I have a whole army out there, dedicated to my personal protection. Flee while you can and don't ever come back."

The doom, whose prospect they had lived under these long years of exile, was now a reality. It was the old bad dream – the fate of nomads that they were always avoiding and fending off – the order to move on from some Local Government official.

The Tennits and fishermen now pleaded with Gobhook. Even Firk himself put on a sorry face and seemed to forget his determined resolve of a short while before.

"There is nowhere for us to go. Will you forget the bad manners that we have shown just now?" he said.

"You have all caused enough trouble. First of all you declare war on the farmers, and then later try to blame them for starting it! Then you say that you have just lost your tempers! You show what an ungrateful a bunch of wretches you are by attempting to ambush me and stab me in the back! Pack up and get off the premises! Be away with you, before I have to call in my men and give you all such a walloping as you will never forget. And take your belongings with you."

Gobhook was shouting in a horrible way. (It was a strange, twisted voice; it might be said to be that of a normally calm, smoothly speaking, middle of the road individual who had, by some twist of the mind caused by professional ambition, become an arrogant, ambitious demagogue, desirous of imposing his dominion over all.)

Economy saw the weeping Tennits and fishermen go on their knees and plead to be left in their homes, but Gobhook was in no mood for mercy. He said that they had already had their last chance. Firk fell down on the ground and prostrated himself.

"Please, just a last chance?"

Gobhook kicked him very hard on the backside. It was an action that, whilst reinforcing the despair felt by the onlookers, made some of them laugh out loud.

"All right," said Jal, intervening, "we will goes quietly."

Economy was thinking how to get down to Gobhook and strike him on the head when there was a loud sound from a pig whistle and the noise of sprightly feet.

The unexpected commotion, in their present distress, only made them all more confused. King Top Carrot walked in and he was dressed in all the regalia of a very important king indeed. He was not alone, but it was almost impossible to make out who were accompanying him – not so much because of the poor light as of the fact that his companions stayed in the background. Economy's heart jumped with surprise at seeing Top Carrot, who was talking to someone Economy couldn't see.

"Hello Gobhook. I have been told that there has been a great rumpus and a good deal of trouble since I have been away. Well of course I wondered why that was so, and why you weren't where you should have been. They said at the village that I would find you here. I brought myself along as quickly as I could. Why are all the people weeping?"

There was authority in Top's voice occasioned by a deep, guttural sound that Economy had never heard before.

"What has brought you back?" asked Gobhook. He had dropped his smile. He was shocked, but not overcome. He stared with intense dislike at his old accomplice and rival.

King Top became less blasé and was now holding the other side of his face with the palm of his hand in a great effort of self-control.

"I have a report of your misdoings, Gobhook," he said.

"You have, have you? Who was the informer? No doubt the relapsed monk, he who was disbarred for telling lies in his own confessional?" said Gobhook.

The 'alter persona' had broken a grave taboo by mentioning what a monk had been excommunicated for. He had that panicky edge of aggrieved anger of someone who knows that the game is up.

Top was appalled by this comment, and made an attempt to lift the tone of the proceedings.

"What happens in the confessional box is under the seal of the Hypocritical Oath. All I know is, I am placing you under arrest and I am taking you back to the prison in Balhop."

"Prison?" said Gobhook querulously.

"A large prison, like they have in Assaland, is just one of the things I have introduced to the island since the commencement of my reign. It is a great way of dealing with troublemakers."

"Reign? You have gone mad, Top Carrot. You have been away too long in a place that is much too big for you. Your ambition has turned your head. Here, get back before I hit you down with this stick."

The onlooking Tennits and Fishermen gasped as he picked up a big stick in his left hand and lifted it high in the air.

There was a stir in the background and Charles, the once-recalcitrant Lasdiac, stepped forward. When Gobhook saw him he stopped in his tracks and the stick fell to the ground with a clatter.

"I am a Lasdiac from Assaland," said Charles speaking to them all in his best acquired island dialect; "and I am the chief leader of all the Lasdiacs who have arrived in your island. I bow down before Top Carrot who is your king, and I hearken to every word he says. I listen especially to his internal locutions. Do not raise arms against him, or I will work a spell of logic on you all that will never leave you. King Top Carrot is now king not just of the Farmers but of everybody in the island."

They had never seen a Lasdiac before. Many there had not even really believed in their existence. Now Gobhook, too, did not feel brave enough to challenge them, or test the mysterious powers that they undoubtedly possessed just to have been able to come all the way there and to be able to look so powerful and wise whilst wearing those sweet smelling, spotless, white garments. Then more Lasdiacs, perhaps ten in all, but more like a thousand to the watching villagers, emerged from the bush behind Charles and Top Carrot. The Lasdiacs walked softly and swiftly into the enclosure, staying closely grouped together and looking neither left or right nor up or down. Economy thought that the sound of their steps was like the cushioned softness of a great, moving forest advancing across the soundless region of night stars.

"This is Gobhook," said Top pointing above his head and ignoring the tyrant standing beside him, "an old acquaintance of mine who, at one time, was a useful administrator. But he has let the privileges of rank and power go to his head. In my absence he has misused the privileges that had been given him. He was once my honoured helper, but he did not know the duties that power bestowed, and now I am king and I would not even consider him for the licking and shining of my boots. He can consider himself a prisoner and he will remain in that hut over there until tomorrow."

He had an impressive expression of stern, calm, responsible authority.

Gobhook opened his mouth to utter a heinous calumny against Top Carrot but Charles stopped him from even speaking by raising his hand in the air, an act that struck terror into Gobhook. He knew that no threat, no appeal would be of any use against the formidable power that was before him.

"Now you lot can stop crying and sulking and pull yourselves together," said the king, addressing the still-gaping assembly, "and put down those sacks and walking sticks and sit down on the ground and listen to me. You will have heard of my name, as I was for long a leader in the farmers' village. But that was when Top Carrot was only an ordinary name, belonging to an ordinary leader. Now I am a very big king. In the past, I was often powerless to do many things, such as to save people from the repercussions of their own mistakes, from social oppression, from death. If I had been a real king then, there would have been no wars. I did not have the power to do many things at the time, and my efforts were often of little avail."

There were grunts of sympathy and murmurs of assent. Top indeed could not to be held personally responsible for all that had happened in the region. As for the murderous acts of Gobhook, he could not have been expected to control them for Gobhook was a far different, and far more invidious personality. Top had not even realised that the fellow was up to no good!

"Gobhook will be punished for that crime. You and the farmers will stop fighting and be friends. You will start organising yourselves for the raising, keeping and maintenance of my stately oins. There will be a great oin farm, spreading all over the neighbourhood and on into the next one and the next one after that and which in fact will never stop growing in extent. You will all be keepers of the king's oins, and nobody will ever have to go wandering or be hungry again but will have proper huts to live in. A group of the farmers are coming over here in a while to discuss the new arrangements with you all."

Firk's Men felt happy and more secure than they had ever done in their lives, in the glow of Top Carrot's new power.

He may indeed have been just a farmers' representative at one time, but now he was something else. Someone great and supreme. Even the Assalanders seemed to respect him! Here at last was someone they could look up to. They were particularly impressed by the manner in which he raised his eyebrows without so much as blinking or having any apparent expression whatsoever on his face. And they were relieved at the way Gobhook seemed to have been put in his place. He looked much smaller now. They were no longer afraid of him.

The delegation of farmers arrived and they sat down on the ground beside Firk's men and listened to the rolling, ringing voice of King Top Carrot. Nobody seemed to notice Gobhook who reclined in disgrace at the side of the hut- more a shadow than a real person now.

"Up in the hills our lesser brothers have collected a good bunch of oins which must be transported at once down to the valleys where they will thrive on much better pasturage. This removal will be done on my orders, but if I hear that even the tiniest hair on the head of one oin has been harmed, the perpetrators will be punished. And remember, everyone is your brother and sister now, especially as we are all in the same business. Come here, Alas, for a moment while I speak to you." Alas, the Relapsed monk, came out of the delegation of farmers and stood before Top Carrot. He was very nervous. He knew that there was nobody worse than the reformed sinner (final forgiveness always had to wait for the deathbed in cases like his).

"Alas, you have been my faithful servant. All your past sins are forgotten. I am appointing you as my Court Jester, and I am making your office the second highest in the land, equal to that of Moth Merrick's and above that of the Chief monk Jalosp himself, for goodness knows we have lacked a jollier and lighter mood in this land for a long time."

This appointment was received with perplexity by Alas and applause by the rest of the crowd.

"And as for the rest of you," Top Carrot continued, "my good friends the Lasdiacs are very keen to stay here and watch over you, to see that you do things the right way and guide you in their ways. You will not need to put them up in your humble abodes, as they have brought their own houses. They also have their own particular oddities of diet. They like to eat oin meat for example, and there will be no shortage of that food in the future! As I said to them on our way here, so famous are my people for their hospitality I would not even have to bother to remind them of the joy to be tasted in caring well for the visitors who are come in our midst. And so now they will take their place amongst you and establish themselves in every part of life in the village. And so it is! Boy, I am hungry!"[1]

Folk went excitedly off in every direction to discuss the new rule of Top Carrot and the children started to play again in the happier atmosphere while the womenfolk, seeing their men preparing yet more madcap enterprises, sucked their lips in disregard and annoyance and went on regardless with their experimental cooking and backyard chats. King Top Carrot walked quietly into the kitchen of Halola's house to get a bite to eat. He went over to the table wall and dipped his hand in a fermenting defunct pie. When he had swallowed a chunk of the pie he fell over with pain. As he slowly raised himself up again from the floor, he spotted the kitchen lad where he was labouring away shining a pot on a stool leg underneath the table.

"Who are you?" asked the king not yet recognising Economy, the very same lad whose household he had visited on numerous occasions, whose earlier fortunes he had overseen, whose now-famous scrawls had had such a controversial influence on recent events in the island, including his own elevation to the kingship.

"Nobody," replied Economy. He did not want to reveal his identity to someone who was the highest leader of all. It might not be a wise thing. Despite this fear, he was still deeply impressed by Top Carrot. The man had a wonderful, powerful personality and Economy felt even more subservient in his presence. Top was the great hero who had been such a kind benefactor in the past, who had come into their home with his arms brimming with good things. It was indeed now a bit disappointing, Economy felt, that Top Carrot had not recognised him. Seeing a quizzical but not unkind frown appear on Top's face, Economy took a deep breath and said:

"I am Economy, the stick gatherer. I lived with my aunt in a hut near your village and to which you brought berries and tans. Once you protected me from a crowd of irate farmers."

"Hm," said Top Carrot, "I can hear him saying something but devil-a-bit of it can I make out or understand. I will see about taking this fellow back to my palace in Balhop, for I can think of some very useful purposes to which he can be put. I will have a word now with Charles about a few things."

Top Carrot, after covering the pie with a broken plate and sticking a piece of ripe fruit into his regal back pocket, strode from the kitchen and did not even notice Economy bowing to him as he left.

The Madness of Eamon Moriarty 225

When he had gone, Economy quickly reset the pie and put a new fruit in place of the old one and then hastily prepared to leave that village for good. There was no point in staying here any longer. The arrival of a seemingly proud, nonchalant Top Carrot, not all that like the old, kind Uncle Top, and who would undoubtedly use him for his new, laborious projects, could be a threat to his freedom. He would take advantage of the hectic activity in the village to make good his escape. As long as Halola did not spot him leaving he should be able to get away. He peered through the chink in the door and did not see anybody in the yard. So he stepped out quietly and cautiously, staying as close as possible to the wall of the house, and trying to keep within the shadows of the undergrowth and the garden tombs of the yet-to-be-dead. He did not even bother to take as much as a scrap of food with him; much less was he in possession of any substantial clothing or public property. He was greatly surprised to hear a voice calling him.

"Come back, where do you think you are going?" said the voice, and when Economy looked around he saw that the speaker was a Lasdiac who had been put on duty by Top Carrot to keep watch. The runaway thought of making a dash for the undergrowth but Firk and Jal, who had now appeared, barred his way. Economy tried to pretend that he hadn't been running away.

"I was going to take a walk in the bush," he said.

"What is the commotion?" asked Top Carrot who had arrived with Charles, the senior Lasdiac.

"This one was walking in a most peculiar way towards the bushes," said the guard.

"As though he was off for good," said Firk and Jal together, anxious to please Top Carrot and his friends.

"It's you," said Top Carrot looking closely at Economy.

"Go back into the house and get some food for yourself. Then go wherever it is your heart is leading you, for I believe your presence in this village is not of further advantage to anyone. You would only be an impediment to my people in view of the new, strict regime I am establishing, and an embarrassment to me in my Balhop palace. Go away and find a wild place in the hills where the nuts will provide you with nourishment and the birds with song."

Economy walked into the house, and then quickly reappeared with a container full of food. He walked slowly to the edge of the enclosure, aware now of a multitude of eyes watching him. In particular, he sensed that the Lasdiacs were studying him closely and scrutinising his every step. He was also aware of Lasdaics speaking urgently to Top Carrot. As he walked into the dark verge he saw their waving arms and heard their coded whispers. Then Top Carrot called him back.

"It is undeniable; there is no doubt," Charles whispered to the king, "but that it is it."

"What did you call it?" asked Top Carrot.

"Hop," replied Charles; "and I never believed in it until I saw it in that man."[2]

"Isn't that what you fell out with your previous leader over?" asked Carrot.

"Oh yes we fell out all right. We had an argument about it and what it all means and that; but none of us really believed in it. And if Usdiark 11 was here now (he 'fell' into the sea) I doubt at all if he would have spotted it in that fellow," said Charles, looking at Economy.

"Lock him up at once," ordered Charles – "you must take him back to Balhop. For he may be used against you if he mixes with the wrong people, and there might be nothing you could do about it at that stage. However with him at your side and not let out of your sight, you will be a lot safer indeed. I myself would also like a long talk with him in private when we get back."

"Is he a prophet, a wise fellow, or just mad then?" asked Carrot.

"I do not know, but he has this thing we call 'hop' which our philosophers make much of, but they were never able to find it in anyone, or get anyone to demonstrate what it really meant."

"But how do you know this one has it?" Top Carrot asked.

"How do I know? I don't know. 'Hop' is not like that. It can only be known in the doing. Nobody else in the island walks like him. What is his name?"

"Economy, he says."

"So he was named after his father or his mother?"

"I would not know."

"Strange."

"I thought he would make a good servant, but then I saw his disquieting manner and I did not want him back in Balhop," said Top Carrot, at a loss to understand, even feeling a bit uneasy, at Charles's interest in the fellow. He himself wanted to put his past life behind him, and the last thing he wanted was for anyone to highlight Economy's part in it.

"You do not have to worry about him. That will be my responsibility. Leave him to me. How would you like to accompany us back to the capital?" Charles asked, turning to Economy and speaking cheerfully yet patronisingly.

"It is a very big place. Is there anything there that you have ever wished to see?"

"There is one thing that I have long wanted to see," replied Economy, "that is the person who fathered me and the mother who left me."

"It is true," said Halola, who had appeared on the scene, "he has never been happy here, for he has always wanted to find those who brought him into the world."

"Interesting," said Charles, giving Economy another close look.

Lasdiacs had a tendency to be very curious as well as suspicious and sceptical.

"Does anyone know this chap here?" he asked the village gathering.

"We have never seen him before in our lives," everyone agreed.

"Sit in that comfortable box over there," ordered Charles, and indeed one had already been obtained for him; "and you will travel in it tomorrow to the place you have always wanted to see. Perhaps we will find what you call your father and mother."

Eamon had been disturbed by the arrival in the village of he whom he called The Bogman and his associates. Up till then he had acquired for himself a very fine niche where nobody paid any attention to him (other than to give him chores) and the more unnoticed he became the more secure he felt. Only Halola ever spoke to him, but even she conversed with him as little as possible, as she knew he really preferred to talk to himself. Then Bogman (this was a nickname for the hated, local busybody), who called himself Mr Fix It, although as far as anybody knew he was by previous profession a minor social worker as well as a local political aspirant and commercial dealer, came around and berated everybody for being 'stick in the mud' and holding back development in the area, telling them to 'get up off your hind legs' and go back to work. He had also got very personal and had a go at one or two individuals in his usual vindictive way that showed he had not learnt from his official Head Office reprimand or begun to lessen his habitual verbal violence in any significant sense. Eamon had fetched a large mallet and put it aside (behind a sack of pumatoes) in case Bogman came in to have a go at him. Then he would silence him for good with that bludgeon.

It was not necessary, for shortly afterwards the old Tom Curran miraculously appeared on the scene, accompanied by some new

The Madness of Eamon Moriarty

acquaintances and colleagues who were impressive for their distinctive dress style and disciplined, even respectable behaviour. There were signs of mental conflict in Tom and that old care-worn look as he struggled with his alter persona and tried to curtail his own, wilder extremities, fighting bravely and putting on a benign face to the world. He tried to persuade Eamon that he had his best interests at heart; however Eamon felt that he was not speaking to the real Tom he had known in the past but that there was now some pretence, some forced characterisation in this Tom's attitude and demeanour. Tom no longer seemed to recognise him, or remember anything about the old days. He kept talking about a better place, palaces and mansions in the capital which he had access to and a lovely home for Eamon where he would be properly cared for. He had only had to sign a form and all would be okay. He did not inquire into Eamon's possible feelings or opinions in the matter. It was as if the lad was just another social statistic along Tom's roller coaster political career. By the end of the consultation, with the whole village looking on, client confidentiality being a rare privilege in these small, isolated communities, the certification form was signed (with an X) by Eamon to the collective sigh of satisfaction, not to mention relief, of the watching crowd. He had more or less resigned himself into their hands, if only because escape was impossible.

Notes

1 - The election of the local man, Tom Curran, as Member of Parliament was a big event in the area, its resonance being felt throughout the neighbourhood. He was a changed man, they said after that, losing the rough corners that had characterised the old man and taking on the airs of a self-made man; indeed even to an extent that of a Prima Donna. He came back from the capital with an entourage of 'assistants' and with the assertion that he was going to be a force for good, for change and for progress not just in the region but in the whole island. Even at that early stage it was clear that his mind was occupied with higher things and the affairs of state; constituency matters in the local villages were simply minutiae to be hastily cleared up. There were

some who said that it was a false Tom Curran they were seeing; that there was something artificial about him, that there was a lack of the old, country-style honesty and gusto. It was even said that he had become slightly eccentric, one or two noting that in some ways he was not really 'himself'. While there was local pride in having 'one of their own' elected to such an august institution as the National Parliament, the area never before having had someone of such prominence in its midst, there was also soon to be disappointment that he was never to be seen around again after that, and had disappeared off into the big world.

2 - Hop – its terms, meaning and implications. The Majority and Minority Reports attempted to give their own interpretations of this controversial phenomenon. It was, they declared, at the centre of the whole business; mysteries would be cleared up if only they could understand it. It was particularly important in explaining Economy's/Eamon's remarkable influence on their society which seems to have been pervasive, if not insidious. Of course it also became the main element in the denouement at the close of the book. There were a variety of suggestions offered by individuals on the board, and contra-suggestions in the Galway Minority Report.

- Hop, it's all in the mind, Dr Crane.
- Hope, the second of the great Christian Virtues, Clerical representative.
- Hop, Step and Jump, his way of walking, which was clearly quite a unique style, Gaelic Athletic Association rep.
- Hop, a type of dance but nobody can remember where, how or when, Musician rep.
- On the hop, catching someone in the act, Garda rep.
- Going on a hop, or a stage in the life-journey of a person, Psychologist rep.
- Hopping in, hopping out, the marked tendency in human nature to absolve oneself of minor responsibilities when appointed to a major position of power and authority, lay member of the panel.
- Hop to it, willingness to take part in public programmes, the Water Company rep. and Chair of the Social Services Committee.

As time went by it became established that the Cork opinion came nearer to the mark on this subject. They upbraided Galway for supercilious definitions of Hop and for not attempting to explain its real significance, instead questioning why anyone should believe that Eamon had some virtue or talent that might be in any way noteworthy. Galway's world-renowned Folk Historian insisted that all it consisted of was that Eamon had a lack of the one ingredient that makes a person normal, a basic structure in nature that each human usually has which 'shows forth the soul' no matter what handicaps or even talents a person has and no matter what vital ingredient is lacking in the personality or what eccentricity is evident; that strange 'hanging together' that we call him or her. In other words Eamon lacked 'soul'. This was seen by some scientific commentators as not merely an extremely interesting secondary feature but actually as a necessary, defining trait in those who have been responsible for mankind's greatest leaps forward, especially if they are to resist the sniggers, mockery and condemnations of their fellow human beings.

chapter FIFTEEN

*E*conomy seemed to have come to accept his fate. He was, after all, going to get to visit the big town and see the sights. Although he had been working away unobtrusively in the kitchen and keeping to himself as much as possible, it seemed that there was no end to the new jobs he was being given. In addition he had the 'attentions' of Halola to deal with, her arms chasing him around so he was constantly having to duck under some piece of furniture or hide in some cupboard. This latter distraction was not welcome. He appreciated her motherly protection but ever since that experience on the couch he had been wary of her more direct physical approaches. Even being near her caused a feeling of suffocation, and when she attempted to encircle him with her arms that suffocation became strangulation. He had never really understood what had happened on the couch. It was said in the book that was written later (about Top's hard, poverty stricken youth which was published at the same time as his committal to a lengthy electoral campaign) that the lad had 'married' Halola. Economy had felt ever since he had moved into the house that Halola was keeping his soul a prisoner. He had become afraid of her, and this was one reason he always obeyed her instructions and did all the work about the place. At least it kept her happy and ensured that there was no time for her to start the other business. Her close presence caused a disturbance in him that could not be mitigated in its excruciating pain. Its accumulated force wreaked havoc both inside him and in his thoughts. It infiltrated every nerve and fibre, and it was as though an evil power was seeking to take over. He acquired an obsession with bodily things and the body's different functions. Yet when Halola went out of his presence all this trouble dissipated and peace returned.

Dr Crane had examined the incarcerated lad later in the asylum. He had questioned Eamon intently on many things, and was mystified by his lack of any human emotion. Moriarty spoke in a highly abstract, symbolic language about many things that Crane, as a doctor, had never heard of before. Eamon did not respond to overtures of affection, or even of anger and impatience, but took all the tricks of interrogation in his stride. He was not receptive to human stimuli or control of any sort; when he did appear to obey instructions it was purely an automatic, robotic response based on some obscure pre-programmed law of nature. It was as if normal human responses were unknown to him.

It was then that Dr Crane got involved in exploring Eamon's peculiar ideas on the nature and functions of the body, and had learnt during deep hypnosis that Eamon believed that the body was essentially the great 'enabler', a facilitator that gave its owner the power to produce, consume, recycle and dispose of goods and services according to his or her own personal wishes. To his mind it was just a sort of commercial entity, rather than the most amazing thing in the world. Its other purpose, apparently, was to enable the individual person to escape from undesirable situations such as death, dissipating off into nowhere and of having to partake of the mysterious, non-material essence of things, which some call the Afterlife. It also enabled the individual to escape the 'non-bodily presence' of others. Hence the relief of waking up in the morning to find that one was still 'in the body'; 'what else were we given these' – *and here he would point to some part of the body, arm, leg, hand- 'for?' They were there, he said, to keep others at bay. As the chief means of production, he continued, the body had many enemies amongst those who wished to see an end to 'laissez faire', individual bodily freedom, and to people working for themselves. This was in order to facilitate the return to slave labour where the body would be kept in check by means of the whip, the chain and the locked door. The body was also filled with a paradoxical self-destructive urge. It was not for nothing that people killed themselves; it was rather to escape for good and all that which even the body was unable to save them from, i.e. the blind, mad urge to life itself, even in some cases to reproduce life itself. Eamon had remembered an 'appalling' experience with a lady in one of the villages he had stayed in; she had entered his body and 'stolen' a part of it which he had never since been able to get back. This trauma on his part might be put down to plain natural debauchery, or even (in his own terms) to some sort of political scheming; (the idea being that by controlling the body's willpower it would be possible to make it generate much commercial wealth, according to the patient's ramblings), but it was very bad for the body politic. He was thereafter extremely wary of the said lady who, according to those investigative biographers and scholars desirous of making a reputation for themselves with a good scandal, became his 'wife'.*

Asked to describe what Eamon felt Dr Crane said that it was difficult to deduce what went on inside his head but by an established procedure of empirical tests, based on his responses to a series of subtly structured ink blobs from their own leaking pens, monitored by a coterie of exiled doctors from the Midlands interested in the undetectable workings of the human mind, it had been eventually formulated that in Eamon the effects of an attempt at an emotional relationship were:

- *a bending of the mind that caused it to become preoccupied with morbid things, such as getting jobs done around the house and a preoccupation with the primeval characteristics and uses of various bodily parts,*
- *an increase in a sense of life's solitude attained paradoxically especially whilst in the company of his closest companions and*

associates. There was a remarkable illustration of the strength of individual will power, to a degree not ever seen before, in his refusal to talk to anybody when released back into human companionship after he had been put in strict quarantine as part of his treatment. Indeed the only result from that experiment in solitary confinement was to stimulate in him an even greater need for, and enjoyment of isolation,
- an inability to look people in the face,
- a sadness exceeding even that of losing his old home, caused by giving up his old, rough lifestyle and having to live in a proper house,
- a deep distrust of his own everyday actions,
- a confusion in thought that prevented him from coming to any coherent conclusion about anything,
- a doubting of the eternal realities,
- a distrust of authority,
- a sense that all is not right in the world, or in the heavens.

These were some of the negative things that resulted from the lady's intervention in Eamon's life, but the strange thing was, although Eamon was not aware at the time of it having happened at the time, he had lost his obsession with chicken stealing.

Halola came to Economy and said that she hoped he would not find his kinfolk in Balhop, as anybody who laid claim to him might demand as much from him as she had. Then he would find himself a poorer man for having had a father or mother than if he had never had them at all. He looked at her quizzically and by his expression it was clear that he did not understand what she was saying.

She had done her best for him. Although he had not known how to respond to her warm words and her expressions of affection, he had always lain there in a quiescent way whenever she had stroked him. He had let her caress the hair on his head and gently stroke his face and lately she had been able to make him forget his great timidity and his doubt about the purpose and even existence of his own body when she had helped him dress and undress before and after sleep.

Economy now said that he had never felt so miserable and exhausted in all his life. He had had enough! He was just glad for the fact that his journey to Balhop did not involve any walking but was to be an easy and carefree ride in a cart with no call for physical strain, the obtaining of food, or having to stop at dodgy wayside places. He could not bring himself to tears (those tears which he had recently discovered) for the leaving of Halola or the village. He watched coldly a single dry tear of Halola's.

In the darkness of the night he heard the loud chanting of the Lasdiacs and the scrimmaging of their feet on the floor. Then a heavy stillness lay over the whole island and try as he did, he could not hear anything, any hum or buzz or whistle in the air or any sort of noise or sign by which he might be able to prophesy; only the sound of the Lasdiac's feet.

He sang to himself.

"I will sing my own song, as deaf as the wall,
and study the heaving forests, dark in this blind room,
and feel the raging sunlight in the dull, black sky.
No one will hear my song, or see my face,
or know what I sing."

He waited for someone to come and complain again about his singing (apparently it always sounded like a high pitched wind), but nobody came. So long was that night and so seemingly endless its transition that Economy thought time itself had ceased to move. Then a light appeared under his feet and he experienced the dawn rise, not on some faraway horizon or distant mountaintop but right there, immediately underneath his own bottom. A kind of darkness remained around him while the day rolled in and up to his chest and then penetrated it seemed to the top of his head and the very extremities of his mind. He was relieved to find himself a little while later in proper daylight, for it had felt like an oven in that box, and it didn't matter too much to him that he was put beside Old Gobhook in the cart. Then, there was King Top Carrot up there as well, addressing the folk gathered in the foreground and all the Lasdiacs in a solemn group looking on.

"I do not want to go but I have to go," Top Carrot was saying; "my heart will remain here with you, and the Lasdiacs will be the custodians of it and of its many hopes, and will see to it that my image is always displayed in a prominent position. Now are you sure you all understand what I have been saying to you?"

"Yes, your Royal Excellency," answered Firk, and Jal nodded as well.

"I'll be off then," said Top Carrot with a wave of his hand; "cheerio to the lot of you!"

Top Carrot, and Charles who was accompanying him back to the city, took their leave with gigantic smiles and, in the opinion of the onlookers, the most incredible, extravagant arm flourishes and hand-waves ever yet seen in the island. The people were glad to see them go, and then they turned to look at their 'custodians', the Lasdiacs. They noticed that these aloof foreigners had never smiled once or shown any emotion as Top Carrot and Charles were taking their leave. Now they realised too that they had never smiled or looked cheerful, or even spoken at all, since they had first arrived in the village.

The journey to Balhop was in Economy's mind not at all like one of those dream-excursions he was accustomed to experiencing in his inspired imaginings, with ease of motion and an effortless, speedy going-over-of-ground but was instead a jerky, bumpy ride as they passed the wrecked mountains, once-bumper fields, shillies and shallies, stored-up rivers and Tennit/fishermen abandoned camps that made up the landscape along the way, down by the soundest route past Inisbay to Balhop. Charles gave his pessimistic opinion as they went along that the island was in a declining state. It was succumbing to a fast-deteriorating environmental condition that, at the rate things were going, might even cause the island to disappear from the face of the earth before too long. Top Carrot reflected on this and then said that he had to agree, while Economy rose out his arm for a drink (Charles and the king were drinking from hour-glasses), but it was not noticed. Gobhook himself seemed to be becoming a shadow of his former self. He had no interest in anything, or in saying anything and it was almost as if he wasn't even there.

They stopped at Inisbay for a drinking song and a speech, but they found that the place was empty of people. An elderly Ebit, who was at least ten years of age, appeared at a corner out of nowhere and nobody noticed him, except Economy, who asked him for a drink. The Ebit gave him a warm pepper drink and also a flash of an enigmatic, shy smile before departing to the nearby burial ground.

"Where are they?" Charles asked Top Carrot in puzzlement.

"This place is supposed to be the second city of our island," Carrot said in wonderment; "now it looks as though there is nobody here to greet the new king,"

"I wonder if they knew you were coming?" asked Charles.

"I am very disappointed," said Top Carrot, "although I am sure that there is a natural explanation. Perhaps they are all out rounding up oins for my plantation. Or they may have gone to Balhop and are awaiting my arrival there."

"It's possible," said Charles.

They left Inisbay more quickly than they came in, and somewhat less jauntily. Only Economy saw the bobbing heads in the background, which Top Carrot and Charles took to be waving trees but were in fact the watching faces of the inhabitants (and Ebits) who had indeed all been out on the beach avoiding the visitors and busying themselves with gathering fallen ludge balls which had been discovered inexplicably floating ashore from some unknown source.

There seemed to be a huge festival going on in Balhop and its vicinity when they arrived there. The first indications of a great carry-on were apparent before they had reached the city, with lines of walking people and batches of quiet, academic and intellectual-driven oins all leading the way to the capital, while everyone casually made room for the galloping ass and cart of Top Carrot and Charles as it passed down the road. Economy had never seen so many people before, and he could not understand the gestures or the shouted remarks they made as they went by. A few people raised bitten sticks in the air and waved them, and he did not know if this was a sign of anger or some sort of jubilant gesture. He thought that the excited shouting and the loud handclaps that greeted their arrival in the city were a further sign of the immense impact that Top Carrot was having as king, although it was also a fact that Top Carrot seemed curiously greatly desirous to share – and even to completely impart by means of generous hand gestures – all the glory on Charles, who was sitting there beside him.

Balhop seemed to Economy to be a very large farmyard and there were strange smells about it that were not unpleasant but were exceedingly strong. The loud shouting and movement of farm machinery made him homesick for the wild woods. He wondered if among all these people – strangely donned in their Sunday best even though it was a weekday – who were trotting urgently about as if they were desperately searching for valuable livestock which had escaped; with the many stables with their open half-doors winding endlessly down the long yards (the proprietor of this farm must have had a plenitude of animals); the tallest, most upright trees he had ever seen running to the heavens with no leaves but emitting screeching whistling noises from their long, thin branches; weird, incomprehensible words and pictures crafted on to the walls and roofs of buildings like the sacred writings on monastery walls (was the farmer practicing some sort of magic in order to ensure a good harvest?), many of which buildings were pigeon lofts for what was obviously a madly pigeon-fancying population; masses of well-replenished chickens strutting about clearly unperturbed by any possibility of there being foxes or rustlers loitering nearby with ill-intent; indeed they looked in their detachment as if they were quite capable of taking care of themselves; tamed ex-bush wild folk now serving this or that man-devised paltry function carried out with strange wooden or stone implements which were stuck in their pockets or their hands and, from the supercilious smiles on their faces, were ignoring the humbling fact of their total servitude here, taking a jaunty pride in their 'civic' sophistication and no-longer-out-of-control desire to kill, injure or eat their neighbours; with sheds full of stone animals and other strange miniature things such as people made of an unusual type of different-coloured stone which he had never seen before, (later he would feel this thing called 'metal' between his fingers and marvel at its softness), or clothing which had for some reason been shed by their wearers lying about in barns in huge piles; something that looked like flying miniature oins going in and out through the windows, strange foods that seemed to be small nuts of every shape and colour of the rainbow and queer vegetables or meats that, like the miniaturised every-day objects, were all 'frozen', wrapped up and laid out, perhaps (like the other goods) for the busy farm workers to take away and eat, consume or wear at their leisure when they felt like it as a reward for all their hard work; the loud clatter of each worker in this farmyard telling the next one of his or her success at this or that fishing or hunting recently accomplished extravaganza; where all the world's goods appeared instantaneously in this wonderful, magically wealth-producing farm of which there were no others like it in the whole world, all without the huge effort or great coming together of communal sowing, weeding and harvesting; the glow of the daytime burning lights which could only have been all the stars which had fallen from the skies (he had never before realized that stars were joined together by long lines of string), and the sight of many angry farmers carousing down the lanes getting in the way of each other in their land ships and sea carts which were heaped high with steaming fruit and vegetables not to mention stinking manure and other things, clogging the thoroughfares as far out as the harbour; asked by Economy how the sea came to be joined to the land, Top explained how the island engineers had moved the sea from a great distance further out, by means of a tremendous effort of engineering skill and ancestral willpower, right up close to the city – he might be able to find someone who would be able to help him discover what his heart had been seeking in the capital.

It was just as well he had come in a comfortable box he thought, since it would not have done to find himself exposed in the middle of that crowd and they perhaps beating him and chasing him through the thoroughfare, as had been his fate in settlements in the past.

The cart left the teeming, noisy highway – where even more crowds had appeared flocking in on their way to or from the markets, abattoirs and pastures – in what felt like something of a hurry and went through a huge gate. Economy noticed that there were no giants standing there holding this gate up but instead its hinges floated freely in the watery air. Gobhook himself was awoken by the noise and he looked around at everything, staring with a grim look at the crowds and now also with some consternation at the gates through which they were going. His frame had become slighter (this was to Economy's relief) and he seemed to be unaware of the others in the cart, even of the regal authority of Top and the incongruous presence of Charles. The gates closed behind them noiselessly with no gust of wind or trace of effort and he heard Gobhook mutter ominously out through the side of his hand that they were 'very fine gates indeed' with a strange note of irony or sarcasm in his voice.

"This must be the palace that Top Carrot was talking about," thought Economy to himself, while Gobhook turned his nose up with a contemptuous air as though he was entering a place that was not worthy of him.

"Put that box in the storeroom," said the king, having forgotten that there were people inside it; "I hope that they've got plenty of food in the pot for us upstairs."

"There is a fellow inside the box," Charles reminded him. He was clearly anxious that Economy, at least, be kept in safe custody. "Oh of course, that talented young man; he reminds me of myself as a boy," said Top, causing Charles to grimace with what appeared to be embarrassment –

"and take Mr Gobhook to our prison."

"Mr Gobhook?" asked Charles.

"Yes, Mr Gobhook," replied Top.

Charles stared down into the box and then gave Top a strange look.

"There is nobody there but the young man," he said in a surprised voice.

Economy found himself in what he believed must have been the best room in the palace, for it was at the top of the building. There was no outlet that allowed the rain or natural elements to get inside; a fine heavy roof was above him, shielding him from the sky and from any watching eyes located in the heavens. There was a magnificent window firmly barred with what appeared to be very hard sticks, (later to be identified as that 'metal'), and from this great height he could see the world outside. There was the massive silver ocean that at first Economy had thought had been the sky, (at ground level in Balhop it had not appeared to be so big), but then after a longer scrutiny he realised was an immense body of water (that which he had once seen before on a childhood visit, causing in him an inexplicable trauma). Now it only gave him a feeling of peace; it had come to represent something in his past, as well as in his future. A thought came to him; perhaps his mother was in that wide, deep sea from whence we all came.[1] For some reason also the words of Top Carrot, as he had placed him in this room, came back to his ears as he stared at what was most certainly the sea:

"Young man, Charles thinks that a great use can be found for you over the water in Assaland, in the schools and expensively equipped laboratories that they do have there; great places of learning and not at all like our own schools here, where you can teach them much by letting them study you in your ways. But it is my own belief that they fear and loath you, both for what you are and what you aren't; and that it is their intention to put you out of sight for good by means of their effusive intellectual optimism, their profuse analysing and their psychological 'assault courses'. They say that the walk you do have is a mighty curiosity which, if all our people copied it, would make our island not a worse place perhaps but nevertheless not the island as they want it to be and a much more intractable place and certainly more difficult to rule. They are afraid of their own teachings. Do you know what a boat is? It is a great thing to ride on. But they are hard to get off once you are on them. Well, I think in hindsight that you would be more useful here, working about the palace, and I can't see what's in your walk that the

Lasdiacs find so important; but we must do as they say at the moment. And whatever you do, don't argue with them."

"My son!" shouted a voice behind Economy.

Economy turned around and saw a wild-looking man standing near him, whom he had never seen before in his life. The man had a very rough appearance, was poorly clad and his face was raw and very strained. His two bloodshot eyes were large and staring. He looked at Economy with a great, warm feeling and a smile came on his face which had a look of much affection in it.

"My son," he repeated, and Economy looked at him – at this meagre, disappointing fellow – with disbelieving eyes.

"Son?"

"You are my son. I am your father. Yes, long-lost. Oh, that rascal. Do you know, my son, the world is full of rascals?"

He ran forward and gripped Economy in a tight squeeze around the neck that almost choked the lad.

"Dad. Son. My father. Can it be the truth?" said Economy, trying to breathe and looking to see if he could recognise his father in the man.

"The truth? It is more than the truth," said Halo enthusiastically.

"Oh, I knew in my heart that I would find you here in Balhop," said Economy as soon as Halo had released him, breathing with relief after the tight hug and thinking that he did indeed see a family likeness in the dingily-dressed, eccentric-looking man who stood before him.

"Did you know that they killed the woman named Na? Why didn't you come to see us? And where is my mother?"

"She whom you called Aunt Na was your mother, lad," said Halo, "and I don't know who told you differently."

"Aunt Na did," said a shocked Economy. "Oh, she did," said Halo, giving nothing away as to what his thoughts were about this.

"She said my mother wanted nothing to do with me and had gone away in the strangeness of her mind. She said that she herself had rescued me from the wilderness, where I had been left in a box."

He was still trying to fathom Halo's words, and absorb the emotions that they engendered in him.

Halo was speaking in a calm, wise, paternal, indeed very sane voice.

"Na was a strange one herself and it is a sad end truly that she came to. You are a doubly ill-starred chap. There is no doubt that she was your mum. She could never bring herself to admit it, I suppose. She was ashamed of you. Look in my hand here, and you will see the look of her eyes in the mirror of your face."

Economy looked in Halo's hand and he saw there the image and likeness of himself, of Na, and of Halo too.

"I always had a feeling that she was more to me than just old Aunt Na," said Economy sadly; "I always looked upon her as my mum."

"One thing is sure, son; you were born of woman, no matter what the cynics say."

Economy sighed as he took in this acknowledgement of his common nature.

"But I never went to see the two of ye," said Halo brusquely, as though he wished to clear up a matter quickly, "because if I left Balhop the whole city would have been taken over by those alien powers. Now they are everywhere. They have won in the end, but it was I who stood for so long between them and their goals. I am afraid that my mission has failed. And indeed I knew that it would, for they all said I was mad."

"I see," said Economy, not knowing what to make of his dad, this Halo.

"And so they killed her, did they?" mused Halo, showing no particular kind of feeling; "did Top Carrot have anything to do with that?"

"He is a king now," said Economy; "he was away at the time, and he came back and arrested the chief culprit and took us both with him to Balhop and put me in here with you."

"He is the chief culprit himself. He is your uncle," said Halo.

"You are not telling the truth," said Economy.

"I will prove to you that I am wise," Halo replied; "if you will sing to me your favourite song."

"All right," said Economy, accustoming himself to the strangeness of Halo.

"Oh, my favourite song is not," he sang,
"the great island song; it is the dirge of the dying woods,
the wild, disappearing clumps, the winding, vanishing tracks
on the ghostly mountain tops, and the sparkle as the night drops
on the silent, hedge bush, and the placid oins humming
in the glow of a friendly sun; oh, give me a bright friend's face,
and if not, the cheering peace of a calm, new-lit moon,
for I know that the day will come, and very, very soon,
of a great, new-shining sun."

"Wonderful words, if in a bad air," said Halo; "I can tell you have been practicing the art of prophecy. Well, it runs in the family and Top Carrot is the best one at it of all, though you wouldn't think so. Now look out the window and you will see what I mean."

As Economy looked out the window he saw the rim of an unknown, large moon appear on the evening horizon over the ocean's edge, bright and creamy in its sphere, portending a revelation.

"I said that it would appear and now here it is," Halo said with wide eyes and a voice become quite hoarse.

"There is more to come than that," said Economy, "for in itself it can be no good to us, not glowing with fire or light or warmth and soon to be easily covered with clouds."

"The very words of a seer," said Halo, "like myself, you can look into the inside of things. But what we observe before us is the very farewell that has been long a-going, a sun or something else that has gone forever into the darkness of our abysmal weather and desolate dreams. What you see out there is the sign of all our past woes, our madness, and of all that is gone."

"It is but a token of what is to come," insisted Economy, "and it is not what it appears to be for it is only the reflection of the coming new sun that will not be weak or dying, but strong and full of life."

"A moon for yesterday," said Halo.

"A sun tomorrow," insisted Economy.

"Perhaps that is the difference between a father and son. Come – let us cease arguing. Do you hear that noise outside?"

There was a great racket going on in the street below, while immediately outside their door there was the silent movement of departing feet and whispered words as Top Carrot, Charles and Jalosp moved away after their eavesdropping.

"They are as mad as humble scholars; I told you so," said Top Carrot; "Halo has clearly passed his folly on to the young fellow. I think you would be wise to leave them both where they are, Charles."

"I found it an interesting debate between the two of them, and while I agree that the old one is eccentric, the younger fellow is still worth studying a bit more; and the best possible place for that is in Assaland," Charles replied.

Deep down what Charles really wanted to explore was Economy's lack of any of the social graces along with his alienated, anarchical disposition. He was curious to know how such an outcast, who was completely indifferent to, or even oblivious of, all aspects of Assaland culture, had yet so easily managed to acquire that admirable, metaphysical 'absence' known as 'Hop', so evident in his personality, which even the best of Assaland philosophers could never aspire to.

There was never any likelihood, however, of the fact of this paradoxical admiration coming to full consciousness, or ever entering into the domain of public debate, (such as those extended correspondences in the letters page of The Balhopian Herald e.g. on the political correctness or incorrectness of locking up people for telling jokes, even good jokes about 'things held dearly', or why should we pay taxes for the upkeep of misfits).

"Mad you say they are? I would agree; they must be mad to be arguing about the sun and the moon, for we seem to be heading into times when every Tom, Dick and Harry believe they can discuss astronomy," said Jalosp angrily.

Charles looked annoyed by Jalosp's outburst. (Soon all such subject matters were to be removed from the monks' remit to become the monopoly of the Lasdiacs themselves).

"Put them into a uniform," said Jalosp, having racked his brains and called up all his reserves of critical judgement and canonical expertise; "that solves all problems."

Then the Chancellor of the Exchequer for the island came into the corridor. His name was Ivan, the companion of Economy in their youth.

"And when are you executing the death sentence on the three fellows whom you say have been causing all the bother?" he asked.

The spectacle of a public killing would take people's minds off disputed financial matters, he added, and Top would surely be only too glad to be rid of these elusive, shadowy fellows who had been causing him all the bother.

"The three fellows?" queried Top Carrot; "oh, you mean Gobhook! Ha ha ha. That fellow! He is called Mister Aloysius Alabaister Gobhook, and he has already gone to meet his Maker."

"The death penalty is certainly a good way of disposing of problems," the Chancellor said; "Professor Sammy assures me that it has great success over in Assaland."[2]

The Madness of Eamon Moriarty

"No," said Top Carrot, "they have not committed the capital offence, which is to go against my will. You know I have this plan for solving the great problem we have with all these wise idiots and stupid but clever people of whom there are so many sitting about the place nowadays, refusing to do any essential work or to dirty their hands in menial employment. That is, to make them work for me and so keep their minds and hands busy for evermore in my service. Well, it is to be implemented immediately by edict. And I wish to see this new law applied to Halo and Economy as well, by making them the official Keepers Of The Inside Of The Royal Prison Rooms. In fact, I have thought of jobs for everyone, even for you, most eminent Jalosp. You are to become my advisor on rocks, stones and dust."

"Thank you," said Jalosp, thinking that he should feel honoured that he would now receive official recognition for an activity he had been doing for nothing for years, the giving of useless, or incorrect advice.

"The boat is ready to leave in the morning with the fellow. It is the best and fastest one we have," Charles said softly to the king, while Jalosp, standing to one side, felt for the first time in his life the unhappiness of being left out of a whispered confidence.

Notes

1 - 'was in that wide, deep sea from whence we all came'; a reference to a surprisingly common human preconception, based on supposed high moral qualities attributed by us earthbound, somewhat self-admiring creatures to ourselves, that we are all linked mysteriously to the great ocean. Are these words, uttered spontaneously from the mouth of a simple, illiterate rustic on contemplating the ocean's omnipotent qualities with the intuition of innocence, proof absolute that we all are indeed greater than our constituent parts? This is what Cork claims, basing their belief perhaps on those meretricious arguments often employed by the southern advocates of

'equality and justice before the law' (see 2 below) to prove their politically biased doctrine (which obsesses the lower classes in that region) that we are all equal. Or so Galway snidely suggests. Emotion and prejudice were to overcome abstract thought even in the refined Galway deliberations when Professor De Waller implied that failure was a Cork trait, saying there is a noticeable propensity especially common to underachievers and failures, to compensate for their inadequate attainments with the claim that they are in some way related or inextricably linked to some external, indestructible power. Examples of these would be the basic elements for example; as in 'he's a down-to-earth fellow all in all, well, his nose is always in the air, his head up in the clouds, he's a fiery, passionate, soulful sort, he has water on the brain, he walks on water, etc. to excuse the worst things.

2 - The case of Professor Sammy, former professor of Greek, Classical Philosopher and expert on Assaland Imperial Military Tactics, should be referred to here. He was famous not so much for his actual achievements as for the mythical status of his amazing intellect, which island gossip endowed with legendary powers. This formerly mild, non-ambitious fellow, as a result of his recent findings from his research into the meaning of life, went on to become an enthusiastic proponent of the Death Penalty. Somewhat getting carried away in the fervour of his new field of study, he had unwisely compromised his intellectual independence by accepting a large research grant from the Conservative Think Tank (CTT). Their candidates in the upcoming election campaign were finding it hard to put solid political arguments against those of the Poor Folks' Party (PFP) in view of the decline in living standards, and were in need of some strong, hard-hitting issues with which to confront their opponents. Sammy was given the task of finding an intellectual basis for proving beyond all doubt that Capital Punishment (the main platform of this party) was an essential requirement for the future welfare of the country and its people. It was in his study of the Death Penalty as practiced in Assaland that Sammy was able to come up with the politically sellable idea that Morality (as upheld by the Conservative Party) and Justice (as demanded by the Poor Folks' party) were irreconcilable concepts. His complex academic theory proving this was set to dispose of once and for all the woolly thinking of the opposition Poor Folk' Party, which allowed them

to propose to the electorate that their poverty, lack of education and absence of any useful skills was somehow an issue of right and wrong and in need of remedying. The whole proposition revolved around the interesting statistic from his research showing that in all of human history more innocent than guilty people had been judiciously or legally killed. 'This should not however foreshadow the end of Capital Punishment', he argued, 'for all of human wisdom shows that the pursuit of justice is irreconcilable with the highest ideals of morality. For the very concept of 'justice' is problematical. It is the exact opposite of what we mean by 'morality'. With the word justice we associate retribution, punishment, revenge, robbery and murder under the name of equalization, taxation, putting wrongs to rights (a contradiction in terms) and overcoming disadvantage, all of which conveyed images to the righteous mind of plain savagery, intimidation and reigns of terror. Justice has always been the cry of the immoral. However, just saying the word 'morality' out loud has a completely different ring to it and the opposite effect. We think of good manners, the gentle virtues, modesty, keeping quiet and not disturbing the peace or the next-door neighbours, decent clothing, hygienic body washing, a quiet mode of talk without curses and dirty words, right as against wrong thoughts, and a satisfying ability to look down on other people so as to make them reform their ways from pure shame and fear of ostracism-respectable behaviour as is recognised by every race, religion and even honest crook in the world. It would seem indeed that the way of the world and the way of virtue were contraposed.

In fact morality was the same thing as the well being of society. It was self-evident that society is made up of different and unequal social groups. Anything that acts against the self-interest of a social group is immoral. Sammy demonstrated with much logical consistency, crystal-clear judgment and brilliant verbal gems delivered with fine oratorical panache, with many impressive allusions to the (inherited) faults of inferior, conquered people as celebrated in all the great classics of ancient literature (with the exception of the disreputable intellectual treatises of the French Revolution) and refutation by the weapon of disdain, and not omitting appeals to man's higher powers of intuitive thought such as the ever-present feeling that everybody else is wrong, the falsity of the contrary suggestions of the opposing party that all men are created equal. For what is more obvious than that some certainly go around with a less than equal capitation in the mental, physical and moral faculties? Therefore it must be in their interests not to be treated equally. It was not without good reason that the greatest civilizations of all sponsored the legalised slavery of the weaker sections of society. For how else would their greatest and longest-lasting achievements, the buildings, roads and monuments for which everyone remembers them and on which their reputation and immortality depend, whilst everything else they achieved has long since disappeared, have been built, or even their armies manned? None of this could have been achieved without inequality. That the mass of powerless people who were judiciously hanged, shot, ducked, burnt, tortured or otherwise put to death by the state over the centuries, whether innocent or guilty of their crimes, were mainly from such lower or 'unequal' classes, could only mean that it was not all of a bad thing, for by sparing the higher classes they had ensured that there was equality of treatment for the unequal.

The pursuit of justice undermines morality by its insistence on disrupting society, and then decent behaviour goes out the window as everybody tries to assert his/her own ideas, opinions and grab a slice of the action. All the wars and crimes of history are caused by this search for justice, he proves in a brilliantly argued chapter in his book that was printed in time for the Conservative candidates to flaunt on the electoral trail. But this scoundrel (as he was described by some) also turned to the Bible to justify his new political beliefs and came up with a new theology (there was no end to his genius). He implied that it was 'the original sense of injustice' (Original Sin) at not being given the 'knowledge' of good and evil (probably the mistaken idea that there was injustice in the world), that led the first man and woman to challenge the Divine prohibition, thereby committing the sin of pride and setting the rest of us up for a lifetime of problems. The truth was, he said, only those people as moral as himself (and the members of the Conservative Party) who believed that everybody should be kept in their place, could ever attain Paradise. Hence there was the awesome prospect that they would most likely be Heaven's only occupants, where they would have the everlasting ecstasy of only ever having to listen to themselves. Some theologians of the I'm All

Right Jack School said that this was the most dazzling spiritual insight of the last two thousand years.

Others claimed that Sammy had finally lost it as a respected academic. They said that he had also made the calamitous mistake, (geniuses are susceptible to relapses in judgement caused by the brain's overheating) of becoming a politician.

For he now had to apply his ideas to real life. The academic went on to a disastrous public career in which he managed, in his pursuit of political enlightenment and good government, to insult and depress the mass of humanity with patronising speeches, to incite ethnic riots, to indulge in the thieving of the state's resources, lying and skulduggery – and all that just in order to secure his parliamentary seat. He then went on to facilitate the legal murder of the opposition and the enslavement, under the yoke of low wages, of most of the populace, all for the sole purpose of establishing a reputation for himself in the field of ministerial expertise.

Later on, when Professor Sammy was himself faced with the death sentence (which had by then become so common that the capital letters had now been dropped from the two words in all printed bulletins), for immorality, by admitting openly in a public debate that there might indeed be justice in the afterlife if people like himself got into heaven, he rescinded his espousal of capital punishment and decreed that it, too, was immoral at the end of the day, as its existence was not conducive any longer to his own well-being.

chapter SIXTEEN

"Look, over there," shouted Halo in the faint pre-dawn light, pointing to the shore, "look at what's making all the noise."

Economy went to look out the window. There was a large number of oins being driven on to a ship, with many more herds of the animals coming in line behind them. It was the supply ship for the Lasdiacs and many, previously unemployed Balhopians holding fire sticks were lighting up the scene. Indeed there appeared to be an immense number of people involved in the whole enterprise. As the oins were being loaded aboard in their twos and threes a junior Lasdiac stood at the side counting them with chalk marks on a writing slate. It was clear that no islanders were being allowed on the ship. They saw Top Carrot sitting astride his big donkey, supervising the whole operation with the help of Charles. The Chancellor of the Exchequer joined them. He was standing to one side, his arms folded and a boozy smile on his face. Charles, too, had a big smile on his own normally sombre face. It portrayed immense satisfaction.

"They are taking away all the oins," said Economy aghast; "what will we be left with now? The oins belong to everybody."

"Top Carrot is everybody now," said Halo."I will see to that," shouted Economy and he tugged at the bars of the window.

"You are the only one who can stop them," Halo encouraged him, "for I would be quickly recognised if I went out there. I will give you a hand at those bars. Pull hard. You are a man after my own heart."

There was a certain deviousness about Halo's enthusiasm, the product of a new sophistication in him caused probably by his return to sanity.

Between the two of them they easily pulled the bars off the window, for the island prison-makers were not yet adept at their art. Halo stood before Economy, the tears streaming down his face.

"I will not embrace you this time, son. I am only an old man now, and it is you who will save the island after all. My son, it all depends on you. Oh, I always knew I had a good son somewhere who would finish the job for me. You alone can stop them taking away our oins. You alone can send those insolent foreigners back to where they came from. I would imagine that they are afraid of you, for you are a person who is not understandable to those educated people. They will be the more superstitious of you, for they cannot comprehend how you have been able to get around without those bodily parts that the rest of mankind takes for granted. Your life is a shameful thing to them, and a wonder. Only you can do it, son. Go to it. And if you don't come back, I'll be the first to say you were my son."

"They will not get past me," said Economy, "nor will they get even the hair of one of our oins, for I will stand on the seashore and block their way."

He dashed out through the window, and Halo did not know how he fared after that, not even if he survived the fall to the ground far below. He did shout out one last piece of advice.

"Don't tell Top Carrot all that I told you," but he did not know if Economy had heard him.

Economy made his way swiftly to the shore, having not even felt the shock of his long drop to the street, and none of the people busily employed on Top Carrot's great scheme paid any attention to the limping 'tramp' approaching the ship. By now the new moon was almost fully risen and was showing itself through the waving clouds and its appearance added to the people's excitement, for the Lasdiacs had been explaining to them all about it. Up on the hilltops and high buildings the monks and scholars too were studying the new planet and shouting their discoveries, though nobody was listening. These obsessive astronomers were not even interested in their king's great enterprise unfolding below them. They were just happy that Top Carrot had promised to get them a new telescope from Assaland – on condition, he said, that they proved either that the strange arrival was be seen from their island alone, or at least that it had been spotted there first. Top Carrot also felt that these tasks would keep them preoccupied and out of politics.

Only one person noticed Economy as he stealthily climbed aboard the first ship, a feat he achieved in full view of the Lasdiacs and all the people. This was the recently dismissed river labourer. He was no longer trusted to convey messages, as only the Lasdiacs were henceforth to be allowed to be in the transport and communications business. The labourer was feeling very bitter about being ignored by everyone, as in the past he it was who had been responsible for all the movements of messages and even oins around the island. He waved at Economy and smiled happily to see one of his own kind up there on the great vessel. Soon the ship was filled with livestock to the satisfaction of its smiling masters, and the lines were pulled up in readiness for the early afternoon sail.

Everybody was heading for home and their tired beds when shouts of great consternation were heard from the shore. A huge commotion was taking place on the big ship and the Lasdiacs and Assaland crew were shouting and jumping into the sea and on to the dock below them, many becoming severely injured in the panic. The ship had been taken over by a mighty, violent 'presence' which no one could see or explain. This 'force', the captain was soon saying to Top Carrot and Charles, was a demon of some kind and it had struck terror into everyone. They must get back to Assaland as soon as possible. They refused to stay in that forsaken island any longer. The oins themselves were a curse, for they seemed to be co-operating with, or obeying the 'presence' and had rushed at the frightened seamen and the astounded Lasdiacs. It was no use trying to identify the cause of the problem. There was something jinxed about the whole thing. The ship had moved off shore for its own safety and the captain said as he boarded the tug to rejoin his ship that on no account would he agree to come back to the shore again. A lifeboat would be sent back for Charles, who had disappeared, but they would have to leave quickly.

"Well, I never," said Top Carrot, scratching his head.

"They are just afraid of the oins," the king concluded, looking at the ship as it lay in front of the new moon. On the shore people were continuing to scramble before the still-stampeding oins; but Charles himself, who had returned to the scene as soon as the captain had left, had a look of resignation on his face and was looking at somebody out on the edge of the dock, where the poor of the island, alerted by the unemployed river labourer, had all now congregated to watch.

"I would not be surprised if he is the cause of your trouble," he said, pointing at a mysterious figure.

"Who is that?" asked Top Carrot.

"That chap you confessed to me was your illegitimate son. I thought he was still supposed to be in that room up at the top of the palace?"

"Call him over here, will you?," said Top Carrot to a courtier.

A triumphant, singing Economy, full of some kind of bubble drink or even something stronger, saw the courtier beckon to him and he went over quite happily to hear what the man had to say. In the distance he could hear the loud singing of Halo in his prison cell. Top Carrot looked depressed and the pride was gone from his face. Economy even felt a bit sorry for him.

"Ah, it is you," said Top Carrot on seeing him close up; "I imagine that you have something to do with this mayhem. Did somebody put you up to it? Was it Halo?"

"Do you mean your brother Halo?" asked Economy, and the small crowd that had now gathered gasped.

"Oh it is a lie; I won't deny it now, for a lie can never be denied. Halo is mad. Do not mind anything he has been saying to you, for he has been trying to destroy me, and you are only his tool. But Halo is also a liar and what he has told you is false."

He looked around and it was evident that nobody believed him, that they knew the king was telling a lie.

Suddenly, in an apparent change of heart, Top Carrot put his arm around Economy and turned to face the gathering crowds of Balhopians and other island folk.

"This slight, weak and distraught fellow is my own son. He has had a tough life in the wilderness, due chiefly to the great hardship that was imposed on him by the government through its past, selfish policies. We must also take into consideration the harsh conditions of the environment in which he and others like him grew up. That would be the explanation for all his tribulations. I had not known of him or his whereabouts for a long time. His mother was dear to me, and yesterday that person who was responsible for her cruel death met the same end himself. I will henceforth amend all that is wrong in the world and in the universe. One day I will take him back to the village with me, and see that he is properly cared for and that he has a home to live in. The Lasdiacs are leaving and so we will have to stick to our own devices and think up solutions for our problems ourselves.

You will all sympathise with me over my poor son, and you will understand the problems brought upon me by having such a child. I ask you all to go home and tell your families about the great trials of he who was your king. I know that some will laugh at me for having got myself into this predicament, but what do I care? I have been wrong. It is enough to recognise that. Here, take away this glorious crown. I am not worthy of it."

He threw his crown at the feet of the crowd, and there was a scramble for it. Top Carrot and a bewildered Economy went away in the rush and excitement, with the people already beginning to call for Top's re-instatement (they had all felt sorry for him during his abdication speech and the call for his re-instatement began as soon as he had stopped speaking) and later, together, they watched the full dawn breaking out over the brow of the bent hill outside Balhop.

"I imagine that they will soon appoint a new king down there, son, and I expect that the Lasdiacs will be back too; and better prepared the next time I bet, with a stronger philosophy. What is the matter son?"

"Halo and yourself – you both have similar features and look alike to me. Which one of you is really my father? I must know."

Top Carrot thought deeply and long before giving his reply.

"Ah, that is the whole matter. He was indeed my brother, but I have long disavowed him. The question of your parenthood is the chief issue between us and was the matter over which we fell out. Do you see? We are both your father. Do not trouble yourself over the matter any more. I have now got to go and tender my resignation officially."

Aemon seemed to be waking up as if from a dream, and he saw and felt a different world about him. He looked around and Tom Curran had left him. He himself was not where he had thought he had been, but lay on a bed in the same room with another man. This man, Harry, looked at him as he awoke, and the wild words of the madman made sense to Emaon and he felt a close kinship with the lunatic.

And now a very bright dawn had appeared, for the clouds of the island had gone in the clear wind and a warm air blew over the sky and the bright sun itself climbed skyward in its full, unblemished glory. The captive Naeom felt at peace and full of a strange wisdom. The island was full of excited folk celebrating the reappearance of the sun and discussing breathlessly the presence of the new, gigantic moon – or planet – at its side. The discontented bird flocks in the valleys and plains meanwhile gathered themselves in more aggressive flocks and began attacking all the villages below them.

Note on the Text

The reason for the setting up of a Board of Inquiry into the affair surrounding Eamon Moriarty and the infamous debacle at the Lord Mayor's Banquet is set out in the preamble.

'Never has there been such an embarrassing and disgraceful scene as took place at the much heralded reception for visiting dignitaries in the City Hall last year. This function was interrupted by a mentally disturbed patient, pursued by white-coated auxiliaries, in a regretful situation where security had not been considered a priority, and the said unfortunate approached and embraced the respected mayor as 'daddy' in a humiliation that was felt not just by the immediately affected party but by everyone there, and meant to the city and county thereafter the loss of yonks of foreign investment and self-respect. The Lord Mayor, recently elected and representing all that is/was best in the region was sadly exposed as a relative of this insane person, leading to the inevitable supposition that he himself was also a possible carrier of the disease. The panic that hit the gathering had to be seen to be believed, and with guests from as far away as Dublin and America among the audience not knowing what was going to transpire next, with an almighty embarrassment and shock in the air, the scene became one of shameful, self-conscious retreat. Everyone fled from the hall, some of the more self-controlled strolling calmly instead of hurrying, their noses held quite high in a denial of all that they had seen. The important, wealthy, invited guests fled Cork forever, their faces red from shame and feelings of unprecedented mortification and pitying empathy on behalf of their host. What with the full blast of publicity in surrounding regions and on the mainland itself, never had the public and private image of Cork become so low. The subsequent publication in the gutter tabloid press of extracts from Moriarty's diary exposed many well-known people to defamation and scandal.'

The tabloid sensationalism had its effect and pretty soon the sexual innuendo and connotations of Eamon's writing became the major talking point of the country's intellectuals, critics and senior high school students. It was not long before 'versions' were appearing in the underground world of 'pass-the-paragraph'. The Censorship Board did its best, but decided at the end that it would be best to let sleeping dogs lie, not to ban the book, and not draw any further attention to the affair. The 'book' would either be unreadable or would soon be forgotten.

Alas, this did not happen. The existence of a sublimated, artistic streak in Cork human nature, possibly based on frustrated imperialistic instincts, emerged as a lasting reality to be celebrated as a hallmark of a now true cultural centre. Nobody was able, thereafter, to remember any of the original details of Eamon's cultural innovations and accepted their new avant-garde status as a product of their own, private genius.

Madness reverted again, after its short period in the cultural (if tabloid) limelight to the twilight world of amnesia and denial.

Tom Curran was never the same again either. He changed his name to its Gaelic version in order that people would either forget his relationship with the mad Currans or else not even know who he was at all.

The University of Galway vowed never again to get involved with its Cork counterparts in the field of literature, medicine or the sciences.

Reverend O'Driscoll's closing words: May he and all the mad ones be blessed forever and ever amen.

THE END